When
The Wind Blows

Take Heed

Earl Snort

A Chief Deputy Barnett™ Novel Book One

TotalRecall Publications, Inc.
1103 Middlecreek
Friendswood, Texas 77546
281-992-3131 Tel
www.totalrecallpress.com

ISBN: 978-1-64883-396-0
UPC: 6-43977-43960-4

Library of Congress Control Number: 2025936715

FIRST EDITION
1 2 3 4 5 6 7 8 9 10

Not a speck of this is true. It's all a pack of lies.

Dedication

To my wife of 53 years
And TJR for sowing the germ of this fable in my mind
And JFW for his friendship, edits, and proofing.

"When I was a kid Uncle Remus would put me to bed
With a picture of Stonewall Jackson above my head
Then Daddy came in to kiss his little man
With gin on his breath and a Bible in his hand
He talked about honor and things I should know
Then he'd stagger a little as he went out the door
I can still hear the soft southern winds in the live oak trees.
*****
I guess we're all gonna be what we're gonna be.
So what do you do with good ole boys like me?
*****
Nothing makes a sound in the night like the wind does,
But you ain't afraid if you're washed in the blood like I was.
*****
So what do you do with good ole boys like me?"

What Do You Do With Good Ole Boys Like Me
Written by Bob McDill
Performed by Don Williams
1979

Illustrations by Susan C. Barnes

Earl Snort - 2025

- Prologue -

I love here it in South Louisiana when we get the subtropical summertime storms, and the wind blows, the lightning flashes, the thunder cracks, and the rain pours; when God reminds us all, natives, coonasses, transplants, visitors, and creatures alike, that He is awesome and in charge. The violence of it all brings us to our knees trembling, but thankful for His majesty and grace.

- *Chapter 1* -
Are Chu Interested?

Wednesday, November 5th, 2003.

Ring. Ring. Pause. Ring. Ring.

"ATF [Alcohol, Tobacco, & Firearms], Special Agent Barnett speaking."

"Marvin Lloyd Barnett. [Pause.] It's Abner. Ain't chu supposed ta say BATFE [Bureau of Alcohol, Tobacco, Firearms, & Explosives] since W [President George W. Bush] transferred chur whole outfit over ta Justice? What kinda DOJ [Department of Justice] employee are chu anyway?"

"Abner, I've been saying ATF since 1978. No way I'm changing my ways now. Besides, I've got my time in and been able to pull the plug for more'n two years. You know that. Maybe I will if they ever really tick me off. Maybe I won't. Why you breaking my stones anyway? What can I do for ya? Oh my gosh! Didja win? Tell me you did!"

"Whadda chu t'ink?"

"I think you did. I think congratulations are in order. Are you unemployed now until January 1st? Need a loan? I gotcha covered. How close was the vote?"

"T'anks. We won by 2,000 votes outta more'n 38,000 cast. Ah still gotta chob, but Ah was awmost erased from da gene pool early dis mornin'. Somebody t'rew a firebomb in mah house las' night chust before Ah went ta bed. We was lucky. Ah put it out before it could do much damage. Chu know who prob'ly done dat, don't chu?"

"Soon to be former Sheriff Alexander L. Neicase?"

"Eidder him or one of his lackeys. All Ah know is, dey was drivin' a black GMC or Cheby pickup."

"You call ATF or the FBI over in Baton Rouge?"

"Whadda chu t'ink?"

"Prob'ly not. You're a hardheaded coonass, Abner Bienville Ladner, Jr. [Besides being a Registered Coonass, Abner was an ex-Marine Corps lance corporal in the heavy weapons platoon - the unit with the heavy machine guns, mortars, and even flame throwers left over from World War II. He served from 1958 to 1962 between wars, so this former second team All State high school offensive and defensive tackle from the 1958 Louisiana Regional Championship football team never had the opportunity to crush the enemies of America in war. He was also the son of a farrier and blacksmith, meaning he was stronger and tougher than raw alligator hide. There is no such human being more hardheaded than a combination Marine and coonass.] So what're you planning to do about it?"

"Mah brudder and mah son an' a few cousins is gonna keep watch. Mah hands are tied until dey swear me in on Chanuary 1st. In da meantime, Ah'm still gonna do my chob. Dat's why Ah'm callin' chu. Ah want chu ta be my chief deputy. Chu'll be in charge of all investigations."

"What? I live in Mississippi! Last time I was a local officer was 25 years ago, and that was back in Kentucky. I couldn't possibly get certified in Louisiana by then. I'm certainly honored though. Besides, I'm not sure Hannah would wanna move. It's gotta be what - 200 miles?"

"Nope. 180. Takes a liddle ober two-and-a-half ahrs if chu take US 190 instead of da innerstate and chu know dat, too. Look, Marvin, Ah really need chu. Da pay's $48 t'ousand. Besides, Ah can turn T'ursday inta Sunday if Ah need to. Ah got all da right connections. Ah'll call Cap'n Boudreaux over in da law officer coitification branch at da Louisiana Bureau of Chustice and woik it all out. Chu take a online course on Louisiana criminal law an' give Boudreaux copies of all chur federal schools. Dat's all she wrote. It's 'wham, bam, t'ank chu ma'am.' Gib 'em a copy of whatcha got from Kentucky, too. Cain't hurt none. Whadda chu say? Come on, man. T'ink about it."

"Marvin, your offer is certainly enticing. You got my head spinning. When I woke up this morning, the last thing on my mind was retiring, let alone moving out of state. Now my mind is going off in a thousand directions, wondering what if? What if? I'll run it by Hannah tonight. If she agrees, I'll put in my papers. I got 25 years. That's 60%. A year's worth of unused sick leave will add 2%. My military time won't count 'cause it was all Army National Guard. Nevertheless, that's about $60,000 before taxes. Add $48,000 and we'd be a little ahead of the game. If Hanna agrees, we're in, but I'm not sure which way she'll tilt. She's pretty happy over here where we are.

"Call you tomorrow, buddy, and let you know. Either way, I do so appreciate the offer. It's huge. I love ya, man. Adiós."

"Adiós chur own self, Marvin. Ah hope Hannah votes fah me. Ah need chu, man."

It was only 9:30 a.m. My heart was thumping. I never saw this freight train headed in my direction. Abner and I had been pals for nearly 20 years. I met him at FLETC [Federal Law Enforcement Training Center] in Glynco, Georgia, when I was a guest instructor for a two-week firearms training seminar for local law enforcement officers.

My POD [post of duty] was, and always has been Gulfport, Mississippi, in Harrison County, although now I live about twenty miles west of there in Bay Saint Louis in Hancock County. Abner has cousins next door in Pass Christian. These are all Mississippi Gulf Coast cities. We both enjoy hunting and fishing, and his wife, Marisol, and Hannah get along like twin sisters. I thought she might be amicable to a potential move and a new adventure, but she was one of only two certified librarians in the Hancock County Public Library, where we've resided for the past 17 years. She loves her job. Our son, Irvin, is a DEA special agent in Dallas, Texas, so he and his family are not a factor if we do decide to make the move. In fact, it would place us about three hours closer to them. The more I thought about it, the more I thought Hannah would probably go for it, but I wasn't sure.

I'm 53 years old. Mandatory retirement for me is the end of the month I turn age 57. That wasn't far down the road. Then what would I do? The last time I checked, getting a captain's job in one of the local law enforcement agencies would pay about $35,000 tops. Chief Deputy in Saint Landry Parish, Louisiana, would be a much better job with substantially more money. Of course, tenure would depend upon Marvin getting reelected. However, even if he didn't, I'd be back in the same place as I would have been, had I stayed on ATF until I aged out.

I got on the horn and called Personnel Division in Headquarters in WDC. They were an hour ahead of us. I asked the personnel specialist to crunch my numbers and send me a printout, assuming I retired on December 31st. I also requested a retirement packet. Then I changed course and took a close look at my open investigations. I was down to three. I wanted to have them all in judicial action by the end of the year. Time to get a move on. It was a paperwork day, but my mind kept switching back to Abner's job offer, and I wasn't as efficient as usual.

I pulled in my driveway about 5:30. Tonight Hannah beat me home. She was checking our mail when I arrived. It was mostly junk. Roscoe, our yellow and white tiger-striped, carnivorous security cat, hunter, slayer and consumer of lizards, small rodents, and at least one bluejay, came up to rub fur all over my trousers. He purred loudly when I scratched his head. Mission accomplished, he moved over to put his scent on Hannah.

Hannah looked up at me and asked, "Good day?"

"Unbelievably good. What say we go over to L'il Ray's restaurant, eat some raw oysters on the half-shell, and drink a pitcher of Miller Lite? You can fill me in on your day and I'll tell you about mine."

"You're twisting my arm, Mr. Barnett. I'm famished, and I forgot to thaw something out for supper. Let me feed Roscoe and I'll be ready to go. I'll drive."

Her driving was an inside joke. I couldn't use my G-Ride [government car], which was a white, 2002 Chevrolet Impala, for personal business. She didn't much care for my old faithful, mint green, 1986 Dodge, D150 pickup truck, especially when she was wearing a dress. I didn't blame her. We compromised in a manner of speaking, and she drove us in her blue, 2001 Dodge Stratus, like usual.

We ate four dozen oysters on the half-shell and drank a pitcher of the coldest beer in town.

I let her go first. She told me all about the problems they were having with their new computer system. Sounded like a nightmare. She was really fired up and went on and on. Good thing the county administrator who mandated this transition was not here to hear this. Finally, she noticed that I was looking at her and grinning like the Joker in the old Batman movie. "You think this is funny, Marvin? It's not! It's frustrating as all get out!"

"No. I don't. Sorry. I know it's a royal pain; however, I also know you'll figure it out, and within a few weeks you all will be standing in tall cotton, operating like you've been using this new software since you emerged from the womb. Oops! We're all out of beer. Let me order us another."

She thought about it and said, "I don't want to spoil this little buzz and ruin the night. I'll deal with it tomorrow. What did you accomplish today?"

I ordered the pitcher and waited for it to arrive. The pitchers were pretty small here. Only four glasses per.

"Well, I got a call from Abner this morning."

"Oh my gosh! Did he win?"

"He did, by 2,000 votes."

"Oh, I'm so happy for him!"

"Me, too. He wants me to be Chief Deputy of the SO [Sheriff's Office]. Be in charge of all the investigations. Pay is $48,000. That's about $15,000 more than any of the jobs I've looked into around here. We'd need to be there by New Year's Day when he'll be sworn in as sheriff. I told him I needed to discuss it with you first, and that I'll let him know tomorrow."

"On my goodness! I never imagined something like this. You know - another move. Is this what you want to do?"

"It is. I called Personnel to see what my annual retirement would be if I retired on December 31st. It's about $64,000 before deductions. They're mailing me a printout. I haven't mentioned this to anyone yet."

"What about our house?"

"Put it on the market and sell it. Buy a house there in Opelousas."

"What about my job? I've got 17 years."

"I know. I'd say take your 401 account and add to it if you find a job you like over there. I'm sure with Marvin's help we could find something suitable. No doubt they have a library too, or something else which would suit your fancy."

"Wow! Embark on another interstate adventure, just like we did when we moved here from Louisville. Back when we were still essentially kids and broke."

"Pretty much, except not so broke now. Otherwise, I keep on doing what I'm doing until I age out. It would add 8% onto the retirement I'd get now. That would probably be about $69,000."

"$69,000 plus $35,000 if you stayed and got a local job here in four years, versus $64,000 plus $48,000 if you retired and took this job now. That's $104,000 versus $112,000, and a job you really want."

"Yep."

"Hmmm. We've been to Opelousas. It's nice there. We're dear friends with Abner and Marisol. Truthfully, my job is boring me to tears. Marvin, let's go for it! I'm really excited for both of us. I was getting stale at work. You know. No longer challenged. No advancement. Same old thing everyday. Same paltry pay. Nothing to look forward to."

"Me too, pretty much. I'll call Abner in the morning. I'll see if he and Marisol would be up for a visit this weekend so we can get the lay of the land. If we're still sold on the idea, we'll put our house on the market. I'll tell Roland [T. Spears, the Resident

Agent in Charge (RAC) in Gulfport] and Mr. [Aaron B.] Woods [the Special Agent in Charge (SAC) in Jackson] that I'm putting in my papers and December 31st will be my last day - at least on the books. I've got some annual leave I'll take at the end."

"Hubba hubba, future Mr. Chief Deputy Sheriff of Saint Landry Parish, Louisiana. We have work to do."

"Ah, there is one more thing you should know."

"What's that?"

"Abner said his house was firebombed last night. He got to it in time and it barely caused any damage. He has good reason to believe it's the outgoing sheriff or one of his associates. At least until he gets sworn in, Abner's extended family is watching his house."

"You've gotta be kidding me! That really riles me up! I'm calling Marisol soon as we get home. Maybe we can help them out. And Marvin, you either get me my own gun or give me that little five-shot Smith & Wesson you carry off duty."

"It's a .38. You can have it. I'm pretty sure Abner issues guns, but if he doesn't, I still have my four-inch .38 Smith I carried on duty in Louisville. Anything else?"

"What kind of shotgun do you have?"

"It's a Remington Model 870, 12-gauge pump with an open cylinder slug barrel."

"They make those without as much kick?"

"Yep. You can get it in 20-gauge. Lot of pre-teen boys and women who hunt or shoot skeet or trap use the 20. Not sure about getting it with a slug barrel, though. I'm sure they will have some with open cylinder barrels and a bead sight.

"Get me one of those with lots of ammo for me to practice. I decided I want my own guns now. I need to defend myself if you're not with me. I want to go to Howard's and Clara's so I can practice with both the .38 and my new shotgun."

"I'll call Howard tonight. In fact, I'm pretty sure he has some 20-gauge pump Remingtons for sale. You really are fired up."

"Told ya! Someone's after our friends! United we stand. Divided we fall."

"I think I read that somewhere - like maybe on the Commonwealth of Kentucky flag. After all these years, you're still a hillbilly through and through."

"I am, and so are you, Mr. Barnett. Come on. We have things to do."

By the time I got around to calling Abner, Hannah had already beat me to the punch. She was on the phone with Marisol.

Abner said, "Hey, Marvin, Ah awready hoid da news! Marisol is gushing. T'anks, man. Chu all are staying wit' us dis weekend. We got lots of room. Marisol can take Hannah around da town ta look at houses and chu and me will stop by da SO. Ah'm still da Chief Deputy an' Cheriff Neicase cain't fire me unless he wants ta make hisself more enemies dan he already has. Besides, when he goes out of office, all his powah will be gone. He doesn't want me ta start goin' tit for tat wit' him. He can't win dat baddle."

"Good deal. This job come with a take-home car?"

"Of course! By all means. Da cheriff, chief deputy, and chief of patrol all has take-home vehicles. We buy marked units for da road deputies, but dey don't get ta take 'em home. We get lease vehicles for da t'ree of us from Poppa Bear Choe Landry's Chrysler-Dodge-Cheep dealership here in town. Pick out whatcha want. We take 'em to da Motorola chop to hab radios installed, and Ledbetter's Custom Chop to get lights and sirens installed. Dey also put on da decals on da doors wit' our badge on it. Chu don't have ta do dat, but we normally do. It saves a lot of problems down da line, so Ah highly recommend it. Cheriff Neicase drives a black Dodge Ram 1500 super cab pickup. Ah got da same t'ing except it's blue and it's four-by-four. Soon as Ah get sworn in, we'll trade 'em in for somet'ing new. Dey got Cheeps, if chu want somet'ing like dat, or chu can stick wit' a sedan or a pickup. Even a van. It's chur choice."

That solved one of my problems. I've had a take-home car since I was a patrolman in Louisville, and it's a major league perk. Drive the 'company car', use their gas, covered by their insurance. It's worth at least $10,000 a year, tax free. Both the PD and ATF had that perk for a very good reason. We were on call for any emergency 24/7/365, and we did get called out fairly frequently.

"What's the population in your bailiwick and how big is your staff?"

"Da county's about 88 t'ousand, including dogs and cats. Opelousas is about 16 t'ousand. We got 54 deputies overall. Besides da cheriff and chief, we got 24 deputies in da chail and 30 deputies on da road, and two of dem have ta cover da courtroom on day chift on weekdays, but dat usually only takes a couple of ahrs. We got a lot of miles ta cover, but we don't have too many problems because most of da folks are law-abiding citizens. Most of ahr arrests are for drunk and disorderly and chit like dat. We also have mutual assistance pacts wit' all da adjacent parishes, but it seldom gets invoked. Mostly for t'ings like high speed chases across parish lines, hurricanes and major storms, and da like. Chu'll see. Usually no difficulties."

"Does Opelousas have a PD?"

"Dey used to, but da mayor disbanded 'em two yeahs ago. Dey only had six guys. Da SO deputies make a lot more dan dey did. Eben so, da city couldn't afford ta pay 'em, so Cheriff Neicase said we'd cober da city fah free since his office was awready in da middle of da city. See, normally, if a incorporated city don't hab a PD, dey hab ta pay da cheriff to do it for dem. Cheriff Neicase hired t'ree of dere guys and da udder guys found woik someplace else. I hoid one ob dem went ta da Louisiana Fish & Wildlife as a game warden.

"What made you decide to run against Sheriff Neicase?"

"He's 76 years old. Been cheriff fah 16 yeahs. Before dat he'd been a reg'lar deputy fah about 15 yeahs. He's got his time in ta retire, an' he's been slipping fah da past four or five. Ah been running t'ings da last ten yeahs or so fah him. It was time fah him ta go, but he couldn't give up da powah. Ever'body could see dat, but he's been a good cheriff overall and most folks didn't want ta hoit his feelings. Da more Ah t'ink of it, Ah don't t'ink he was involved wit' da firebombing. Ah 'spect it was one of da hard-cases Ah busted. Sooner or later Ah'll find out. Somebody will talk. Den Ah'll deal wit' him my own way. Don't worry. It'll all be legal and by da book. Anyt'ing else?"

"Nope. That about covers it. See you all Saturday morning. We'll bring some guns. Hannah wants to shoot."

"No problem. Gotcha covered. We'll go ta our range. Don't forget ta get online and take dat Louisiana law course fah officers. Maght take chu a few days ta complete it."

"I'll start on that first thing tomorrow. Call me if anything comes up before Saturday."

"You got it. Bye."

"Bye."

- *Chapter 2* -

Working Like a Hebrew Slave in Ancient Rome

November 2003

There were hundreds of things Hannah and I needed to accomplish before New Year's Day. I submitted my retirement papers through my boss, RAC Roland T. Spears, to the big boss up in Jackson, SAC Aaron B. Woods. Hannah notified Clarice Pendleton, the director of the Hancock County Public Library, of our pending relocation. We scurried around and buffed up our house to make it look new just like it was back when we bought it, except even better. We had already taken care of some major renovations, including the installation of hardwood floors, a new air conditioner and furnace, and repainting the interior walls a pale shade of blue. Our yard was shaded by six large live oak trees. Everything looked nice; everything worked; nothing was broken; and, we had been very content here.

We cleaned out the house and the garage, making a couple of used furniture and junk dealers extremely happy. We hired an energetic realtor, Anna Hobbs, whom we knew from church. We contracted with a local moving company to move our belongings to Opelousas once we were ready. We already located a house in Opelousas we were interested in, hoping it wouldn't sell before we sold our house. I spent a week off and on, successfully completing the online Louisiana law enforcement officers' course. Abner personally presented my packet to Louisiana Bureau of Justice Captain Percival Boudreaux, his old pal, who approved it while Abner was waiting, and then had his clerk drop it in the mail to me while Abner was still there schmoozing. Talk about service with a smile!

I quickly completed and assembled my oldest case file. The malefactor was Gerard D. Snodgrass. The charge was for being a convicted felon in possession of a firearm. It's the easiest charge to prove in ATF's 'bag of tricks'. I presented it over the phone to AUSA [Assistant United States Attorney] Dennis G. Buchholz for prosecution.

He approved it, but threw me a curveball. He only authorized a criminal complaint. That allowed me to obtain an arrest warrant from our U.S. Magistrate Judge Winthrop K. Hanson, U.S. District Court, Southern District of Mississippi, in Biloxi; however, it also meant after his arrest, he was entitled to a preliminary hearing if we couldn't get him indicted first. Now that I knew I was retiring and moving out-of-state, time was of the essence.

Snodgrass was 'caught with his hand in the cookie jar' so I considered a complaint as lame. I had expected to present his case for an indictment. Complaints are usually reserved for weak cases because they are easily dismissed. Indictments are nearly 'til death do us part'. Difficult to quash, but not impossible.

Snodgrass was a twice convicted felon. He got busted by the Biloxi Police Department [BPD] in a barroom brawl carrying a loaded revolver in his pocket. They charged him with the misdemeanor charges of carrying a concealed deadly weapon and simple assault. BPD seized the revolver and notified me. I notified Dennis. In the interim, Snodgrass paid a $150 fine to Biloxi City Court and was released from the Harrison County Jail the next day. That was another sore point.

I had requested that the jail notify me before releasing Snodgrass, knowing Dennis had agreed to prosecute. (I didn't have the warrant when Snodgrass was lodged in jail.) This is standard operating procedure between the Feds and locals in nearly all jurisdictions, and I had never encountered a problem in the past. That being said, the jail lieutenant supervising the front desk, Clovis J. Mudd, let Snodgrass have a two-day head start before notifying me of his release. Think maybe someone 'greased his palms'? The Harrison County Jail had always been more helpful than this. It came as an unpleasant surprise to me.

I made a note to self to speak to Sheriff Hobgood personally about this, and I did the very first chance I got. Former Lieutenant Mudd is now Deputy Mudd on the midnight shift. It was either take the demotion and shift change or resign. I bet that took most of the starch out of Mr. Mudd's britches.

I finally discovered the reason I couldn't get Dennis to indict Snodgrass from the get-go. Besides being too busy at the moment, it was because Snodgrass was a card-carrying member of the Bandidos Motorcycle Club. He was back 'in the wind' the minute he got released. Dennis was afraid I couldn't lay hands on him before I retired. Ergo, he didn't want the case to languish for years, waiting for some cop to pull Snodgrass over for a traffic violation and learn then by happenstance that he was a fugitive.

This was a little insulting. Nevertheless, I didn't voice my dismay, although I did feel sorely aggrieved. Instead, I 'put on my big boy pants' and set about to scoop up Snodgrass forthwith, thus quietly demonstrating to Dennis that he had made an incorrect assumption about my skill and/or dedication to duty. I collared the oxygen thief the same day I obtained the signed warrant. (I knew I could. I had an informant who was the brother-in-law of Snodgrass's main squeeze. He tipped me off while the star-crossed fornicators were shacking up in the sleazy Long Beach No Tell Motel, otherwise known as the Sleepytime Lodge.) Dennis was duly impressed, and somewhat sheepish while 'licking the egg off his face'.

We indicted Snodgrass the day after his initial appearance in U.S. Circuit Court in Biloxi. He was detained without bond because Magistrate Judge Hanson ruled he was an escape risk. The sentence he was facing was fairly light - capped at five years; however, a conviction was steamrolling his direction just as sure as rain is a major factor during a hurricane. Besides, nobody wants to do any amount of time in prison. Snodgrass knew with his past, he was screwed and would receive the full five years. It was time for him to 'cowboy up'.

Next up, I called our Forensic Services Laboratory in Headquarters and prodded them to giddy-up just a little bit on my second open case. I had submitted 14 [all paper in those days] ATF Forms 4473 [Firearms Transaction Record] regarding a suspect named Craig F. Elwood. He was a convicted felon too, and his conviction was for a serious crime. He had committed an armed robbery of a liquor store in Pascagoula, Mississippi, in which shots were fired but no one was injured. He was finally paroled after serving 11 very long years of a 15-year beef in the Mississippi State Penitentiary in Parchman. The prison is uncomfortably situated in the stifling, flat, vacuous delta of rural Northwest Mississippi in Sunflower County. You can see for miles there in any direction. Nothing in sight, except for cotton fields and a few shanties.

The prison has more than 30,000 acres of cotton, with something like 26 fenced-in work camps scattered throughout.

Some of the prison guards even live with their families in little state-owned cottages located on the prison property! It's a novel concept. Not only that, most of the inmates roam about the prison grounds freely during the day, going about their work until after supper, when they're locked down in the little compound to which they are assigned. Of course, the Death Row and other hard-case inmates are locked down full time in small concrete cells in the main, brick prison building, and they don't have this freedom.

Bet you can guess how most inmates spend their time in Parchman during the daylight hours. That's right. Somebody's got to plow the fields, till, plant, weed, and harvest all that cotton. The profit from cotton sales really helps the state to recover the costs of operating a prison, especially when you don't have to pay your laborers, AND they stay busy year around! It's hard work too, but at least they're not confined in dimly lit, eight-by-ten concrete block cells. It actually isn't all that bad for the average inmate, so long as he doesn't object to farm work. What if he does? The obvious question then, is why don't the prisoners escape? What keeps them there? After all, they are convicts.

It's simple. Some of the guards ride mules, and others drive off-road pickup trucks with bloodhounds, and they roam freely all over the prison. They're armed with radios and shotguns, with chiseled-in-stone orders to shoot any convict who attempts to escape.

I know. I've been there and seen the proof for myself. I saw a dozen or more eight-by-ten, glossy color photographs of dead inmates who attempted escape, framed and hanging on the walls of one of the cafeterias open to both inmates and staff. I ate there after interviewing an inmate on Death Row, who at one time had been one of my documented snitches. He murdered a woman in cold blood while robbing a gas station late at night. Neither the judge nor the jury had any sympathy. Nor did I, but it was a real tragedy to both the victim and to ATF. He always had good information. Now he was done for - a dead duck - a dead man walking, as they say.

Summing up, the odds of surviving an escape attempt from Parchman are probably statistically the same as trying to escape from Alcatraz. To say the odds are slim would be a gross understatement.

Getting back to Craig F. Elwood, he had acquired or manufactured, not sure which, a very excellent counterfeit Mississippi driver's license in the name of Jonah K. Burke. He used said counterfeit license to purchase 14 handguns from nine different licensed and reputable firearms dealers in South Mississippi. I got him on video at three of them.

My unsupported supposition was that he sells most of the guns at a profit to other convicted felons, but I had no proof. Why else would he take the risk, unless he were smuggling guns into Mexico or Canada where handguns are illegal? I considered that highly doubtful. He was 'too small potatoes'. Not enough 'jingle'.

Actually it didn't matter why. Falsification of a Form 4473 in an effort to acquire a firearm unlawfully is a felony no matter the reason, and it carries a penalty of up to five years imprisonment per purchase. He was looking at 70 years potentially. Of course, he'd never draw that much time, but he'd get at least ten. In the Federal system, that worked out to be 8-1/2 years with good behavior.

Elwood was a pretty devious character. He thought he was 'flying under the radar', but he wasn't. The way I got onto him was by performing routine Form 4473 checks at the various gun dealerships on the Mississippi Gulf Coast. We do this periodically just to keep the dealers honest, and sometimes, just like 'the blind hog who finds an acorn ever once in awhile', we recognize the name of a convicted felon we know.

It was a little different this time. I spotted the name Jonah K. Burke twice, then three times, then four. I thought to myself, "Jonah, like the Book of Jonah in the Bible, where he gets swallowed by a whale and survives? Who names his kid Jonah?" I checked with the Mississippi Department of Motor Vehicles [DMV] and learned there was no such licensed driver in Mississippi. Just what I thought. No one names a kid Jonah.

This energized me to keep on digging. One of the gun dealers happened to notice the vehicle Jonah K. Burke was driving. It was a fully restored, bright yellow, 1953 Ford F100 pickup truck. Absolutely cherry! Showroom quality. This turned out to be a pivotal observation. I requested that DMV check for registrations on all 1953 Ford F100s. There were only three. No way to tell from the registration if any were cherry. Two were in North Mississippi and one was in Ocean Springs, in Jackson County, directly across the bay from Biloxi, which is in Harrison County, same as Gulfport. That one was yellow, too! I got the printout on all three, but I knew where I was going to look first.

The yellow truck was registered to a Craig F. Elwood, at 1604 Harper Street, Apartment 2, in Ocean Springs. I sat up on the apartment, off and on for a day and a half before I finally saw the vehicle or the driver. I got a pretty good look at him from a distance. His appearance was similar to the photograph on Elwood's Mississippi driver's license; however, I was too busy snapping pictures to tell for sure. Later, by studying my photographs, I could tell it was him. That's when I did a deep dive on Elwood's background. I continued checking at all the licensed gun dealerships on the Mississippi Gulf Coast, which is how I wound up with 14 ATF Forms 4473 signed by the fictitious Jonah K. Burke.

Craig F. Elwood had never seen or spoken with me, but it didn't mean he was 'slip sliding away' in the words of Paul Simon. He was on my radar screen. Elwood's legitimate occupation was with a local pest control company, poisoning bugs and other pests. This allowed him lawful entrance into the homes of unwitting clients. The company was called Gulf Coast Exterminators. Question: How would you like a convicted armed robber who traded shots with the victim, spraying your house for bugs while your wife was home by herself? Food for thought.

Elwood was completely oblivious to my investigation. That was part of the challenge which made it more interesting to me. Imagine his surprise when I show up unannounced with a warrant in one hand and my handcuffs in the other. I had conducted numerous surveillances on him and so far, had never been 'burned'. I had also interviewed clerks and owners of gun stores he had deceived, but no one ever tipped him off. I had been waiting patiently for the past seven weeks up until now that I was retiring, for both the latent fingerprint and questioned handwriting examinations to be completed on all 14 ATF Forms 4473 that I had seized as evidence and submitted for analysis.

I spoke with the fingerprint expert first. She confirmed recovering Burke's latent prints on each Form 4473. The handwriting expert said he had examined 12 documents thus far. Of those, he had one highly probable opinion, six probables, and five no opinions that the person who signed the fictitious driver's license was also the same person who signed the Forms 4473. He said he would complete the last two examinations by COB. He would mail his report together with the latent print report forthwith. I should have them within a week.

The videos and latent prints alone were damning enough to secure 14 convictions. The handwriting examinations were done to 'slam the door shut on the foot' of his lawyer, assuming he decided to muddy the water by claiming someone other than Elwood actually signed the forms.

I spoke with AUSA Dennis Buchholz on this case. He said to bring him a case report as soon as the laboratory reports were in. He would place Elwood on the docket for presentation to the Grand Jury. Once the indictment came down, I could put the 'habeas grabbis' on him. His 'goose was cooked', but doing time in Club Fed is a much better deal in every aspect than going back to Parchman to be a cotton-picker.

That left my last open case. It was based upon information received from the Stone County Sheriff's Office [SCSO] on an old time moonshiner named Merlin J. Beauchamp. In fact, he was 67 years old. Most crooks are much younger. He was an inveterate moonshiner, having been convicted four times by ATF with three other near misses.

With respect to the near misses, the only legal action ATF could take was to blow up his stills, because nobody was present at the time they were discovered operating full bore; however, the kicker was that all three near misses were on Merlin Beauchamp's 30 acres of cracker peckerwood paradise, deep within the scruffy, piney woods of Stone County.

The various AUSAs on those cases declined prosecution because in their opinions, ATF could not prove beyond a reasonable doubt that Beauchamp was the distiller, since he wasn't caught red-handed. I suppose they were correct. Knowing is not proving; however, stills cost quite a bit to make. Copper tubing and the copper sheet metal to make the cooker ain't cheap. Then there's all the barrels (which are usually 55-gallon metal drums), the sugar, which is also not cheap, and the corn. Blowing up a 10-barrel moonshine rig back in 1982, was somewhere between a $1,000 to $2,000 loss for a moonshiner who probably didn't earn more'n $6,000 or $8,000 per annum. Some would say that was penalty enough.

ATF's cases on Beauchamp went back to 1956. Merlin was only 18 years old then, yet he was already an accomplished distiller. He'd learned at his daddy's knee, who had learned from his daddy. Merlin's file ran all the way up to 1997. Now six years later, I had a new file on him. His four convictions occurred between 1956 and 1982. The last near miss was in 1997. The convictions resulted in sentences of 18 months twice, 2 years, and 30 months. I remembered his last arrest in 1982, because I was in on the raid. (I was not the case agent.)

Every case against him took place on land he owns. At first, I made the assumption his current still is on his land, but maybe it's not. Maybe it is. Before I went prowling around in the woods, I needed to check with the Stone County Real Property Tax Assessor to see if he'd acquired some more real property since 1982.

How does SCSO know he's making white lightning now? Because he's been selling it to the blacks around Wiggins in half pint bottles for three bucks a bottle. The Wiggins Police Department [WPD] and SCSO have both arrested several of Beauchamp's recent clients. What they haven't done so far, is see

Beauchamp actually make a sale. Being caught up on my other two cases, I decided I better go up there and take a look-see for myself on Beauchamp's property, and depending upon circumstances, maybe conduct a few interviews. I checked out $500 in buy/informant money just in case someone with useful information were talking. I decided to take our newest rookie, Joel B. Red Horse with.

Interesting background on Joel. He's a full-blooded Navaho Indian from Window Rock, Arizona, which is located on the northeast border with New Mexico. Like all his male relatives going back to World War II, save for one, he enlisted in the Army after he graduated from school. The lone hold-out was an independent cuss and well-known hardhead. He enlisted in the Marine Corps instead. The rumor was, his parents weren't married, so the Army wouldn't accept him. Everyone knows the Marines are a bunch of bastards anyway, or so I've been told. That was the joke.

The thing which made Joel stand out from all his other veteran relatives is, he didn't join the Army right after he graduated from high school. He waited until he got a bachelor's degree in anthropology from Arizona State University in 1991. Then he dutifully signed up. [Note to self. Native Americans are very patriotic and truly love America. It stands to reason. They were here first.]

Joel was exceptionally physically fit, but he didn't participate in team sports, so he slipped through high school generally unnoticed. Just another kid on the rez. Therefore, surprising to many who knew him, Army Basic Combat Training [BCT] and Infantry Advanced Individual Training [AIT] at Fort Benning, Georgia, were pretty much a cakewalk for him. 'No heavy lifting' as they say. He volunteered for Airborne School, which is also located at Fort Benning, and Ranger School, which has a phase there, too. He successfully completed both, graduating at the top of his class in Ranger School. He was selected to join the elite 75th Ranger Regiment, assigned to B Company, 3rd Battalion. Not long thereafter, while he was a new private first class, B Company deployed to Somalia. In October of 1993, Joel was a combatant in the Battle of Mogadishu, sometimes referred to as the Black Hawk Down Incident. He was awarded the Bronze Star with V device (for valor), Purple Heart for injuries sustained in combat, and the Combat Infantryman's Badge.

He was honorably discharged from the Army in 1995 as a specialist [E-4]. He returned home, and hired on with the Bureau of Indian Affairs [BIA] Police as a GS-1801 patrol officer. [GS stands for Government Series.] After one year, he applied for, and was promoted to special agent GS-1811 criminal investigator. That's the exact same position description as special agents with the FBI, Secret Service, DEA, ATF, etc. Both patrol officer and criminal investigator positions require successful completion of their own specific courses of training at FLETC. Joel went to the former at FLETC-West, located in Artesia, New Mexico, and to the latter at FLETC, located in Glynco, Georgia.

In 2002, Joel applied for a lateral transfer as a special agent to ATF. He was in pay grade GS-11. He was selected to fill a slot in Gulfport, beginning in January of 2003. Uncle Sam paid for his move. He graduated from the ATF Academy, back in Glynco in July. He was 34 years old, married, with two small daughters.

We don't have many Native Americans in Mississippi. A small population of Cherokee Indians do live up in the northeast corner. Considerably more Choctaw live in Neshoba County near

Philadelphia, and also in Lauderdale County on the Alabama border. What I'm pointing out is, Joel was isolated from all Native Americans by living here on the Mississippi Gulf Coast, not just from his own Navaho tribe. However, it didn't seem to slow him down. He's a great fellow, extremely competent, good-natured, and someone you can trust with your life. Joel 'didn't wear race on his sleeve.' He blended in with everybody, and was well-liked.

Joel was excited to go with me. This was his first opportunity to investigate something not situated on the Mississippi Gulf Coast. Besides, nobody had worked a moonshine case culminating in a prosecution since 1982. This could well be the last one ever worked. Very few ATF agents on the job in 2003 had ever even seen moonshine, let alone bust a still. Most of those who had were senior to me or retired. Nobody outside of the Southeast Region had worked a still case since the 1960s. Back then, moonshine cases were ATF's bread and butter. This opportunity would give Joel bragging rights with his peers for years to come.

I told Joel to wear woods clothes and bring a pack with enough to eat for a day or two in case we needed to stake out a still. Include toilet paper, extra socks, poncho, compass, bug spray, space blanket, small first aid kit, sturdy knife, extra ammo, and 50 feet of sturdy cord or rope - basically everything he needed when he was in the Army. Let his wife know we might have to RON [remain overnight].

I said I would do likewise, plus I would bring the case file, a 1:25,000 topographic map of the area, DL photo of our suspect, and in an abundance of caution, my issued pump shotgun. As an afterthought, I told him to bring his issued assault rifle with a couple of extra mags. I said the weaponry was more than we'd normally take going walkabout looking for a whiskey still, but it never hurt to be over-prepared. Finally, I told him to meet me at the office parking lot the next morning at 0600.

That night I told Hannah what I had going on and said I expected to be home late in the evening, but didn't know for sure. At a minimum I would call her to let her know either way.

Now I'm going back down a rabbit hole, but you'll see the connection. I was honorably discharged from the Army National Guard in 1974 after my six-year enlistment expired. That was four years before I was picked up by ATF. My full-time job from 1972 until 1978, was as a county police officer assigned to patrol. In the National Guard, I was an assistant gunner in an M101 field artillery battery. We had six howitzers [tubes], which fired the 105 millimeter HE [high explosive] ammunition, although there were two other rounds available, which I had fired in Field Artillery AIT at Fort Sill: HEAT [high explosive anti-tank], and smoke. Each tube has two wheels with a split trail for towing and setting up. We towed it behind a deuce-and-a-half [M35 6x6, 2-1/2 ton cargo truck].

In AIT, we fired hundreds of rounds, but in the National Guard, we only fired our tubes four times a year, and then with substantially less ammo. Ergo, we weren't nearly as proficient as the Regular Army, but we did our best. At least our battery didn't blow up someone's house like some unfortunate second lieutenant did from another unit elsewhere in the state. In gunnery practice at Fort Knox, he was responsible for a salvo which went wide right of the range limits. The mistake was made in the Fire Direction Control center, where he was in command. (The math was calculated manually back then with slide rules.

No computers.) The salvo demolished the house! Fortunately, this occurred on a Saturday and the family had gone to town shopping. There were no casualties, but what a shit storm! The lieutenant was convicted of negligence in a General Court Martial, dishonorably discharged, and incarcerated for five years.

The segue is this. When I went hunting whiskey stills as a newbie, my woods clothes were my old combat boots and OD green Army fatigues. They are long since worn out, so now I wear my hunting camo. I didn't realize all of Joel's military gear was sand-colored, so he went out and spent money he really didn't have, buying hunting clothes he would never wear again unless he took up hunting. I felt like a jerk. Blue jeans and a work shirt would have been just fine.

Joel's eagerness to comply with vague instructions was in sharp contrast to what one of my FLETC classmates assigned to our parent office in Jackson did. He was a Florida State graduate from Tampa. We went through the ATF Academy in the summer when it was hot. He showed up for his first official whiskey still hunt as a new agent, in December, wearing dress slacks, a white shirt, loafers, and a thin nylon jacket. That was his swan song. Did I mention besides freezing his ass off, he didn't make it through his probationary period? He should have known better.

In training, we learned how to locate, dismantle, and set explosive charges on moonshine stills in the piney woods of FLETC in South Georgia. We also learned how to make moonshine and determine when the fermenting mash was ready to distill. He had to have worn appropriate clothing for training there, or he wouldn't have graduated. I don't remember anything out of the ordinary about him. Anyway, ATF fired him right after they returned from busting the still, basically for exercising poor judgment. He returned to Tampa, never to be heard from again.

No more rabbit holes. Joel showed up a few minutes early. We took my G-Ride. First thing we did was stop by Hardy's for a couple of country ham biscuits and a large coffee. While we ate, I went over my case file with him. Then I took out the topo map and showed him the area where I thought the still was located. Joel studied it carefully with an intensity that only a combat infantryman going into battle does.

I laid out my plan of attack. Touch base with the SCSO and WPD first. Check the courthouse records to see if Merlin Beauchamp had acquired any new acreage. Interview any of his clients who got busted, maybe with someone from the PD or SO to assist since they know the locals and we don't. Stop by the two groceries to see if Beauchamp had been purchasing unusually large amounts of sugar. Then, head out of town and try to locate both his still and stash of unsold moonshine.

The first stop was at the SO. We had a cordial, impromptu meeting with Sheriff Enos L. Ledbetter. He brought in Captain Donald J. West, a solid guy, whom I also knew from my many previous trips up here.

I asked Sheriff Ledbetter how the election went. He replied, "Well, I didn't have no real competition. Chief Enright [WPD] ran against me again but he didn't draw many votes. If his daddy-in-law wasn't on the County Board of Supervisors, he wouldn't even be a county dog catcher."

"Well, nevertheless, congratulations are in order and we salute you, Sheriff.

"By the way, this is my new partner, Joel B. Red Horse. Pretty sure the B stands for badass. He hails from Arizona, where he was a special agent with the Bureau of Indian Affairs. He's also a combat Army Ranger vet with both a Bronze Star and a Purple Heart. He hasn't been told yet, but he'll be taking over for me in this neck of the woods after I retire at the end of the year."

Sheriff Ledbetter smiled. He and Captain West both reached over to shake Joel's hand vigorously and to welcome him aboard. Then Sheriff Ledbetter said, "Gee, Marvin. How many years has it been?"

"25-plus, all here in South Mississippi. A dear friend of mine in Opelousas over in Saint Landry Parish, who used to be the chief deputy, just got elected sheriff. He asked me to be his chief deputy and I accepted. I'm really looking forward to it."

"Well gol darn! Congratulations to you too! We're really gonna miss you too, Marvin. Best wishes. This'll be a fitting way to cap off an illustrious career."

"Thanks. I truly appreciate it, Sheriff. Once I'm gone, you all call Joel. He'll take very good care of you.

"Anyway, I'm sure you all know we're here about Merlin Beauchamp. From what Captain West reported, we understand he's gone back to his wicked ways. Got any information that might help us to send him back on his merry way to Club Fed for a little vacation?"

Captain West replied, "Well to get caught up, Merlin drives a decrepit old green '60 Ford Econoline van with a cracked windshield and a broken left taillight. Rings is shot and it belches black smoke like a forest fire. His oldest boy, Gomer, is his right hand man. Gomer's probably about 45 now. Never been arrested so far as I know. He used to be in the 226th Transportation Company in the National Guard over in Hattiesburg. He done real good there. Made sergeant E-5. Lot of local boys served in it, including me. Gomer makes a living as a pulpwood hauler. Drives an old red Diamond Rio tractor most of the time, but he also has a gray primered '69 Camaro with a black hood that his old lady, Trudy, drives.

"Merlin's been moonshinin' his whole life since he was a boy, and he's gotten pretty tricky selling his product so's he don't get caught. He normally sells it at an old run-down tavern called Uncle Nemo's which caters ta blacks. In fact, all his customers is black. It's over on the old cut-through called Lucedale Road, about six miles west of Wiggins. We can show you where it's at if you all don't know. Howsomever, he has also been known to sell at Lucky Willy's Social Club over on the east side of Highway 49. It's on the north side of town near the intersection of Smith's Corner. It's also a black establishment.

In the past three or four months, we've arrested three, no, make it four shiftless blacks who spend more time imbibing alcohol and fornicating with other men's wives than they do earnin' an honest livin'. Bad as that is, there's a good side to it. They ain't got no money ta pay a fine nor bond outta jail, so whenever we do arrest 'em, they plead guilty and Judge Wilson Roberts sentences 'em to jail for a few months. They ain't hard-cases nor escape risks - they ain't got nowheres else to go, neither - sose we put 'em on the road gang and feed 'em good and give 'em a warm bunk and they do their civic duty by cleaning up litter or mowing grass or painting buildings or whatever else we have that needs doin'. In fact, we got six of them guys on the road gang as we speak. Two of 'em were busted by the PD.

"You're free ta talk ta any or all of 'em, but word'll get back ta Merlin and he'll be harder ta catch. Besides, we done talked to 'em, and ain't none of 'em knows where his still's at."

I responded, "You're probably right. Besides, these fellas know you, and it sounds like you all take pretty good care of 'em. Why would they want to speak to an outsider? You all feed 'em and give 'em meaningful work. We could give 'em a few bucks for information, but they'd probably just turn around and buy more hootch with it.

"Do you all know if Merlin's acquired any property in the past few years that nobody knows about where he could set up his still?"

Sheriff Ledbetter said, "I'm pretty sure he hasn't. He basically lives hand to mouth. You might want to check at the tax assessor's office when you're through here just to be sure. We're probably a little derelict in our lawman duties, because we ain't walked off his property but once since I been sheriff, and we didn't find diddly squat then. That was oh . . . . five or six years ago. You all fixin' ta walk it off?"

I replied, "That's the plan. We certainly came prepared to do that. You got any suggestions? It's been years since I've been out there and walked off his property. Things have probably changed since then."

"Well, probably not as much as you think. Merlin and his old lady, Hilda, still live in that old shack what was his daddy's before him. He's got a redbone and four or five blue tick hounds runnin' around what he hunts deer with. They ain't vicious, but they will stir up a ruckus if they scent you. His kids is all grown up and scattered about, but Gomer and Trudy and their passel of kids live in that old white house trailer with the mint green stripe runnin' across the middle just a quarter-mile down the road past Merlin's driveway. You all plannin' on going in through the woods road off Carter's Road?"

"That's what I thought."

"What about this? Let me know what time you all wanna head over there. I'll get one of my deputies to take you over in one of our work trucks. He can drop you all off and keep on going. That'll help to keep the local CB radio grapevine chatter down was someone to see a strange car driving or parked in the vicinity."

"Great idea. We accept. I don't need the air let out of all four tires, which happened to me over in Greene County a number of years ago. I had to walk three miles each way just to borrow a bicycle pump from the family who owned the still I was hunting for, which I never did find, but do know they had. Anyway, they had a good laugh at my expense. We didn't have any tower coverage for our police radios over there back then."

"Tell you what. I'll loan you all one of our handhelds, but it would be better to set a time in advance when ya think y'all are ready to come out. My deputy will swing by and pick you all up at the drop site. You'll have the radio as a backup if something comes up before then. Use the call sign Stone 28. Folks monitoring on police scanners will think we done hired a new deputy. Ha! The joke'll be on them."

"Sheriff, it's almost 9. What say Joel and I hook up with your deputy over at your garage at 10?"

"Suits you. Suits me. Good luck. By the way, I heard Merlin's got some serious dental issues. He could probably get hisself some new dentures in Club Fed if he got convicted of moonshining again. You all might be doin' him a huge favor if you do catch him."

"Now that's a kind thought. Thanks a million. We'll let you know how this turns out, assuming we don't find ourselves engaged in World War III with Merlin and all his kin and have to call for reinforcements before the pick-up time."

"Merlin ain't no rocket scientist, but I doubt he's dumb enough to try and take on the Feds. At least he never did in the past. Talk to y'all later. Nice to meet ya, Joel. Don't be a stranger. My door is open any time."

"Much obliged, Sheriff. That's a two-way street. Adiós."

- Chapter 3 -
One Last Hurrah

When Joel and I left the SO, we walked straight to the tax assessor's office. Nobody with the last name Beauchamp had acquired any new holdings in the past ten years.

I decided against checking the two grocery stores for large quantity sugar sales. It was too risky. Someone would probably drop a dime on us; however, I did purchase a package of eight hamburgers to bribe Merlin's canine patrol force if it became necessary. Joel laughed like a hyena. Said I was an old softy.

Next, we stopped at a Texaco filling station. Joel refueled while I went to the restroom and urged Mother Nature along. I'm not a bear. I hate doing bear business in the woods. Then we went to the county garage to meet our ride to the drop site.

All during the while we were looking for potential leads, Joel maintained a steady stream of chatter. I'd never known him to be so conversant. Usually he was observant but quiet. I felt us bonding. Too bad I was moving along. It had been a long time since I had a partner who was as close as kin.

Joel thanked me for investing the time to learn his background and provide the SO with a detailed recitation. He knew it was designed to add to his stature with the SO, which would then spread to all the other lawmen here in Stone County.

He asked if I received any awards while I was in the National Guard. I told him yes, but they were very minor. The first was an Expert Rifleman's Badge in basic training, which I maintained throughout my service. (We qualified annually, and you wore whatever you qualified for until the next qualification. They even amended it in pencil on your personnel file every year. The lowest rating was Marksman, followed by Sharpshooter, and topped by Expert.) My other award was the Army Reserve Components Achievement Medal [ARCAM] which I received a month or two before I was discharged. They awarded them to everyone in our field artillery battery with at least four years of service who never got into trouble, or had an unexcused absence for drill or annual training camp. In essence, it was like a Good Conduct Medal, except commissioned officers were eligible, too.

I told him that in an act of vanity, just before my ETS [expiration of term of service], I went to a photographer's studio and had a portrait made standing next to the American flag, wearing my Class A summer khaki uniform with the full medal and expert rifleman's badge. It's hanging on the wall in my office at home, just to the right of my basic training photograph in dress greens. I call them my before and after pictures. A photograph of me in my police uniform hangs to the right of that. They're all for posterity, depictions of when I was a young man full of piss and vinegar. Those days are long behind me now. Middle age has caught up with me, and boy do I know it.

He asked if I received any decorations while I was a cop. I told him the only thing the PD did there was to give you a typewritten citation signed by the chief, which could be suitable for framing, I suppose.

I received four, which were in a file in my desk drawer at home. One was for arresting an armed bank robber as he was fleeing on foot. Shots were exchanged; the second was for saving a woman's life with CPR after her family thought she was dead; the third was for rescuing a dozen or so apartment dwellers in the middle of the night when someone tossed a Molotov cocktail in a window and burned the place down; and, the last was for my participation (along with all our other officers) in the rescue efforts after a tornado wiped out a 100-house subdivision. These were all good deeds, but only the first was because of derring-do when I thought my life was in peril.

Then he asked about ATF and if they have awards. I told him, yes, but not many and they aren't very visible. They have a citation sometimes awarded for valor as I understand it, but I don't know anyone who ever got it. I think it's called the Secretary's Honor Award or Meritorious Service Award. Something like that. Probably the agents who were involved in the Waco incident with the Branch Davidians back in 1993 got it. I've never seen one.

The main award they have is the Albert Gallatin Award. He was the longest serving Secretary of Treasury, and he apparently set the example for statesmanship. (ATF was a Treasury Department agency until sometime after 9-11.) They award this at your retirement if you have 20 or more years of high fidelity service. It's a nice framed certificate, but you only ever see one if a retiree hangs it up in his home. I expect to receive one when I retire.

Then they have two types of fiduciary awards which come with a cheap certificate.

The better of the two is the Quality Step Increase, called the QSI. They call it the gift which keeps on giving. Essentially, it's an immediate in-grade step increase. If you are at the upper end of your pay grade where it's three years between step increases, it's a nice shot in the arm. For example, you could go from a grade 13, step 8, to a step 9, receiving a sizeable bump in pay up to three years earlier than normal. They don't hand out many of those. I never got one.

The more common of the two is the Performance Award. You normally see them right at the end of the fiscal year. If you've had an unusually productive year, they normally give you this award. It comes with a one-time lump sum payment. The first one I ever got was worth $750. The last one was for $2,000.

Working stiffs don't get them all that often. Supervisors get one almost every year. They say 'It's all on the level' but it's not! Go figure. Making a lot of cases in a year or one really significant, newsworthy case is how you usually get one. Being a boss is the other way. It's a whole lot easier and pays much bigger dividends.

Joel listened but didn't comment. Then he said he appreciated me tipping him off to the responsibilities he would inherit once I retired. I replied that Roland had only informed me yesterday, and to keep it to himself because our in-house slacker, Carlos Martinez with 11 years on the job, has been pestering Roland for my territory upon my departure. Everyone in the office knows Carlos is deadwood, and that's why he's assigned the territory he has. You can't flub big cases if they're not in your territory. Like the slugs say, "Big cases. Big problems. Little cases. Little problems. No cases. No problems." Carlos was a no problem kind of guy.

Stone County Deputy Sheriff Harold Eckley was waiting for us when we arrived at the county garage. He was sitting in a white, 1994, Ford F350 crew cab pickup with the standard (non-law enforcement) Stone County emblem on the door, and yellow emergency flashing lights mounted on the roof. This was one of the trucks they used for the local Department of Transportation work crews. We pulled our packs and long guns out of my trunk, and climbed in. Harold handed me a portable Motorola radio with six channels. It was preset to Frequency 2. Soon as we were ready, he took off.

Deputy Eckley wanted to know what time we wanted a pick-up. I told him 4 o'clock. It took about 20 minutes to get to the drop site. He slowed down when we got close. The two-lane blacktop road with no shoulders was absent of other motor vehicles or pedestrians. He stopped just long enough for us to unass the truck and run into the tree line. Less than 30 seconds later he was back on his way. You could say it was a successful clandestine entry. (I've had a couple which weren't.) It took me a minute to reorient myself.

I whispered, "Merlin has 30 acres, but as you can see, there's a lot more than that around here where he could set up. There's a small branch which runs mostly in an east-west direction. (I pulled out the topo map so he could see). You know he has to have water to operate a still, but around here, most moonshiners have a pump and use a black rubber hose from the water source to the still. His house is back over this way (pointing northeast). It's been several years since I've been here. I suggest we find the branch and look for a hose first."

Joel nodded.

"In deference to your Ranger skills, you can lead and I'll follow. Look out for snakes. We have a lot of rattlers around here and some of 'em are pure ornery. I'll let you know if I think we need to search in another direction. And oh, if we come up on any dogs, let's feed 'em to hush 'em up."

I handed him the map, and doubled-checked my bearings with my compass. He did likewise. Then we began creeping through the woods, doing everything possible to be quiet, such as walking flatfooted to avoid making noise by stepping on a dead branch. It was slow going because the woods were thick with scrubby bushes, vines, hidden holes, large stones, and gnats which were a real nuisance. He stopped and put on more Army issue bug repellent. He handed it to me and I did the same. It really helped. The temperature was only in the mid-60s, but the humidity and density of the tangle of growth made it very cloying. If you're breathing in South Mississippi, you're working up a sweat.

He found the branch (for some reason Mississippians refer to creeks as branches) and stopped. We decided to follow it towards the west. Nearly an hour later after no success, I pointed east, and we backtracked and continued past our starting point. Then we found it. We should've gone that way first. We paused for a water break, looking for the best avenue to cross without getting our feet wet while we sipped on water from our canteens. It really sucks stomping around the woods for a day or two in wet boots, and we were doing our best to avoid that.

We followed the hose northeast until we heard a noise not indigenous to Mother Nature. Joel motioned for me to sit tight. I did. He continued north very stealthily, creeping through the woods. In 30 seconds, he was lost to my sight. He returned about 20 minutes later. He whispered, "He's alone. He's got a 12-barrel rig, and he's starting to fill some milk jugs. Looks like he's already filled 10 or 12."

"Great. See any dogs?"

"Nope, but hand me the hamburgers in case they do show up."

I turned over our canine bribes. Then I whispered, "Let's let him run off this entire batch before we bust him. It'll take him a couple of hours. Do you have a good place to watch him without being spotted?"

"Yep. You can watch from the tree-line behind a big rock and some bushes. He doesn't seem to be wiggy. He's in a clearing. You want I should take the first watch?"

"You found it. You get to decide."

"I'll take the first hour. It's 12:25. See you at 1:25. From here, you're about 75 yards south."

"See you then. I won't move up much closer unless I hear a commotion."

"Roger that." Then he left.

I set to, eating my beanie weinies and both of my bologna and mustard sandwiches, washed down with 20 ounces of warm lime Gator Aid. (Got to replace those electrolytes!) I was famished and felt like I hadn't eaten in a week.

Soon it was my time to take up the eyeball. I crouched down, walked, and crawled up behind Joel. He pointed to the growing circle of full moonshine jugs. There were about 50, and equally that many empties. Mervin was hard at it. This was going to be a pretty decent bust. Joel pointed to his watch, signaling that he'd be back in an hour. He left, and I stuffed some Copenhagen between my lip and lower gum. Then I settled in to watch.

By the time Joel returned, the operation had slowed down. Most of the jugs were full and the amount of shine coming out of the condenser had slowed down to a trickle. I motioned for Joel to join me.

Finally all the distillation for today was done. Merlin began putting full jugs into a wheelbarrow and pushing them up towards his house out of our sight. We waited until he had collected most of the jugs. Then I motioned to Joel that it was time to make the arrest. While Merlin was loading more jugs into the wheelbarrow with his back towards us, we stood and began walking slowly towards him. We got within 15 yards. Merlin put the very last jug in the wheelbarrow that it could possibly hold, and then he looked up and saw us. It literally scared the bejesus out of him. He fouled his britches. He wanted to run, but he already knew without a doubt it was hopeless. He was busted. Time to pay the piper.

He sat down on a stump and lit his corncob pipe with a small wooden kitchen match. His hands were shaking. He drew in a few puffs to get it going good and asked, "How long you all been watching?"

Joel replied, "Oh, more'n two hours."

"Can I ask who ratted me out?"

I responded, "Actually, no one, but with the uptick of moonshine flooding the area we decided to check you out first before all of the other known violators since you're the most notorious moonshiner in this area."

"Officer, a man's got to make a living if he's a man. I ain't on the dole and never will be. Look fellers, I ain't gonna run. I know I'm caught. I'll come along peaceable. Please, will you all let me go up ta the house and clean myself up and get me some clean underwear and 'over-halls'. You all done skeert the shit plumb outta me."

"Who's up there now?"

"Just the old lady. She been washin' clothes. She's gonna love this."

I said, "Joel, why don't we walk up and let him do what he needs to do? Once we see it's all clear, I'll stay behind and keep an eye on him. I'll also call the SO for some assistance. Then you can start taking photographs and making an inventory. I'll get them to bring my G-Ride so we can get the rest of our gear. If you can pick up any tower, call your wife and let her know you're gonna be late, but you will be home tonight."

"You got it."

Merlin said, "Officer, you all can use my phone to call home. Cellphones don't work that good around here."

"Thanks, Merlin. We'll take you up on that."

We strolled up to the house. Mrs. Beauchamp was taking the dry clothes off her clotheslines and folding and placing them in pastel-colored, plastic baskets. She took one look at us and said, "Merlin, I done told you this would happen if you got too greedy. Now you done bought yourself another vacation back in that Federal prison in Florida. This time tell 'em you need some new chompers, you hear me? Your teeth is all wore out. Who be you officers?"

Merlin continued into the house to the bathroom. I followed him inside that far. I saw the telephone on the kitchen wall, and raised my voice and told him and his wife at the same time I was gonna make a call. I heard his wife tell Joel, "My name is Hilda. I'm a Beanblossom from the Beanblossoms down the way. Me and Merlin's been married 48 years. He ain't got a fuck left in him, but he still keeps me warm of a night. What are you all doin' with that package of all them raw hamburgers?"

Joel replied, "Nice to make your acquaintance, Miss Hilda. I'm Joel B. Red Horse. I'm also the new ATF agent assigned to this area. My partner's Marvin L. Barnett. He's known Merlin for 20 years or so. We brought the hamburgers for the dogs in case they stirred up a ruckus."

"Here, let me have 'em. Them dogs eat dog food. I'll eat up them hamburgers for ya. That's several days worth for me, especially now that Merlin won't be here to feed at the trough for a while."

Joel handed her the meat. He asked, "Where are the dogs?"

"Our oldest boy, Gomer, done took 'em deer hunting. He won't be back afore nightfall. We could sure use the meat, too. We's nearly out."

While they were getting acquainted, I called Sheriff Ledbetter. I told him of our success and that my car keys were on the front left tire of my car. He agreed to get a deputy to bring it. Then he said, "Besides bringing some deputies to he'p you all out, I'm bringing a reporter and photographer from the *Herald Press.* You don't mind do ya? We could use the publicity and it wouldn't do you all no harm neither, bein' that this is your last hurrah."

"I think that's a swell idea. I never even considered it."

Merlin was all done cleaning himself. He was wearing clean Sears & Roebuck bib overalls and a long-sleeve white shirt buttoned up to the neck. He even buffed his brown boondockers, cleaning off the dust. I said, "Sheriff Ledbetter's coming. He's bringing the press for a photo op. You got time to put on your Sunday clothes or comb your hair if you want to. I'm gonna tell Hilda, too."

"Why for he wanna go an' do that? Me and the old lady don't need our 'pitchers' took for the paper. Dern! That's embarrassin'!"

"You'll have to ask him when they get here. Hilda, you hear that? Want to put on your Sunday clothes for the picture?"

"I believe I will. Comb your hair, Merlin." She quit folding laundry and went in the bedroom and shut the door. A little while later she emerged with her brown hair done up nicely in a bun, wearing a pink and yellow floral dress and a white knitted shawl and some new sneakers. You could tell back in the day she was a real pretty woman. She still had all her teeth and they were white!

In the meantime Joel took photos and began inventorying all the shine. There were 121 full plastic gallon milk jugs, plus 62 full, glass half-pint bottles stored upright in old cardboard longneck beer bottle cases in the shed. It took nearly an hour, but Sheriff Ledbetter, Captain West, Deputies Beaver, Quick, and Eckley all showed up. Eckley was driving the same truck he dropped us off with. The press, consisting of reporter Donald 'Duck' Dobbs and photographer Mary Lou Van Winkle, arrived in a pale yellow, 2002 Volkswagen Beetle with a white plastic daisy standing tall like an anteater's erection (and emission) next to the steering wheel. This was obviously a chick's automobile. Donald Duck looked more like a worn out, rusty, 1978 Ford Pinto with bald tires and burnt rings kinda guy.

The chick, Mary Lou Van Winkle, was quite attractive. She smiled a lot and took dozens of photographs including several with Merlin and Hilda centered in the middle, flanked by Joel and me next to Hilda and Sheriff Ledbetter and Captain West flanked next to Merlin. (What did it cost ATF if the photograph suggested that the SO were the lead agency in the bust?) The three deputies were positioned on the end. The moonshine was artfully placed in front of us. Before she started shooting, Mary Lou insisted that being the guest of honor, Merlin put on a tie, which she helped tuck in under his bib overalls, and straighten his fedora, which was just about as disreputable as Jed Clampett's in the 1960s television series *The Beverly Hillbillies.*

When the newsies were done and on their merry way, and had enough time to be out of earshot, Joel and I retrieved the explosives from the trunk of my car. It included a cardboard box with 24 sticks of 40% dynamite, a small wooden box with checkerboard sectioning to isolate each blasting cap, and a roll of non-electric fuse to blow up the still.

Sheriff Ledbetter rushed over and said, "Marvin, I got a huge favor to ask. The Board of Supervisors and the Stone County Historical Society and I been upscaling the Stone County Museum. They asked me to ask if you could let us put this still in the museum. We don't want his 55-gallon drums. We have some real oak barrels which ain't been used to ferment mash, so they don't have an odor. What say you? This would mean more to us than you would ever know. We're doin' our best to make folks proud of their heritage."

"Just so that copper cooker and coil don't grow legs and walk. There's quite a few folks in this neck of the woods who'd love to have 'em for their own unlawful purposes. Merlin paid a pretty penny for all that copper, not to mention the work involved to make everything exactly the way he wanted it. He's a true artisan in the manufacture of distilling cookers and coils. It deserves to be on display for historical purposes and Merlin should get credit for making it."

"You're so right. If any lowlife ever tried to do something like that, some of those characters who've put so much time and money into the improvement of the museum would no doubt track him down and lynch him - whilst I was out of town down at the Gulf Coast on vacation, of course. You can bet the body would never turn up. Follow me? This moonshine still will be a huge attraction for us."

"I do. Agreed. We're still gonna blow the barrels after we dump 'em. Could you get your deputies to start pouring out the jugs - all except for three for us, which we need for court? Ditto for the cases of half pints. I need three full bottles in a case full of empties."

We shook hands. Then everybody got down to business. Joel placed the charges and blew the drums. He took before and after photos. When we were all done, Merlin hugged and kissed Hilda goodbye. She was silently weeping. I felt kinda bad for her, but she knew how Merlin made a living and all the risks it entailed. Besides, moonshiners never draw much time, and on top of that, maybe he could get his rotten teeth pulled and receive some dentures. The Federal prisons do stuff like that for inmates all the time. Then we were done and said goodbye.

Joel and I brought Merlin back to our office to complete ATF's booking procedures: three sets of inked, and rolled fingerprint impressions; one card for each hand with palm prints and finger tips; one R-84 Final Disposition fingerprint card; plus, eight 35-millimeter mugshots. Joel drafted the the affidavit for the complaint and I approved it. Then we lodged Merlin at the Harrison County Jail.

I called AUSA Dennis Buchholz to give him a heads up regarding Merlin's initial appearance in court tomorrow on our probable cause [PC] arrest. (AUSAs hate PC arrests because they have no control over them. They must either accept the case for prosecution, or dismiss it at the initial appearance, the latter of which, besides both offending the arresting agent and his agency, also counts against the AUSA's conviction stats, which is their true motivator to prosecute. Therefore, to maintain peace, we at ATF only make PC arrests when it's absolutely essential.)

Finally, I called Roland and later he called SAC Woods. I filled him in with the particulars. Then I told him there would probably be an article in the *Herald Press.* He seemed pleased and we rang off.

I looked at my watch. It was nearly 9 o'clock. It had been a fun day. This was Joel's first ATF arrest. He was ecstatic and I was pleased. Besides this possibly being ATF's very last whiskey still case, it meant I now had two of my three pending cases in judicial action.

It was doubtful any of my three defendants would go to trial. Guilty pleas result in lower penalties due to the Federal sentencing guidelines and they all knew it, and so did their court-appointed attorneys. Therefore, I planned to spend the remainder of my time working with Joel to finish up my Elwood case, and if I had any time leftover, we'd move onto his cases. No new cases for this short-timer.

The *Herald Press* article was picked up by the Associated Press. It was in all the regional newspapers. SAC Woods wasn't especially pleased with the 'family photograph' but he did like the positive press. In fact, this did turn out to be the very last whiskey still case ever prosecuted, at least as of now. On my way out the door, I got a $2,500 Performance Award for this case. It was a nice 'pat on the back.' Joel received one for $1,000. I also received my ATF badge, number 1179, in a clear lucite square, as a retirement souvenir.

Before I got too distracted with personal matters, I needed to present my case against Craig F. Elwood, a/k/a Jonah K. Burke, to the Grand Jury. He was indicted on 14 counts of falsifying ATF documents in furtherance of unlawfully purchasing 14 firearms, one count of possessing a counterfeit or fictitious driver's license, and one count of being a felon in possession of a firearm. I was in and out in 20 minutes.

The next day when I received the arrest warrant, Joel and I got our heads together to apply for search warrants for Elwood's apartment and his truck. We went over there to see his apartment, 1604 Harper Street, Unit 2, in Ocean Springs, so Joel could 'get a lay of the land' before putting pen to paper. I had taken scores of photographs of both the apartment and his truck, but nothing is as good as 'boots on the ground'.

We returned to the office to write up the affidavits. I pulled up several from past cases so he would could get a feel for writing 'the Real McCoy'. The one for the truck was easy. The one for the apartment was pretty easy. When I thought they would fly, I took Joel to meet with AUSA Dennis Buchholz. He made some minor corrections, and sent us to see U.S. Magistrate Judge Winthrop K. Hanson. He studied both applications. Then he had Joel, as the affiant, sign both affidavits. Then he signed and put seals on the search warrants.

We returned to the office and met with Roland to schedule the raid. He told us to draw up a raid plan. He would get Special Agents Roger Schenk, Carl Smithers, and Alex Taylor to come help. Roland said he would be there too.

The earliest the government can execute a search warrant is 0600 hours, and the latest is 2200 hours, absent judicial approval due to exigent circumstances. Roland told us to meet at the all night Krispy Kreme Donut Shop in Ocean Springs no later than 0530.

It was a late night and very early morning. We planned the raid early to catch Elwood before he left for work. We were successful in our endeavor. At 0605 we woke up Elwood by banging on his door. Talk about catching someone flatfooted! He was so overwhelmed with surprise that he had been caught, he signed his rights waiver immediately and couldn't be helpful enough. He had eight of the 14 guns he had purchased in his apartment and he took us to them. They were even in the original boxes with receipts! His favorite, a Smith & Wesson Model 29, .44 Magnum revolver, was in the glovebox of the truck. He readily provided the names and addresses of the five felons he made purchases for (and sold guns to).

We were wrapped up by 0730, but Joel and I stayed behind with Elwood so he could complete his signed, sworn statement before we left. (Never stop when you're ahead.) Roger and Carl took the seized guns and Alex drove the seized truck back to the office. Roland went back to make coffee. Joel and I brought Elwood about 30 minutes later.

Joel got another hands-on lesson in processing prisoners. We took Elwood before Magistrate Judge Hanson at 2 p.m. for his initial appearance and arraignment. Because of Elwood's excellent false identification card, AUSA Buchholz told the court he considered Elwood a flight risk. Judge Hanson agreed, and set bond at $100,000 cash or security. Elwood didn't have the dough, so the deputy U.S. Marshals hauled him off to the Harrison County Jail.

Essentially, though it all took place in very short order, I had done about all I could do to mentor Joel. He was a quick study, and I was proud of him. He took over all three of my cases when I said goodbye for the last time as an ATF special agent. It started his new year off with three convictions, plus new spinoff cases against the five felons to whom Elwood sold guns. 2004 should be a productive year for him. Joel would probably receive another cash award at the end of next year.

Thanksgiving came and went. Irvin and his family joined us from Dallas. We all had a lot to be thankful for. As they say, 'a good time was had by all.'

Our house sold the first week in December. Closing was set for Friday, December 26th.

The house we liked in Opelousas had sold, but Marisa found us an even nicer one. It was built in 1918, and sat on a one-acre lot. It was a stately, white clapboard, two-story Victorian house with a wrap around verandah on three sides. It was 2,380 square feet, not including the cellar. The roofing consisted of forest green asphalt shingles, which were only four years old. The trim, including the wooden shutters on all the windows, were also forest green. It had four bedrooms with the master downstairs.

The house had been completely modernized with new wiring and lights, new copper plumbing for the 2-1/2 bathrooms, and a new, modern kitchen. The central air conditioning was only two years old. The house boasted 14-foot ceilings. It was located on LA Highway 182, the main drag heading north out of town. It came with a detached wooden, two-car garage and a large shed. The backyard had a farm fence. The front yard had a white picket fence. The original owner had been the proprietor of the local sawmill. His granddaughter was the last owner. She was a widow, moving to New Orleans to live with her daughter and family.

The house was in move-in condition, plus it was well within our price range. Closing was set for Monday, December 29th. The movers were scheduled to bring our household goods on the 30th. We were both ready to begin our new adventure on time.

- *Chapter 4* -
A New Era

I can't say the move was painless, but it wasn't bad. We obviously weren't a hundred percent operational by New Year's Day, but we were making progress.

The swearing-in ceremony was casual by yesteryear's standards - suit and tie for men and dresses for women, but no tuxedos or ballroom gowns. It was also just for newly elected parish (county) and municipal officials and their families. The public was not invited, but they weren't turned away either, if someone did decide to attend. None did; nevertheless, both the press and the parish had a professional photographer present to record the event for posterity.

Nobody made a windy speech. It was a dignified affair, but not stilted. It didn't last more than an hour, soup to nuts. We were sworn in by the eldest, retired senior Saint Landry Parish Judge, Oscar T. Bergeron III, and blessed by Father Thurman C. Bledsoe of Saint Aloysius Roman Catholic Church. There were discreet alcoholic libations and light hors d'oeurves served afterwards.

Abner Bienville Ladner, Jr. was presented with a framed certificate from the State of Louisiana affirming his newly elected position as Saint Landry Parish Sheriff; a new, laminated identification card signed by Judge Bergeron III as the authorizing parish official; and the new badge he ordered for himself. It was gold-plated six-point star, and it shined like a sunbeam at noon in the desert.

I was sworn in with all the elected officials for one reason only. I was an out-of-stater being appointed as the chief deputy, the second highest position in the sheriff's office. Abner wanted the public to know without a doubt that I had not bypassed any state requirements. The ceremony 'legitimized' it for those who had hoped to receive this appointment. As such, I, Marvin Lloyd Barnett, also received a framed, state-issued certificate, a gold-plated, six-point star badge, and laminated identification card, except Abner as sheriff, had signed mine. Both of our badges were fitted into a customized leather belt clip.

Once the event was over, Abner exclaimed, "Come on. Hoiey up, chu all. Follow me. Ah've got Poppa Bear Choe Landry on standby so we can pick up ahr new vehicles. Chu figure out what chu want?"

"Is a Jeep still on the table?"

"It most coitainly is."

"I think that's what I want."

Hannah and I followed Abner and Marisol in Hannah's car. Poppa Bear seemed excited to see us. He ought to be. The parish did a lot of business with him, as in always purchasing their entire fleet of vehicles from his dealership. Abner selected a 2004, Dodge Ram 2500 super cab pickup, just like his old one, except this year he picked white.

I selected a 2004, two-door Jeep Wrangler, white with a black fiberglass roof. (They didn't make 4-door Wranglers back then.) It had air conditioning, an AM/FM stereo, a V-6 engine, and a 4-wheel drive manual transmission. The seats were gray cloth. The mag wheels were modestly oversized with off-road tires - not like jumbo tractor wheels, but bigger than the standard el cheapo wheels and tires. The Jeep was both appealing to the eye and rugged. It ran like a scalded jack rabbit.

Once we made our selections and were about to go our separate ways, Abner said, "Ah almost fuhgot." He handed me a bright blue, sturdy, hard plastic case with a substantial hole in the handle for locking with a stout padlock (not included). He said, "Dis here is chu new duty weapon, but Ah highly recommend chu carry it off duty too. It's a 9-millimeter Glock G17, Gen 3, wit' a 4-1/2-inch barrel, comes wit' t'ree 17-round magazines. Follow me ta da office and Ah'll get chu some ammo, holster, and everyt'ing else chu s'pose ta have. It's all laid out fah chu. Marisol, why don't chu and Hannah go back ta ahr house and we'll meet chu dere when we get all done? Prob'ly take an ahr."

That's what we did. Abner was excited to get the ball rolling and so was I.

He gave me a set of office keys and took me to my office. It was larger than I had expected, situated directly across the hall from the radio room. A nameplate with my rank and name was already positioned front and center on my desk. That's where all my gear was laid out with military precision, just like an Army SAMI [Saturday Morning Inspection].

Besides the Glock 9 millimeter pistol, my issue equipment included a black polymer, Blackhawk brand holster, and a double ammo pouch (which was a first for me. I've always had leather gear); a handheld police radio with a black leather carrier; expandable metal asp (thumper) with a black canvas carrier; Peerless brand handcuffs with two keys and a Blackhawk polymer case; miniature AA flashlight and black canvas carrier; Remington Model 870HD, 12-gauge, matte finish pump shotgun with an 18-1/4-inch open choke barrel, and a black polymer stock; pistol and shotgun cleaning kits; and uniforms.

The uniforms included three pairs of 511 brand khaki trousers, black 511 brand combat boots with soft soles, six blue pullover shirts, two blue baseball caps, one blue cotton pullover sweater, one blue nylon jacket, and a blue bulletproof vest emblazoned with SHERIFFS OFFICE in yellow (front and back). All the garments and hats, minus the trousers, had the embroidered SLPSO badge.

In addition, he gave me four boxes (50 rounds each) of Federal 9mm, 124-grain copper ball ammo, two boxes (25 each), of Federal 12-gauge shotgun shells in double-aught buck, and four boxes (5 each), of Federal rifled, one-ounce shotgun slugs.

I was impressed, and asked, "How'd you do it? How'd you know all my sizes?"

"Chu gotta wife, don't chu? Dey good for more'n chust cookin'. (Then he winked.) Che told Marisol. Come on. Da Citrus Bowl be on TV soon. LSU is playin' Iowa."

The next four workdays were devoted to getting our units set up with a police radio, spotlight, blue, roof-mounted Visibar, Federal siren hidden under the hood, SLPSO door decals, and a locked rack for my issued Remington, 12-gauge pump shotgun. It held five rounds in the tubular magazine. (I purchased a nylon sling with 15 loops for additional shells, which I filled with buckshot. I also purchased an elastic stock sleeve with five loops, which I filled with slugs. I kept the magazine loaded with buckshot, but no round in the chamber.)

Abner didn't require me to wear a uniform since I was both the chief deputy and sole investigator, but I did anyway. He paid for them; they were high quality; looked good; and besides, everyone knew who I was anyway. Why not?

Abner wore the uniform too, except his shirt was a white, long sleeve dress shirt with the SLPSO badge and his name embroidered on the chest. The baseball hat was optional. You could buy your own beige Stetson. Abner had already selected the authorized beige color and model. He had a contact, so you could buy one at a substantial savings, or you could wear the baseball cap. His only requirement was that you wore one or the other while you were on duty. No bare heads.

Abner wore a Stetson all the time. I bought one too, but mostly I wore the baseball cap. The headrest in the Jeep conflicted a little bit with the back brim on the Stetson, plus if you got in a scuffle, the Stetson might get damaged. I usually wore it for dress up or off duty. I never wore it if I knew I was going to arrest someone.

It didn't take long to learn my job. All criminal incident and arrest reports came to me for review, and assignment if necessary. Also, I investigated all the serious felonies personally. All the misdemeanor arrests, traffic citations, non-criminal incident reports, and accident reports went to Captain Harold R. 'Hal' Hebert (pronounced Ā'-Bear), who was third in our hierarchy as Captain of Patrol. He had overall supervision of every deputy, be he assigned to the road or the jail. That being said, Lieutenant Leon A. Caldwell supervised the jail deputies on a day-to-day basis. He made out their schedule, whereas Hal made out the schedule for road deputies. Hal had been on the SO for 23 years and he was a solid guy. Did four years in the Air Force in the Security Police. Very helpful to me.

It did take me some time to grow accustomed to once again being a local officer. Our jurisdiction stopped at the county line for all misdemeanors unless we were in hot pursuit. We did have authority to make felony arrests throughout the state, but normally that was only done after gaining approval from the other jurisdiction. This was something which I never worried about as a Fed. My ATF badge was good anywhere in the USA.

Another significant distinction between the locals versus the state or federal authorities, is that local law enforcement is on the hook for all crimes committed within it's jurisdiction. That could be anything from a stolen tricycle, dog bite, armed robbery, aggravated rape, or murder. (Thankfully, murders were one crime we had very few of.) Being an officer of the primary law enforcement agency within a parish, we were far more visible and accessible than a Fed in a dark suit. We had significantly more personal contacts on any given day within our jurisdiction. We were not anonymous lawmen. You couldn't 'pass the buck' on a political hot potato because everything within our jurisdiction landed in our lap. As they say, "You da Man!"

Another adjustment was, I hadn't made a misdemeanor arrest since I became a Fed. Feds never get involved in domestic disputes, vandalism, or barroom brawls. They can't arrest an obnoxious loudmouth for public drunkenness, disorderly conduct, or disturbing the peace. They have to walk away. It was nice to once again have this authority. I had six years of local law enforcement experience, but that was 25 years in the past in another state. During the interim, I had largely forgotten about just how close a local officer is connected to the public. Once I made this mental adjustment, I much preferred it over being a secondary source of law enforcement assistance.

Two weeks into my new job and I had my daily routine down pat. Absent anything more pressing, I spent the mornings reviewing reports. Then I went out in the field to follow up on new or pending investigations, and more times than not, investigate the criminal violations myself no matter how minor.

Each complaint received a follow-up.

In many respects, it's easier to investigate felonies than misdemeanors. Nobody has to witness a felony. As an example, if someone defaces a building by spraying graffiti on it, normally that's a misdemeanor violation. Misdemeanors are punishable by up to a year of incarceration in the local jail and/or payment of a moderate fine, usually no more than $5,000. They're classified as minor crimes, not life or death situations. You don't lose your right to vote. Without an eyewitness you are generally SOL [shit out of luck]. Sometimes you do get lucky by catching the culprit with the paint can in his possession. Sometimes a guilty conscience will induce the perpetrator to 'fess up', but usually not. All you can do then is let the victim know the agency is sympathetic, and will notify the beat officer to be on the lookout for someone committing those types of crimes in that vicinity.

I was wrapping my mind and my arms around my new responsibilities with the different parameters (local versus federal) when Abner blew into my office with all the force of a Cat 5 hurricane, but the positive energy of a bottom of the ninth inning, two out, come from behind home run to win the game. It was first thing Monday morning, February 2nd, meaning it was also Groundhog Day.

"What chu got goin' on today, Sunchine?"

"Besides finishing my first cuppa joe? Let me think. Would you believe it if I said I was wondering if Punxsutawney Phil would see his shadow today? Or, how about getting ready to gird myself up in full battle gear to venture forth fighting crime and corruption, tooth and nail, no holds barred?"

"Don't chu worry about all dat. Chu and me got impoitant woik ta do. Chu gotta loin how ta separate da fly chit from da peppah. What Ah'm talking about is peppah. We're on a tight deadline. Put evert'ing chu got goin' on, on da back burner."

"You're the boss. How can I be of assistance, Sheriff?"

"Chu ever ride a horse?"

"A few times, but I'm not Roy Rogers."

"Chu fall off or hurt chuself?"

"No, of course not, but I wasn't going hell for leather chasing The Riddler or Geronimo, either."

"Chu got any cowboy boots?"

"I do. They're a little worn, though. They're Justins, the type with the lower heel and a rounded toe - not the type with the pointy, kicking-cockroaches-in-the-corner toe. They're made for comfort. Not for looking at."

"Dat'll do. No sneakers or flip-flops.

"Da Opelousas Mardi Gras Parade is on Saturday da 21st. Dat's da Saturday befōe Mardis Gras. We gotta cheriff's posse chere. It's mostly ceremonial, but anyone who isn't a reg'lar deputy who's on da posse is a special deputy. We got anywheres between 9 and 15 members of da posse. Dis year we got 13 plus chu and me. We ride in da very front of da parade. It's a big deal. Chu can borrow a horse from Elmer Duplechain, same as me. He got some nice mules, too, if chu prefer dat. I provide da French blue cowboy shoits and red silk scarves.

"Chu eat breakfast yet?"

"Nope."

"Me neider. Let's take a walk over ta Grand-mère Benoit's diner. Ah'll fill chu in on da rest."

We walked down the town square to the corner and found a seat by the window. Grand-mère fed us well. I had French toast with a rasher of bacon and cranberry juice. Abner had scrambled eggs, boudin, grits, biscuits, and orange juice.

He filled me in on all the routine festivities on parade day. I was no stranger to Mardi Gras, having lived in Gulfport and Bay Saint Louis for all those years. Bay Saint Louis was situated halfway between Gulfport and New Orleans, where Mardi Gras is a way of life, just like Christmas or mowing grass. Opelousas was just far enough north and west that I was surprised to learn they had a parade. I shouldn't have been. Most communities in the area with a dense Cajun population have at least one parade, if not their own Mardi Gras krewes and festivals. The Opelousas parade was always scheduled the Saturday before Mardi Gras, so it wouldn't interfere with those planning to make the trek to New Orleans.

The other topic, besides practicing our horseback riding skills, centered around traffic control for the parade. They'd been using the same route for years, so everyone except for Hannah and me had it down pat. That was Captain Hebert's responsibility. Mine was handling any criminal investigations which might crop up. I just needed to pay attention to road closures where traffic was to be rerouted and at what times.

After breakfast, we went over to Elmer's ranch to select mounts and tack, and then to practice riding. Of course Elmer was a lifelong member of the posse. Abner selected the same mare he rode every year. She was all white with a gray mane and tail. She was 15 years old and her name was Molly. I decided on a 7-year-old red mule named Scarlet. Elmer said his granddaughter, Judith, sometimes rode Scarlet in barrel racing competitions, and that Scarlet had amassed quite a few ribbons. Who knew a mule could compete against horses in a race and win? I certainly didn't. I just liked her long ears and the way she looked. She turned out to have a soft ride, too.

Abner used Elmer's old dress tack. It included a hand tooled black saddle with silver conchae, boot cups for stirrups, chest straps, and a fancy bridle. I thought it had a Roy Rogers or Gene Autry or even Hopalong Cassidy look - a little on the pimpish side for my tastes. Using a fancy saddle like that, you should be wearing a pair of nickel-plated Peacemakers with mother of pearl grips, a hand-tooled gun belt with a row of shiny brass cartridges, and wearing baby blue skintight trousers and matching shirt like *The Lone Ranger* on TV. Oh yeah, sterling silver spurs that spin. Ergo, I selected a plain brown saddle and bridle with no gee-haws. Very Clint Eastwood as in the 1992 movie *Unforgiven*. Everyone in the posse used matching saddle blankets with the SLPSO star embroidered on each side.

We rode for more than two hours on dirt roads and paths throughout the area. I had a great time. Abner declared that we'd practice twice a week up to the parade. He said I'd be sore after what we did today and he was not wrong.

Hell's bells! Being a chief deputy was a lot more fun than being a Fed, even if I were carrying an Austrian-made plastic gun which was uglier than a sackful of assholes. However, between a full magazine in the grip plus the two spares, it had 52 bullets (including the one in the pipe). That's more than a full box of ammo, and it shot well, too! I suppose classic beauty isn't everything.

The entire community was pumped up about the parade. I learned that it wasn't uncommon for 60,000 folks to show up. The excitement was infectious.

It was during this time that Hannah landed the perfect job. She got on as the children's librarian at the Saint Landry Parish

Library. It was part-time, Monday through Thursday, from 8:00 to 4:30. Now we both had rewarding, but fun jobs.

It had taken me a month to adapt to the slower pace of life here. It was rare for me to spend more than eight hours a day at work. The commute to and fro was five minutes. We had time to eat our meals without rushing. If you needed to take fifteen minutes to drop your shoes off at a repair shop to get them half-soled, it was okay. Nobody cared or complained that you were abusing the government car at the taxpayer's expense. I could even use it for personal use. Even Hannah liked to ride in the Jeep. Driving it made me feel 20 years younger.

My load of both administrative and criminal paperwork had been cut by at least half. Not only that, I'd been here just long enough to see that the local court was both judicious and fair in dispensing justice. It was an absolute marvel in today's world. The guilty were reasonably punished and the innocent were exonerated. I had time to devote to parade prep and still do all my criminal work. Hannah and I were both making friends in the community. In other words, we were 'living large'. We were happy.

Parade prep was extremely important to many residents. Any business or social entity could sign up to enter a float. They were built in someone's garage or barn. Most of them were small enough they could be pulled by a tractor or 3/4 ton pickup truck. The Saint Landry Parish High School Marching Band was busy working on some new music. The Opelousas Volunteer Fire Department planned to showcase their trucks. Alpha Company, 2nd Battalion, 163rd Quartermaster Brigade of the Louisiana Army National Guard located in Opelousas, planned to march in full battle gear. (Quietly, they were always looking to recruit some new troops. It was a given that most rural boys and young men are fascinated with guns and things which go bang.) The list of parade participant's kept growing.

Nearly everyone in Opelousas and most of Saint Landry Parish at large were preparing for the big day. That included Abner and me. We rode horses at least twice a week. I was getting into it. When I was a kid, I always wanted to be a cowboy. It occurred to me that Hannah and I could turn this into a hobby if she were so inclined. Elmer Duplechain rented horses and mules as a side job to folks who like to ride. That could be us.

In the back of my mind, I kept thinking about Derby Day when I was a cop. We worked our asses off. I don't think I ever went through a Derby without making at least one arrest. I hoped this would be more relaxed.

The universe of Saint Landry Parish was up and at 'em by 0530 Parade Day. There were 131 entities in the parade, including 91 floats. I never considered that the Louisiana State Police would have a float, nor the Louisiana Department of Wildlife and Fisheries. There were many other surprises, too. For one, this was the most family-friendly Mardi Gras Parade I had ever witnessed. No drunks yelling, "Hey lady! Show me your tits!"

The parade chairman, Isabelle Croft, signaled to Sheriff Ladner it was time to begin. He was 'the tip of the spear' up at the front of the posse, leading the parade. The honor was all his. He nodded his head, clicked his cheeks, and Molly stepped forth. The parade began regally with the posse 'strutting its stuff'. I thought we all looked resplendent in our bright blue satin cowboy shirts with mother-of-pearl snap buttons, red satin scarves, identical beige cowboy hats, shiny star badges pinned to our chests, and law enforcement hardware strapped to our waists. I could see Hannah snapping pictures with her 35 mm camera and extended lens. This was the first time either one of us were in a Mardi Gras Parade.

It took nearly two hours for us to walk the route. Then I circled back and watched the rest of the parade from my mount. What a hoot!

There were some minor hiccups throughout the day, but only one arrest, regarding a reveler who had one too many Hurricanes or Squalls and got loud, obnoxious, and rowdy. He was from Baton Rouge. Cost him two nights in jail and a hundred bucks fine. That was the sum total of law enforcement issues until much later in the day.

Hannah and I had just returned home. We were changing clothes, getting ready to relax with a few libations and a charcoal-grilled steak for supper. Then I received a call from Deputy Henri LeBlanc, a solid patrolman working the afternoon shift. He said he had responded to take reports of five separate house burglaries in Eunice (located on US Highway 190 on the west side of the county). 'While the cats were away (at the parade) the mice did play.'

The fun times were over. Time to get to work. This is what they pay me for. I wouldn't have it any other way.

- Chapter 5 -

A Major Crime Spree

The five houses were all on the same dead-end street. I met Henri at 1014 Robert [pronounced Rō'-Bear] Lane. A white, 1995 Ford F-150 and a blue, 2000 Ford Crown Victoria were parked in the driveway.

This was a blue collar working man's neighborhood. The houses were all small, 60-year-old, single-story clapboard houses with a single car asphalt driveway and a matching, unattached single car garage. Almost all the houses were in good repair. Most were painted white. The homeowners on this street took pride in their little slice of the American Dream. Several houses were flying the American flag. Two were flying the purple and yellow LSU flag. Would you expect anything less? You better believe this was in the heart of Bengal Tiger country!

Henri introduced me to Mr. and Mrs. Oscar T. Rowan. Mrs. Rowan's first name was Beulah. He was 41. She was 36. Their two kids, Rachel, age 9, and Willy, age 7 were also present, along with Bud, their blue tick hound. After introductions, I said, "Show me what happened."

Oscar said, "Come inside."

We went inside. I could see where the door jam had given way with force by a hard flatfooted kick. You could see the scuff mark but no discernible tread. As soon as I entered, I noticed the wooden-framed, glass doors on the oak gun cabinet in the living room were ajar. It didn't have a lock. Just a latch.

Oscar pointed at the empty cabinet and said, "They took my

guns. All of them. One of them was passed down to me by my grandfather. It was an LC Smith, 16-gauge, side-by-side. Chief, that gun was worth at least a thousand bucks. It was my most expensive, and my most precious. I seldom shoot it because of its value to me as a family heirloom. That's how important it is to me.

"Then they took my Remington Model 1100 12-gauge. That's my everyday bird gun. It's probably worth $200. Then they took my Marlin Model 336 .30-30 lever-action. Depending on where I hunt deer, I use it. Also worth about $200.

"They also got my Winchester Model 70, bolt-action .30-06, with a Redfield 3x9 variable scope. Worth about $500 altogether. I use that deer hunting when we're out in the plains. Also my Savage single-shot .22 caliber rifle. I got it when I was 12. I don't even know if it had a model number. It's probably not worth 50 bucks today, but it's worth a whole lot more than that to me. Of course they took all the ammo. That in itself is worth probably $150. I'm sick to my stomach!"

"Do you have the serial numbers of the guns, or any photographs?"

"Yep. I got all the serial numbers. I've got plenty of hunting pictures with most of the guns. The one with my grandpa and the LC Smith is probably at least 30 years old."

"Good. Pictures are helpful for those who wouldn't know an LC Smith from a refrigerator. Was anything else taken?"

"Nope, but what they stole were my most precious, personal, material, possessions. Hell! Why couldn't they have stolen my TV or truck? I could replace them without giving it another thought."

"Do you have insurance?"

"Sure do. The loss for firearms is capped at $500, but I don't want their stinking money! I want my guns back!"

"I don't blame you. Do you have any idea who could have stolen them? You know, someone who's shady and knew you had 'em?"

"No. Sorry. Of course all my neighbors and hunting buddies did. It wasn't a big secret. Everyone here's a gun owner, and most of them are hunters. If I had any idea, I'd run you right over to their house right now."

"Understood. Henri, do you have all this information in the police report?"

"You bet."

"Mr. Rowan, we will do all we can to catch the thieves and return your guns. Wait a little bit before reporting this to your insurance company. If you accept their money and we recover your guns, the insurance company owns them. Understand? I'm really sorry this happened to you."

"Thanks, Chief. Accepting a pay-out from the insurance claim would be like getting robbed again. You can't win. If I hear anything that might help, I'll give you all a call."

"That would be most appreciated. Thank you."

Next stop was at 1017, catercorner across the street. Henri introduced me to Mr. and Mrs. Antoine G. and Hélène Dubois. He was 59 and she was 57. Their black and white pit bull named PeeWee was present as well. Gain of entry was the same as it was for the Rowans' house. After introductions I asked, "Could you all show me what happened?"

Mrs. Dubois burst into tears. She led us into the kitchen. The refrigerator, stove, and dishwasher were obviously missing. She exclaimed, "Look what they did! Just last week Antoine bought me all new appliances - oven, cooktop, fridge, dishwasher, and microwave oven. They were all white enamel, matching GE. Exactly what I wanted. Got them from D'Iberville Appliances downtown. I hadn't even learned how to use all of them! We haven't made the first monthly payment yet! I can't even cook Antoine's supper tonight! We have to go over to our daughter's house."

"Did they take anything else?"

"We checked the house. So far as we can tell, the answer's no. Chief Barnett, we paid over $1,800 for all this!"

"Do you all have insurance?"

"Yes, from Elton Moreau. He's got the Eunice All State Insurance Agency downtown. I called him. He said to come see him Monday morning and he would take our claim and write us a check. Problem is, we have $500 deductible so we'll have to make up the difference. I'm just heartbroken."

"Mr. Dubois, do you have any idea who could have done this?"

"Not exackly. Ah dribe a bread truck fah Bunny Bread. Hab fah 17 yeahs. Mah route takes me all t'rough dis region - Saint Landry, Acadia, Evangeline, Allen, Beauregard, and Jefferson Davis Parishes. Lotta good folks dere, but trut' is, in Ville Platte, over dere in Evangeline Parish, dey got a rotten bunch of t'ieves, chop shop specialists, fences, boiglars, t'ugs - chu name it.

"Dey's run by a old man name of Noé Arceneaux. Gotta 50-year-old, run down, doity white, concrete block auto soivice garage wit' a dozen or so chunk cars in da lot. It's called Noé's and it's on LA Highway 10, chust west of Ville Platte before chu get ta Vidrine. He's got seben or eight convicts woiking for 'im - Darnell Guillory, Claude Martinez, Delphin Somebody-or-Udder and some udders whose names Ah don't know.

"Noé is da top crime lord in dis neck of da woods, but he's protected. See, his uncle is Odette Arceneaux, who's da Evangeline Parish Coicuit Court chudge. Da biggest catfish in da pond. Cheriff Pascal Rousseau hates Noé's guts, but he hab ta tread lightly. Da rumor is, so long as Noé and his band of t'ugs don't commit no crimes in Evangeline Parish, Cheriff Rousseau looks da udder way. If somet'ing must be done, den he normally calls LSP [Louisiana State Police] ta woik da case."

"Thanks for the insight, but the thing is, they had to have a panel truck to steal all your appliances, and you're only the second victim I've spoken with so far."

"Dat's true, but dat's w'at Ah been telling chu. Noé's got da men and da trucks ta pull dis off, and da market ta fence 'em in."

"I think you may be right. I'll look into this, but keep this to yourself, huh? I don't want to tip my hand, and I certainly don't want you to face any reprisals."

"Ah appreciate dat Chief. Ah really do. Dey don't even know who Ah am, but dey better keep dere distance. Me, Ah was an 11-Bravo [rifleman] in da 101st Airboine Division in Vietnam. Dey made me da M-60 macheen gunner in mah squad due to mah size. Ah wuz a liddle bigger dan da udder guys. Dat meant Ah was trained wit' da Colt .45 pistol too, and Ah carried one ever' single day Ah was over dere. Ah chot expoit wit' it. Ah don't hunt much anymōe, but Ah still got mah old 12-gauge H&R chotgun from when Ah wuz a young man. Surprised dey didn't steal it, but maybe it wudn't good enough for dem.

"Ah do still have dat Army .45, w'ich somehow managed ta find it's way all da way from dere to chere in Louisiana. Dey said it wuz lost in action. Ah got a conceal carry poimit, and Ah carry it wit' me ever'day wit' a loaded spare clip. If one a dem try ta do me or mah fambly harm, Ah will send dem straight ta Hell, so he'p me God! Same as Ah did more gooks dan Ah could even count. Dat M-60 macheen gun didn't axe no querstions nor take no names when da chit hit da fan. It chust do its chob, like me."

"I have no doubt. Thank you for your service, Mr. Dubois.

"Henri, did you get the model numbers and serial numbers from all these appliances?"

"Sure did, Chief."

"Good. Mr. Dubois, we will do all we can to recover your appliances and to arrest the culprits. I appreciate your insight and confidence. We will let you know if we hit pay dirt."

"T'anks, Chief. If Ah loin anyt'ing else, Ah'll let chu know."

"Appreciate it.

"Henri, who's next?"

"Over here at 1021, two doors down."

Henri introduced me to Mr. Joel S. and Mrs. Blanche Auguste. He was 36 and she was 35. I also met their three children, Ernie, age 10, Clarice, age 9, Buster, age 7, their beagle, Fatso, and their cat, Jennifer.

I said, "Tell me what happened."

Mr. Auguste replied, "You see that area along the outside of the driveway up near the garage where the grass is worn off and where those two ruts are?"

"Yes."

"That's where I back in my work trailer every night when I get off work. It's a white, metal, 8x12-foot, hard side trailer, which I keep double-locked with two padlocks. I'm a finish carpenter by trade. Everything I need to do my job is in that trailer - two table saws, electric nail guns, planer, sanders, measuring instruments, hand tools, extension cords, variety of wooden boards, router, workbench, stains, brushes, cleansers, shop vac, you name it. If you've seen any type of carpentry tool in Home Depot, I have at least one in there.

"Someone hooked it up and drove off with it while we were at the parade. My whole livelihood was in it. I couldn't even begin to estimate the loss - at least $12,000 for the trailer and $15,000 in tools and supplies. Maybe more. I'm in the middle of a home restoration - I'm just one tradesman involved - but I can't even go to work Monday. You think my old '84 Dodge work truck has enough room in the bed to carry all the stuff I need? Not hardly. Besides, I'm still making payments on the trailer."

"Mr. Auguste, did the trailer have your company name or logo painted on it anywhere?"

"Nope. Just plain white. It was only a year old."

"How about anything which would make it easy to identify?"

"Well, Ernie is the LSU fan-in-chief here. He put a small LSU Tiger decal on the bottom right side of the rear bumper."

"That'll help. Have you got any idea who could have taken it?"

"My best guess is the same sons a bitches who stole all my neighbors' stuff. Other than that, no. And before you ask, yes I was insured, but what I'll get will only cover about half of my loss."

"We'll do our very best to find it for you. If you can wait at least 'til Tuesday to start replacing items, maybe we can find it for you and save you some money."

"You have absolutely no idea how much that would mean to us."

"Well, we'll do our very best. Guess we need to head down to your neighbor, Mrs. Caldwell's house. We'll be in touch."

"You bet. Take care. We're keeping our fingers crossed."

Next stop was at 1024 at the Mrs. Naomi A. Caldwell residence. She was a 78-year-old widow woman. Henri knocked and she let us in.

Henri said, "Miss Naomi, this is Chief Deputy Marvin Barnett. He's here to learn about your burglary."

"Welcome, Chief Barnett. Could I entice you all to drink a cup of coffee and have a slice of pecan pie with me?"

I replied, "That would be very sweet of you."

She led us to the kitchen where we took seats around her wooden kitchen table. Once we began eating, I asked, "Miss Naomi, tell me about your burglary."

"Well, I must have left the door unlocked by accident. My daughter and her family stopped by and took me to the parade. We had such a lovely time. Chief Barnett, I saw you up there with Sheriff Ladner leading the procession! My, didn't you all look fine in your bright blue shirts and white cowboy hats. I'd have never imagined you would be here visiting with me the very first day I ever laid eyes on you."

"Thank you, Ma'am."

"Anyway, they brought me home, and at first I didn't notice anything. My departed husband, Walter B. Caldwell, Junior, was somewhat of a numismatist. He had a very nice coin collection. His interest was in Indian head pennies, wheat pennies, and buffalo head nickels. He had at least two from each year they were struck. Some years ago, he took them to a numismatist shop on Royal Street in New Orleans, where they appraised the collection at $3,000. That was back in 1984, I believe. Anyway, they were mounted and framed, and hung right up there next to that curio cabinet. If you look carefully, you can see a slight fading on the wall paper where they hung."

"I do. Do you have insurance?"

"Yes, but it wouldn't begin to cover the true value of those coins."

"Just what I thought. Is anything else missing?"

"I don't think so. Wait a minute! Let me see if Walter's revolver is missing. Be right back."

She returned in less than a minute, holding a well-worn, reddish-brown leather cartridge belt full of brass .44-40 cartridges with an Army cavalry-style holster with a flap, housing a blue steel, Colt Peacemaker with a 5-1/2-inch barrel and real ivory grips. She handed it to me to examine. It was very well preserved. I could smell the fine coating of gun oil and the leather wax. What a magnificent specimen of Mr. Samuel Colt's most famous firearm!

She said, "I would have died if they had stolen this. Walter was from Laredo, Texas. His daddy, Walter B. Caldwell, Senior, was a Texas Ranger for 34 years. Walter didn't move here until after the war (which she pronounced wō'wah) when he was discharged from the Army. I met him at a dance at Camp Claiborne in 1943. We courted while he was in training there. He asked me to wait for him, and I said I would. I was 17 and he was 21. He looked so dashing in his uniform! He was a sergeant in the 3rd Armor Division. Was awarded a Purple Heart, too. That's his photograph on the mantel standing next to his tank. That photograph was taken in Normandy after D-Day. We were married on November 13, 1945."

"You must be very proud, Miss Naomi. Thank goodness they didn't steal Mr. Caldwell's revolver.

"Okay. We will get to work on Walter's stolen coin collection right away. We will be in touch. Thanks for the coffee and pecan pie. It was first class."

"You are very welcome Chief Barnett and Deputy LeBlanc. Stop by anytime you all are in our neighborhood. It's always nice to see our lawmen."

The final stop was at 1029. This was the Mr. Colin B. and Mrs. Monique Reese residence. He was 26 and she was 24. After introductions, Mr. Reese said, "Thanks for coming out in person today, Chief Barnett. We saw you in the parade. Sorry to interrupt the rest of your day off."

"Thanks, Mr. Reese. It's all part of the job. Sorry we had to meet under these circumstances. What all did these scoundrels steal from you?"

"They got my 2003 Harley Davidson Road King. It's bright yellow. I had it covered under a tarp in the garage but the outline was unmistakable. We went to the parade in my wife's Camaro.

"I'm one of the two full-time technicians in the Army National Guard unit here. We're the 223rd Military Police Company. I'm an E-6 (staff sergeant) squad leader when we drill, and basically one of the two full-time 'shoe clerks' who keep us operational during the rest of the month. Monique is an elementary school teacher in Church Point. She commutes in her Camaro. I commute to the National Guard Armory here on my Harley. We don't have any other vehicles, so we're kind of in a bind. We've never had any problems on this street before. Henri can confirm that, can't you?"

"You got that right. This has always been a quiet neighborhood. Chief, Colin and I've known each other since grade school. We were both on the 1994 Regional Championship

Football team here in Eunice, and I served with him for eight years in the 223rd."

I responded, "That's quite a distinction here, smack dab in the middle of football country. I know you're both very proud and I don't blame you. Also, just so you know, I did my time in the Army National Guard too, back in the Dark Ages. My unit was a 105-millimeter Field Artillery Battery, so Colin, as a fellow National Guardsman, I am very simpatico to your loss. Henri, you got all the particulars on the motorcycle in your report, right?"

"I do."

"Good. Mr. Reese, we are going to do everything we can to recover your bike. If you have a color snapshot of it we can have, that will help. I know what Harley's look like, but I wouldn't know a pan-head from a knucklehead. If they don't change the color before we locate it, it should be easy to identify from a hundred yards away. Don't lose hope yet. We will be in touch."

"Thanks, Chief. Really appreciate everything you all do. Don't be a stranger, Henri."

Monique ran up and handed me a great color 35-millimeter shot of the bike.

As we were returning to our units, I told Henri to meet me at the Texaco filling station. Henri bought a Pepsi and I bought a bottle of water.

I said, "Henri, Mr. Dubois gave us a huge lead. I don't want that information leaking out just yet. How long have you been on the SO?"

"Three years."

"Have you always been in Patrol?"

"Yes, once I graduated from the Police Academy."

"What's your work schedule for the next four or five days look like?"

"Off tomorrow and Monday. Work afternoons Tuesday through Saturday."

"Do you have any other obligations like a part-time job or college classes, or watching the kids while your wife's at work?"

"No Sir. I graduated from LSU before I joined the SO. Got a bachelor's degree in law enforcement. I have a fiancé. Her name is Misty. No kids. Just a dog named Goofy. No part-time jobs."

"You wanna work this case with me? I think we can resolve it in a few days. It would mean putting in some extra hours without extra pay. It's not an obligation. I fully understand if you need to take care of other matters."

"I'm in, Chief. Whaddaya need?"

"Great. I'll run this by Sheriff Ladner later today. You touch base with Captain Hebert, too. As you already know, we don't have any true undercover vehicles. What type of POV [personally owned vehicle] do you have?"

"A silver, 1999 Chevy, 1500 Silverado standard cab, blue interior, with a short bed."

"Perfect. Mine is a 1986, faded mint green, Dodge D150, standard cab, probably a little more the worse for wear than yours, but no dents or rust. You live here in Eunice?"

"Yep."

"Let's drive over to your house. Leave our units and take your truck to Ville Platte. When we get ready to go, I'll call us both out of service on a special project."

"What will we do in Ville Platte?"

"Check out Noé's garage. See if we can spot any of the stolen items without getting caught. Also log in vehicles which appear to be in use by Noé and his band of thieves. Maybe spot some of the villains so we know what they look like next time we see them. Anything else which comes to mind once we get there."

"Need me to change into civies?"

"Probably not. It's starting to get dark. Maybe if it's not dark enough, just take off your badge. We should be back within a couple of hours. This sound okay to you?"

"Right as rain, Chief."

"Good."

It was dark by the time we found Noé's business. The address was 10045 LA Highway 10, Ville Platte. Everything was dark inside the building, all locked up tighter than a crypt in a mausoleum. There was one outside pole light in the front parking lot. The back lot was protected by a six-foot tall chainlink fence. It looked like Mr. Auguste's trailer could be parked back there, pulled in just a few feet to the right of the building inside the fence. I started to have Henri drop me off so I could see for sure, but I noticed two junkyard dogs roaming around behind the fence.

I said, "Did you see a house nearby?"

"Nope."

"Me neither. Good. Take me back to town. We passed a MacDonald's. I need to buy a sack of hamburgers."

"What for? You hungry? I know a better place."

"Not me. To feed those dogs. I want to creep up and see if I can ID the trailer. If so, I'll take some photos. If it's Mr. Auguste's, these photos will get us a search warrant. I'll work on it tomorrow and get the judge to sign it. We'll be back first thing Monday morning to execute it. That trailer should give us enough probable cause to get inside the garage and search it. If all I can get is a warrant for the back lot, the garage should be open for business, so we'll have to rely on 'plain sight' inside the building until we spot something we know is stolen. We'll call that into the judge for a verbal warrant. All we need to find is one stolen item in the building, and then 'we'll be in like Flynn.' We can make probable cause arrests on everyone there for being in possession of stolen property, especially if we recover the stolen guns. If it's true that they're all convicted felons, we can send all of them 'up the river'. This could wind up being a really big case."

"What about the local sheriff?"

"We can't pull this off without Sheriff Ladner on board. His presence alone will either stiffen up Sheriff Pascal M. Rousseau's backbone, or put him in a blind rage. If that happens, we call the Captain of Troop I and get some state troopers to assist. One way or another, we raid Noé's garage as soon as it opens for business Monday morning 'before the loot sprouts wings and disappears.'

"This how you all did things in ATF?"

"Very similar."

"That must've been a great job."

"I loved it, but I love this job too. I was a patrolman on the Jefferson County Police Department in Louisville, Kentucky, for six years and change. There, all the sheriff has is the jail, courtroom security, and collecting taxes. Maybe serving the occasional civil process or arrest warrant. We had the same jurisdiction as you have here, except we didn't make arrests inside the city limits unless we had to. We covered everything outside of the city limits. Besides, the city had 800 officers and we only had 400. The really sweet part was, we made more money than the city.

"I enjoyed working there too, but I jumped ship to make more money with the Feds. The job offer came with me paying for my own move to Gulfport, with only a very slight chance I'd ever get back to Kentucky. That's usually the way the Feds do it. You almost always have to move, and sometimes it's to a great big city like New York or Los Angeles.

"I was lucky. They offered me a choice of Gulfport, Jackson, or Miami. I jumped on Gulfport. I knew I was one of the lucky ones, especially when I went to the ATF Academy in Georgia. At least half of the guys were in places I'd never want to live - Chicago, Detroit, Philadelphia, Atlanta, etc. You get the idea. 'The grass isn't always greener on the other side of the fence' so 'be careful what you wish for'.

"If you have an itch to go Federal, come see me. Maybe I can help. If you like living here in your hometown, about the most you could hope for would be an assignment in New Orleans, Shreveport, or maybe Baton Rouge, and that would probably be with the U.S. Marshals Service. They're a great agency, but to get hired by them, you usually have to have a hook on the inside."

"I appreciate your insight, Chief. I don't really have that wanderlust. That was a major consideration for me when I went into the National Guard instead of joining the Army, because the enlistment in the Guard was for eight years! I just ETSed [expiration of term of service] two years ago. It enabled me to serve both my state and the nation for the most part right here in Louisiana. We only got deployed once while I was in, and that was for Hurricane Floyd over in Cape Fear, North Carolina. We were gone about six weeks. That was it. I'm fascinated by your law enforcement career, and I certainly appreciate your insight."

"I'm happy you won't be leaving us anytime soon."

I bought four hamburgers and we returned to the garage.

Henri parked in the shadows of the front parking lot, concealed between two junkers. I got out with my flashlight, camera, and sack full of burgers.

The dogs started to kick up a ruckus before I even approached the fence, so I unwrapped the burgers and tossed them eight or ten feet deep into the lot. They ran over to wolf down the food, and from then on, we were semi-friends only separated by the Berlin Wall, except it was chain link instead of concrete. The dogs shut up. I squatted down to get a closer look at the trailer. It had the LSU Tiger sticker on the right rear bumper! I snapped six photos and looked deeper in the lot. What do you know? A stake bed truck with some white appliances in the bed was parked towards the other side of the lot. I took more photos. Then I returned to Henri's truck and we headed back to his house.

En route, he asked, "How can I help you tomorrow?"

"Well, it's up to me to write the affidavit and get the warrant signed. Also to get Sheriff Ladner and Captain Hebert on board. What I'd like you to do is check on this garage once in the morning and once in the evening. Hopefully they won't be back until Monday. Draw me a diagram of the building and lot so we can brief the deputies who will be involved in the raid."

"Won't Evangeline SO be involved?"

"I certainly hope so. They won't need a schematic, but our guys, or LSP if that's who we have to use, will appreciate it, having never been here before."

"Roger that. Consider it done."

- Chapter 6 -
Lining Everything Up

It was past 8 o'clock when I returned home. Hannah had baked the potatoes and made the salad earlier. She had also been nipping on the Mondavi Cabernet Sauvignon in the fridge. I poured myself a splash of Wild Turkey 101, and started the charcoal fire. The steaks turned out perfectly. We cleaned up and sat out on the back patio getting mellow and watching all the stars. A few even twinkled. I lit up an H. Upmann Maduro Churchill cigar, enjoying Hannah's company and allowing the cares of the world to drift away in the aromatic smoke and the taste of premium sour mash bourbon.

I told her all about my afternoon. Then I remembered to call Abner! I interrupted one of the West Coast college basketball games on TV he was watching in his man cave while he imbibed on his frosty Miller Lites. He 'didn't have a dog in the fight' because it was not football, and it wasn't LSU or the Saints, so he didn't care very much whether he was interrupted or not.

"Why chu boddering me while Ah'm busy painting mah fingernails? Dey ain't had time ta dry yet. Chu ought ta be gettin' chu some poontang and leabe me alone."

"That's next order of business, Abner. You need to do the same."

"How chu know Ah ain't already done dat?"

"Touché.

"Hey, we got something really big going on and you need to know."

"What's dat? I'm all ears."

"True. You're always all ears, just like Bugs Bunny."

"Wiseass."

"Henri LeBlanc called me right after I got home from the parade. He had just taken five separate dwelling house burglary reports from the same block in Eunice. Seems like everyone on that street had been to see our parade. He took me to each house, and I interviewed all the victims. The loot consisted of guns, new appliances, trailer full of carpentry machinery and tools, a coin collection worth at least $3,000, and a Harley Davidson motorcycle. You still listening?"

"It's gettin' real hard ta hear chu because mah head is boilin' wit' da steam comin' outta mah ears. It's makin' too much noise in mah head. What did chu find out?"

"Well, one of the victims is a bread truck driver who covers all the parishes around that area. He said there's a local crime lord named Noé Arceneaux, who owns an automotive garage in Ville Platte. All of Arceneaux's employees are supposedly convicted felons. He gave me three names - Darnell Guillory, Claude Martinez, and another dude named Delphin LNU [Last Name Unknown].

"Anyway, Arceneaux's uncle is Odette D. Arceneaux, who's the circuit court judge in Evangeline Parish. He protects Noé. Allegedly, Sheriff Pascal Rousseau has a deal with Noé Arceneaux that he will leave his operation unmolested so long as all his thieving occurs anywhere except for in Evangeline Parish.

"So, today Henri and I rode over to Ville Platte in his POV. We located the garage. It's at 10045 Highway 10. It was closed and nobody was around. I sneaked up and took a look inside the fenced-in back lot. I positively identified the stolen carpentry trailer because of a tiny LSU sticker on the bumper. I also saw a stake bed truck with some white appliances in it. Of course, I couldn't be sure they're the stolen appliances, but I bet they are. I took half a roll of photographs.

"I plan to write the affidavit for a search warrant and get it signed tomorrow. Henri's off tomorrow, but I told him to make a pass-by in the morning and again in the evening, just to make sure the LSU trailer is still there. You can see it from the street.

"My idea is this. You and I and a half-dozen deputies, to include a couple who work in the jail, meet at 0600 Monday morning. The jail deputies drive the prisoner van and take a truckload of leg-irons and handcuffs to haul back arrestees. We stage them at the Flying J Truck Stop at I-49 and LA Highway 10, except for one unmarked car to watch the shop. That plum assignment should go to Henri.

"You and I go together to meet Sheriff Rousseau. You work your sheriff-to-sheriff charm to get him on board; allow him to save face; receive all the credit for the bust if he's not too scared. Otherwise, we do it alone or with LSP. If we're lucky, we'll recover everything AND bust the thieves. We can at least charge them with receiving stolen property. Also, once we have everything wrapped up, we should get the local press out there to take photos. You could make a joint press release if Sheriff Rousseau's on board. 'Turn chicken shit into chicken salad.' We give them a huge inside story wrapped in a fancy box with a big red bow. Let the public see that their sheriff's office is working around the clock to keep them all safe.

"Whaddaya think?"

"Ah t'ink chu're wort' ever' penny Saint Landry Parish pays chu, Marvin. Ah can't remember da last time we hadda big case like dis, or even da last time when Cheriff Neicase made a press release. People will sit up and pay attention. Ah'm 'all over dis like white on rice.' Chu goin' ta da office tomorrow before choich or after?"

"Probably about the time it starts. I got a boatload of stuff to do."

"See chu dere. Good night."

"Good night, Sheriff."

The first thing I did Sunday morning at the office after making coffee was to make myself a personal file with copies of all five item numbers. [Most law enforcement agencies in Louisiana refer to their incident or crime reports as item numbers. Each report, or item, has it's own distinct number. Usually item numbers begin with the last two digits of the year - in this case 04 - followed by a hyphen, then however many 0s the agency thinks it needs before beginning with one, and numbering sequentially for as many numbers as it takes until the end of the year. The radio room, sometimes referred to as dispatch or headquarters, issues the item numbers, maintaining a log, whenever an officer calls in a new report. It's how we keep track.] My new case incorporated item numbers 04-0071 through 04-0075.

I began writing the affidavit explaining the probable cause as to why I believed the property stolen from our five victims was located at Noé's Automotive Shop in Evangeline Parish. It included the postal address, a detailed description of the premises, date of thefts (to establish timeliness of the request), each stolen article, including brands and serial numbers if known, specifically referenced to the five item numbers. It took four pages and two-and-a-half hours to write.

In the meantime, Abner had Thelma Vidrine, one of our radio dispatchers, to run each of the potential suspect names. These included Noé Arceneaux, Darnell Guillory, Claude Martinez, and Delphin LNU. We were plugged in with NCIC [National Crime Information Center], NLETS [National Law Enforcement Telecommunications System], EPIC [El Paso Intelligence Center (which monitors drug trafficking and unlawful entry by illegal aliens)], and Louisiana OMV [Office of Motor Vehicles]. What we didn't have were any of the private data bases you had to pay for monthly, Auto Track being the main one. LSP did, and Thelma had a contact.

Thelma performed her magic both within and outside her tiny office, and provided us with a clearer understanding of whom we were up against.

First, Noé René Arceneaux, age 54, had two felony convictions. In 1971, he was convicted of grand larceny (auto) in Fort Riley, Kansas, where he was a draftee diesel mechanic/private first class in the Army in the 1st Infantry Division. He was dishonorably discharged, and sentenced to serve five years in the federal penitentiary in Fort Leavenworth, Kansas. Then in 1978, he was arrested in Caddo Parish up near Shreveport on I-20 by LSP during a traffic stop. The vehicle he was driving was stolen. Besides speeding, he was charged with grand larceny (auto). He got another five years in the Louisiana State Penitentiary in Angola. He was released on parole after serving three. He was no longer on parole.

Second, Darnell T. Guillory, age 39, had three felony convictions. The first was in 1985 when he stole his neighbor's television. He got off with two years on probation, which he completed. Then he was convicted of armed robbery and felony murder in Jefferson Parish in 1987 when he shot and killed a liquor store employee in Metairie during a heist. He got 20 years to serve in Angola. He was released on parole in 2000. He's still on parole now. Parole violation would be yet another charge.

Third, Claude F. Martinez, age 64, had three felony convictions. In 1958, he was arrested for possession of marijuana in Jackson, Hinds County, Mississippi. He had two ounces of weed. (Possession of any type of illegal drugs was a big deal back then.) He was sentenced to 10 years in the Mississippi State Penitentiary, where he served seven before he was released on parole. (He was lucky he didn't get 20 years.) In 1971, he was arrested in Tallulah, in Madison Parish, Louisiana, for murder - specifically, for strangling his live-in girlfriend when he caught her cheating on him. He was sentenced to 25 years at hard labor in Angola. He served 21 and was released on parole. Within two weeks, he was arrested again in Madison County for dwelling house burglary. He was sentenced to serve five years, which ran concurrent with the remainder of his parole. He was released on a serve-out in 1996.

Fourth, Delphin LNU was Delphin S. Robard, age 25. He had one felony conviction from Houma, in Terrebonne Parish in the bayous of South Louisiana in 1998, for receiving stolen property, which happened to be 26 stolen firearms found in his possession from the local Ace Hardware store. He absolutely refused to identify the person(s) for whom he was holding them, so he was sentenced by the livid judge to five years of incarceration in Angola without benefit of parole. He was released upon his serve-out four months ago.

Fifth, in addition, other persons listed as affiliated with Noé's Automotive Repair Shop included Clarence A. Lockwood, age 32, convicted of burglary in Jennings in Jefferson Davis Parish in 1998. He was sentenced to three years on probation, which has since elapsed.

Sixth, Enrico M. Lambert, age 44, convicted of grand larceny (auto) in Baton Rouge in East Baton Rouge Parish in 1985, for which he served two years in Angola.

Seventh and last, was Lawrence G. Smith, age 34. He had two arrests for grand larceny (auto) in Ville Platte in Evangeline Parish, both in 2001. Both charges were summarily dismissed by Judge Odette D. Arceneaux. Hmmm!

Thelma had full-page, color copies of the driver's license photographs for all seven suspects.

Abner and I waited impatiently until 1 o'clock before calling Judge Calvin M. DesHotel at home. Abner told his wife, Miss Loretta, that we wanted to stop by so he could review my application for a search warrant in Evangeline Parish. She told her husband, who said for Abner and me to hurry on over, so we did. Miss Loretta ushered us into his well-appointed study, where he was engrossed working on his coin collection. He looked up and said, "Abner, Marvin, come in. Have a seat. You all have my undivided attention. Something's up. I can smell it. I want to know what it is before I review any paperwork."

I replied, "Something is up, your honor." Then I recited the very same facts I related to Abner Saturday evening.

Judge DesHotel stopped me as soon as I mentioned the stolen coin collection belonging to Mrs. Naomi A. Caldwell. "What does she collect?"

"Well, Sir, it was actually her deceased husband, Walter's collection. He collected Indian head pennies, wheat pennies, and buffalo nickels. As I understand it, the collection was appraised by a reputable firm on Royal Street back in the mid-1980s for $3,000."

"Outrageous! They must be recovered intact! Please continue."

When I was through reciting all the facts, he took a lengthy pause to collect his thoughts, or perhaps to make me even more anxious, finally stating, "You know, it's not an everyday occurrence for a circuit court judge in one parish to sign a search warrant for a property located within another parish. It's akin to 'fishing in another man's pond'. It usually causes ruffled feathers, as it were.

"I completely understand your problem, Abner, as I do Sheriff Rousseau's.

"As it turns out, after I completed undergraduate studies at Tulane, I went to LSU Law School, where I became acquainted with Odette D. Arceneaux, who was a fellow first-year pupil. He had a reputation for being shady even back then. His daddy owned the largest plantation in all of Evangeline Parish back in those days, but he lost it, beginning with some bad investments and culminating with a losing hand in a cutthroat poker game. As I recall, he relocated somewhere in Texas, I believe, in utter disgrace. I don't know whatever became of him, although there was a rumor he drowned in a lake under suspicious circumstances. True or not, Odette was never the quite same after that.

"Hand me your affidavit so I can review it."

He went through it thoroughly. I held my breath. Then he looked up and asked, "Did you get Onslow Trudeau [the District Attorney] to review this?"

I replied, "No, Sir."

He responded, "Splendid job! ATF trained you well. Better let him know what's on his horizon."

Then he signed it with a flourish. "Happy hunting, fellows. I'll be sorely disappointed with both of you if you don't recover that coin collection. Good day, sirs."

Abner and I returned to his office. I called Mr. Trudeau and filled him in. He told me to put a copy of the affidavit and search warrant in an envelope and shove it under the door to his office. Then he wished us luck.

Abner waited before calling Hal Hebert, Captain of Patrol. I heard him ask, "Hal, Ah catch chu at a bad time? No? Good. Can chu meet me and Marvin up here in da office? Good. Bye."

Hal showed up ten minutes later, all out of breath.

Abner said, "Hal, Henri LeBlanc took five boiglary reports from da same street in Eunice yestidy. Him and Marvin went ta woik and located w'ere at least some of da loot is located, in a automotive chop named Noé's in Ville Platte. We got a soich warrant and we're gonna execute it tomorrow at 0800. Ah'm goin' too, so chu'll be in charge chere tomorrow. Besides Henri, Ah need two corrections deputies and t'ree more road deputies. Who can chu kick loose for me?"

"Let me look at da schedule. Chu t'ink chu'll be done by afternoon chift?"

I replied, "I do. Soon as we hook up the suspects, we'll send them on their merry way here in the paddy wagon. We should also be able to break one or two road deputies loose after we complete the search."

"Dat's not too bad. Chu can have Otis D'Orleans and Bruce Winkler from da chail and Chohnny Carpenter, Dennis DeWalt, and LeRoy Washington from Patrol besides Henri."

Abner said, "Great. Tell dem ta be standin' tall in full gear including vests, here by 0600 in da morning for da briefing. Da chail guys drive da paddy wagon and da patrol deputies double up in two-man cars, full of gas, and ready ta go. Make chur dey got either a chotgun or an M-16 in bot' patrol units."

"Consider it done, Cheriff."

Hal left and Abner and I discussed our options. I asked, "How well do you know Sheriff Rousseau?"

"So-so. Ah always liked 'im. Ah didn't know nuttin' about his problem wit' his chudge. He's in a trick bag. Ah t'ink his heart be in da right place. If Ah can convince 'im he can weadder dis storm and come out ahead, Ah t'ink he'll choin us. Ah coirtainly hope so."

"You want to ride together tomorrow?"

"Ah do. Two heads is better dan one."

"I'll meet you here in the morning. Tomorrow is D-Day for us."

"Chu got dat right. See chu tomorrow. Tell Hannah hey for me."

"Right back at you with Marisol."

I went home. While we were eating supper, I told Hannah what Abner and I planned to do in the morning. She said, "Sounds like you and Abner have been busy beavers today. I'm sure you realize Abner's putting his reputation on the line by agreeing to kick over a hornet's nest in some other sheriff's backyard."

"I most certainly do, but you do realize that if we don't resolve these five burglaries quickly, especially this early in his tenure, his star won't shine anywhere nearly as brightly as it did the day he was sworn in, and for that matter, neither will mine."

"I do understand, and that's why he has you.

"Finish up. Go smoke your cigar. Sip on your bourbon and

get to bed. I'll set the alarm for 4:30, and get the coffee maker ready. That should give you more than enough time to get you there early."

"You always know what to do and what to say."

"That's because I know you better than you know yourself, Mr. Barnett."

After my taste of bourbon and my smoke, I undressed and crawled into bed. Roscoe followed me in, and curled up beside me. He was purring like a Singer sewing machine when I fell asleep. All was right in the world.

- Chapter 7 -
Hitting Pay Dirt

We didn't waste any time Monday morning, February 23rd. Henri LeBlanc and LeRoy Washington rode together. They departed in a gold, 1996, Ford Crown Victoria, four-door sedan, a 'plain brown wrapper' in cop lingo, seized from a drug dealer, which we use for surveillances, radar enforcement, and any other time a marked unit would be inappropriate. They made a beeline to set up on Noé's Automotive Shop before any of the villains showed up for work.

Johnny Carpenter and Dennis DeWalt rode together in a marked unit. They staged at the Flying J with Otis D'Orleans and Bruce Winkler in the paddy wagon, which was a seized, 2002 Ford F-350 delivery van we repainted and repurposed. Abner and I boogied straight to the Evangeline County Sheriff's Office. We were there at 0700, before Sheriff Rousseau arrived. The dispatcher called him at home, and he met us there at 0715.

He walked in and said, "Hey, Abner. Dis must be really impōtant for chu to be here so early. Chu all want some coffee?"

"Dat would be nice. Pascal, dis is my chief deputy, Marvin Barnett."

We all shook hands. He said, "Glad ta meet chu, Marvin. Call me Pascal. W'at's up?"

Abner said, "Pascal, we need chur help. Saturday when we wuz havin' ahr Mardi Gras Parade in Opelousas, some rascals broke inta five houses on da same block in Eunice. Ahr investigation revealed dat da t'ieves ahr da Noé Arceneaux gang. We found a stolen carpenter's trailer parked in his back lot. Also, a truck wit' appliances w'ich look like da appliances from one of ahr udder victims, is also parked dere, too. We got a signed soich warrant, w'ich we wanna execute w'en dey open up at 8. I know dis is a sticky wicket for chu because of Chudge Arceneaux. Want to woik dis wit' us?"

"Ahr chu kidding? Fuckin' A! Chu have no idee how bad Ah want ta do dis wit' chu. Chudge Arceneaux hab been a royal pain in mah ass from day one. Noé, too. I hate dos rat bastids. What chu need from us?"

"Well, besides Marvin and me, Ah got six deputies standing by. We'll take as much he'p as chu can spare. We got ahr paddy wagon, and we plan to haul off however many t'ieves we identify dat's involved."

"Tell chu w'at. Get on da horn and tell chur guys ta meet us here, soon as possible. Me and all six of mah guys on day chift will help out. Dis day has been a long time in comin'. Chu hab no idee. Dis is lahk Christmas ta me."

"Let's do it. Ah already got a unmarked unit wit' da eyeball on the chop. Da udder guys can be here in 15 minutes."

"We'll do a briefing in da parking lot den."

It was almost like a pep rally. The EPSO deputies were energized to finally be turned loose on Noé and his despicable band of villains, like hungry sharks circling a wounded whale. We waited for Henri to let us know when the shop was open and it looked like all the workers were there.

We got the call at 0805. Then we swarmed like hornets, descending on the shop at 0810. It was chaotic like firemen responding to a five-alarm fire. We caught Noé with his pants down literally. He was in the middle of his morning constitutional when we raided his empire. We had Darnell T.

Guillory, Claude F. Martinez, Delphin S. Robard, Enrico M. Lambert, and Lawrence G. Smith in handcuffs by the time Noé finished fumigating his one-hole lavatory and the attendant paperwork. Sheriff Rousseau and Abner had waited in the hallway for him to finish because Noé was peeling the paint off the walls. A wooden door was insufficient to contain the odor. Geez Louise! A three-day-old roadkill skunk never smelled this bad!

After all the chaos, Clarence A. Lockwood finally showed up. He was running late. Had he been smarter, he'd have kept on going and never come back. His tardiness actually worked to our advantage. He had yet to step foot inside a prison cell. The closest he had come was getting sentenced to probation for a burglary. I figured he'd be the easiest nut to crack and I was right. This was who I had been waiting for all along. Henri scooped him up and was waiting for me.

Backing up, upon our arrival, Delphin S. Robard was observed by deputies fondling and cooing over Oscar Rowan's LC Smith shotgun. All Oscar's guns were on a table in the back room of the garage where he was arrested. They also saw Darnell T. Guillory sighting through the scoped Winchester when they hooked him up. (Jackpot! Felons in possession!)

Lawrence G. Smith had been observed pulling the tarp off Colin Reese's Harley and and sitting on it. He was stroking it like his pud while watching a porn flick.

Deputies also saw Claude F. Martinez pop the first lock off Joel Auguste's carpentry trailer with a bolt cutter. Enrico M. Lambert was standing there next to Claude with his thumb us his ass, licking his chops, impatient to unwrap his purloined Christmas presents.

Henri had confirmed the serial numbers of Hélène Dubois's appliances in the back of the stake bed truck. The only loot not located was Walter and Naomi Caldwell's coin collection. This was extremely disappointing.

I borrowed Abner's truck keys, and told Henri to put Clarence Lockwood in the backseat. I had Henri switch Lockwood's handcuffs from the rear to the front. Then Henri and I climbed into the front seat. I surreptitiously switched on my pocket tape recorder. Even Henri didn't know I had it. (By state law, only one party needs to consent to the recording and I was that party, although I knew Henri wouldn't care. I used it for two reasons. First, to confirm Lockwood's consent on the rights waiver. Second, so I wouldn't make a mistake in reporting what he said.)

I read the Miranda Warning and asked Lockwood to sign it. He did. Then I wrote the date and time on it. Henri and I signed as witnesses.

I said, "Clarence, we know quite a bit about you already. You've managed to escape a stay in prison thus far, but I'm afraid you're not going to be that lucky this time. On your second time around, getting busted for committing more felonies, you're bound to draw some time. The question is, how much - a year, three, five? None of us knows. What I do know is, this time you won't appear before that pushover judge in Jefferson Davis Parish.

"This time you're going before Judge Calvin M. DesHotel in Saint Landry Parish. He's a stickler for the law. He's like that old time hanging judge over in Fort Smith, Arkansas, Judge Isaac C. Parker. He sentenced 160 people to death by hanging. You know the rhyme. 'Can't do the time? Don't do the crime.'

"Sheriff Ladner and I met with Judge DesHotel yesterday - on a Sunday, no less! We told him everything we knew about this criminal nest of vipers, of which you are one. We have five Saint Landry Parish families in Eunice who are victims of felony grand larceny because of this protected band of outlaws you belong to over here in Evangeline Parish. That really chaffed Judge DesHotel's ass!

"He signed a search warrant so we could come over here and recover all the stolen property and arrest all the vile villains. That's what he called you all. Vile villains. [I lied about that.] Looks like we've recovered most of it, too. You, Clarence, and all the other vile villains, including Mr. Big Shot Noé Arceneaux, are on a one-way express train headed straight for Angola.

"You know what? You actually look like a Jennings cowboy to me instead of a thief. You ride horses, Clarence? Maybe you can get yourself a slot on Angola's prison rodeo circuit.

"So, if you have anything you want to say to mitigate your guilt, throw yourself on the mercy of the law, this is your one shot. Once we put you in the paddy wagon to take you to Opelousas, your fate is sealed. Get ready to do some serious time. This is no joking matter."

"Sir, can I say something?"

"Of course. I was hoping you would."

"Sir, I'm not like all the others. I never kilt nobody like some of 'em has. I got a wife and a four-year-old son. I lost my job in the canning factory. I was about to lose my truck because I'd missed two payments. I had been a mechanic before that. I couldn't find another job anywhere. I did whatever I could to pay the bills.

"About a year ago I heard Noé was looking for some help. I came over and he hired me. All I was looking for was a job as a wrench making the standard rate - $6 an hour. He gave me $7. It wasn't 'til later on I learned about all the stealing from other parishes and fencing the stuff from here. All the locals know Noé's protected here, so long as we don't rob anyone in Evangeline Parish.

"The first time they took me with them, we stole four cars off the big used car lot over in Church Point. That was in April of last year. Mostly cars and other types of motor vehicles is what Noé is interested in. In May, we broke into an auto parts store in Jennings, and pretty much cleaned it out. Then on July 4th, we broke into another auto parts store in Kinder, but I wasn't involved in that one because I had to take my wife to the hospital. We thought she was having an attack of appendicitis, but it turns out she wasn't. On Labor Day, we pretty much picked a street clean in Lake Charles like we done Saturday in Saint Landry. Thanksgiving evening we broke into a pawn shop in Broussard. We done real good there. We got 28 guns, all nice ones too. That was the last job before this one."

"What was the divvy on this last job?"

"Well, we was gonna decide that today, except for the coin collection. Noé laid dibs on that. What Noé says goes."

"Where did he take it?"

"Oh, it's in his house. He said he was hanging it up in his family room over the fireplace."

"Okay. I'll check that out. You be willing to testify against these guys?"

"I can't. They'd kill me."

"You think none of them has noticed that you're not sitting on the floor handcuffed next to them? They're gonna be looking for someone to blame. You were late getting here today. They'll think this was a set up. They'll all be looking to exact some payback on you. You really think we can toss you back in amongst them and you'll be safe?"

"I don't know. Geez, I never wanted any part of this. I'm screwed no matter what I do. I'll end up losing my family and my life. For what? Because I lost my job and hired on with this asshole? He had me over a barrel because I'm broke."

"Henri, you stay here and keep an eye on Clarence. I need to have a little tête-à-tête with the sheriff."

Abner and Pascal were having their own little pow-wow when I walked up. I asked, "What's up?"

Abner said, "We got everyt'ing but da coin collection."

"Anyone talking?"

"Nope."

"What about our victims? Have you been able to reach any of them?

"Yep. Antoine Dubois is on his way ta get his appliances. Ditto for Joel Auguste and his trailer, and Colin Reese and his Harley. I got Oscar Rowan's guns. We'll return dem on da way home. All we need is the Caldwell coin collection."

"I may be able to help you with that. The coin collection is hanging over the mantle in Noé's family room. I'll call Judge DesHotel for a verbal search warrant. Pascal, do you know his street address?"

"Chur do. 108 East Main Street. Ah'll send a car over dere ta keep an eye on it. Hopefully, his wife ain't hoid wat's happened yet."

Abner said, "Ah'll send a couple of ahr guys, too."

It was 9:05. Court wouldn't start 'til 10. I figured Judge DesHotel should be in his chambers. I called and he answered.

"Judge DesHotel speaking."

"Judge, this is Chief Marvin Barnett. We executed the search warrant. We recovered everything except for the coin collection. I flipped one of the thieves. He said it's hanging on the wall over the mantel in Noé Arceneaux's family room in his house at 108 East Main Street, Ville Platte. I'm calling to request a telephonic search warrant for that address."

"Chief Barnett, the time is now 9:11 according to my watch. Search warrant granted. Call me back as soon as you execute it."

"Yes, Sir. Thanks, Judge. Will do. Bye."

I walked back over to both sheriffs. "Judge signed off on a verbal search warrant for the coin collection."

Abner said, "Marvin, chu keep an eye on t'ings here. Pascal and me are headed over dere ta execute it. Anyt'ing else chu can t'ink of we chould look for if it's in plain sight?"

"Yes. Thanksgiving evening they stole 28 firearms from a pawn shop in Broussard. If you call the SO before you go, maybe they could fax you all a list of the stolen guns. If you see one in plain sight, stop what you're doing and call me. I'll request another telephonic search warrant for the rest of them. We don't want to overstep and get the whole thing tossed."

"Chu got dat right. Call chu soon as we get t'rough."

It took almost 30 minutes. My phone rang. I hurried to answer it. "Marvin! We got da coin collection! Not only dat, we seen four of da stolen pistols still in da boxes on a end table in da family room. Da serial numbers are eben on a label on da outside of da box! Call da chudge."

"Cutting it close. He'll be in court in five more minutes, but I'll try."

My heart was pounding. I made the call. The judge answered

again.

"Judge, Chief Barnett again. We recovered the coin collection intact. Also, we saw four stolen pistols in plain sight, still in the boxes on an end table in the family room. The serial numbers were written on the outside of the boxes. We have a list of 28 stolen firearms from a pawn shop in Broussard and these match. I'm calling again to request another telephonic search warrant to look for the other 24 stolen guns."

"Granted. The time is 9:58. I'll be in court, but I want you to call back as soon as you know what you have. My secretary, Mrs. Enright, will take a message. Understood?"

"Yes, Sir. Understood. Thank you."

I called Abner. "Sheriff, I got the warrant, but I need to run some things by you before you execute it."

"Choot."

"First, we have six men in handcuffs. I flipped Clarence Lockwood. He's provided all the information I've given you, and a whole lot more we need to take a look at. If I put him in custody, he's a dead man. The only harm he did us was to participate in the thefts in Eunice, but we've wrapped up everyone else who was involved. He doesn't want to testify, but I don't think we need him. I want to cut him loose and keep his name out of this."

"Do it. What else?"

"I want to send the other six arrestees on their way to our jail. We've got all the photographs we need of this site. The trailer, appliances, and Harley have all been picked up. I want to lock up and send the others back too, just as soon as I can. However, I still suggest we do a press release in the front yard of Noe's house, to include a photo with all our guys and Pascal's. This is the time for both you and Pascal to toot your horns. It should render

Pascal beaucoup goodwill points with the locals, to include the press, and it could even lead to Judge Arceneaux losing his next election."

"Agreed. Lock it up. Den chu and all our guys, including da paddy wagon crew wit' da prisoners head over here for da news release."

"Thanks, Sheriff. Be there in a few."

We locked up and left within ten minutes. Before Henri and I left, I told Henri to un-cuff Clarence.

I surreptitiously turned on my recorder again and said, "Clarence, Sheriff Ladner told me to cut you loose. You've probably got a 24-hour head-start before some of your criminal associates bond out of jail. You and your family need to get the hell out of Dodge. Comprenden? You need to find someplace else to live, and I mean now! If these thugs find you, you're a dead man and you know it. If one of the other sheriffs whose venues you helped to rob finds out your name, he will probably arrest you along with the others. Running away is your only chance.

"Do you have any kinfolk out of state who could help you find a job there?"

"Well, I got a brother who lives in Hattiesburg. My wife's step-mother lives in Beaumont, Texas. We could call one of them."

"Okay. I'm not kidding you. You and your family better cut a chogy before Noé gets out of jail. He will kill you himself or pay someone else to do it. He definitely has the money to contract a hit. Your disappearance without a trace is your only chance. I'm writing my phone number on this piece of paper. Call me once you find a new home. Promise?"

"I promise. I think we'll go to my brother's. Thanks Chief.

You've given me and my family a new lease on life. I'll never forget it. I promise from here on out, I'll fly the straight and narrow. Thanks again. Bye."

"Bye."

Once every law enforcement officer who was working this case was at Noé's house, Pascal and Abner made a joint press release in the front yard, backed up by deputies from both agencies. They had set up a table in the front yard with the coin collection and 15 stolen handguns on it. Both the TV press and the ink press were there. The sheriffs even made our six prisoners' line up for a group photograph. Noé had his photo taken in handcuffs standing in front of his own house! It was priceless. This was Abner's and Pascal's day in the sun, and they shined brightly like the northern lights [aurora borealis]. When it was all over, each of the deputies from both SOs were bonafide 'blood-brothers'. In the meantime, I called Judge DesHotel's chambers and updated Mrs. Enright.

Abner and I returned Mr. Rowan's guns and ammo to his wife. We also returned Mrs. Caldwell's coin collection. Both ladies expressed their gratitude profusely. Then we stopped in Eunice at Victor's Saloon for a red beans, rice, and smoked sausage meal, topped off with French bread, iced tea, and bread pudding for dessert. (Note to self. Commit this restaurant to memory.)

We were back at the office by 1:30. I had a mountain of paperwork to complete on this file. I told each of the six deputies to write a report for me detailing everything he saw and did in the execution of all search warrants and the arrests; further, that I needed them by COB. I knew we had to tie in specific arrestees with specific thefts for successful prosecutions.

When I was a Fed, we would have tacked on a charge of conspiracy against each defendant. To prove conspiracy, one must establish an agreement between two or more persons to commit a crime, with any co-conspirator committing one overt act in furtherance of it. For example, if two people agree to commit a bank robbery, and one of them procures a gun to do it, that's conspiracy. Both culprits are guilty, facing up to five-years of incarceration each. Not only that, co-conspirators can join and withdraw from the conspiracy at any time and still be guilty. 'In for a penny, in for a pound.' The bar is low to convict. It's a powerful law enforcement tool, and one of my favorites.

The problem with many state prosecutors is, even when conspiracy is a viable statute in their code books, they still won't charge it. They consider it as unethical or unsportsmanlike. Go figure. Conspiracy always made my job a whole lot easier.

I had a lot to accomplish before the six initial appearances set for 10 o'clock Tuesday morning. In particular, I needed to write a criminal complaint for each defendant. I decided to push my luck. I called Judge DesHotel again. Mrs. Enright patched me though.

"How may I be of assistance, Chief Barnett?"

"Judge, I was wondering if you have prohibited the district attorney's office from charging defendants with conspiracy."

"Hmmm. Let me think. Is it listed in the *Louisiana Criminal Code 2003: Title 14 of the Louisiana Revised Statutes by LLC?*"

"Yes, Sir."

"Then it's fair game. You may even inform Mr. Trudeau I said so. Is there anything else?"

"No, Sir. Thank you. Good day."

"Chief Barnett, you may have to arm wrestle Mr. Trudeau,

but I believe that a man of your many talents will prevail. In fact, I fully expect it of you. Are we clear, Chief?"

"Crystal clear, Judge. Thanks."

That substantially lightened my load. I got down to business. I drafted one lengthy indictment including all six defendants. From that I created an individual charging document for each defendant for their initial appearances, because I couldn't present the proposed indictment before the Grand Jury until Thursday. The indictment began with Count 1 charging all six defendants with conspiracy.

Sometimes the most difficult aspect in establishing conspiracy is to prove the agreement. I got lucky in this case.

It seems that when Antoine G. Dubois came to pick up his stolen appliances at Noé's Automotive Repair Shop, he saw both Claude F. Martinez and Enrico M. Lambert, the latter of whom he knew on sight but not by name, sitting on the floor all handcuffed together along with the other four arrestees. He pointed them out to Deputy LeRoy Washington.

Specifically, Mr. Dubois said he saw both of them in the 1975, white-over-green, Pontiac LeMans, which was parked in the front lot of Noé's business, on his street on Friday, February 20th about 6 o'clock in the evening. It was right after he returned from work. Martinez was the driver and Lambert was in the right front seat. First, they cruised slowly down the dead-end street all the way to the end, and then they turned around and came back. Their front windows were rolled down, and Martinez pointed at two houses, one of which was Oscar T. Rowan's burgled house, and the other was his own. Mr. Dubois recognized them as thugs from Ville Platte who didn't belong there, but thought maybe they had just made a wrong turn. It was seeing them together in handcuffs this morning after his house and others on his street had been burgled that he realized they were 'casing the joint.'

That was my overt act - casing houses to burgle the evening before they did it!

Charges 2 through 4 included three counts of felons in possession of a firearm - Noé René Arceneaux, Delphin S. Robard, and Darnell T. Guillory.

Charge 5 was on Darnell T. Guillory for violation of his parole.

Charges 6 through 11 included a count of receiving stolen property [RSP] for each defendant, based upon witness statements by each of the participating deputies. Specifically, Noé R. Arceneaux was charged with the coin collection recovered from his house; Darnell T. Guillory was charged with the scoped Winchester rifle; Claude F. Martinez was charged with the carpentry trailer; Delphin S. Robard was charged with the LC Smith shotgun; Enrico M. Lambert was also charged with the carpentry trailer; and, Lawrence G. Smith was charged with the Harley Davidson.

Soon as I finished, I hustled over to the Office of the Saint Landry Parish District Attorney, Onslow K. Trudeau, knowing I was about to face ferocious resistance. I knocked and he told me to enter.

"What have you got, Chief?"

"This is a draft of a proposed indictment for Thursday for all six jaybirds we brought back from Ville Platte. I also included individual charging documents for their initial appearances tomorrow.

"We don't need to indict yet. We'll have a preliminary hearing first on Thursday. The indictment will follow the following week.

That's how we do it here. We've always done it this way."

"No disrespect, Sir, regarding past practices, but there's a better way 'to build a mousetrap'. Besides saving time, we won't have to give the defense too much early discovery."

"That may all be true, but it's not our normal procedure here. The defense attorneys need more time so they can get paid before going to trial."

"Sir, the only defendant in this entire gang who has the money to pay for private counsel is Noé Arceneaux, the ringleader. He's the nephew of Circuit Court Judge Odette Arceneaux over in Evangeline Parish. The other five defendants work for him and 'don't have two nickels to rub together'. The judge will assign them appointed counsel and we both know it.

"I know very well who Odette Arceneaux is."

"Good. Then you probably know his nephew already has two separate and distinct felony convictions. This will be his third. It may be time to consider going for the 'high bitch' after he gets convicted this time." [Slang term for the Habitual Offender Act regarding offenders with three or more separate felony convictions. The mandated penalty for conviction is 25 years without parole, consecutive to any other sentence, hence the slang term.]

"You're getting way ahead of yourself, Chief. Not only that, I see you added a charge of conspiracy for each defendant. We do not ever charge anyone with conspiracy in Louisiana. It isn't done. I'll chalk this up to your lack of experience in law enforcement in the 'Sportsman's Paradise'. [State motto emblazoned on all Louisiana license plates.]

"Sir, I'm not your enemy. I'm trying to help you win convictions in court. I'm here face-to-face with you to ask you to present this indictment with these charges to the Grand Jury. Please, Sir. Judge DesHotel himself told me he wants to see conspiracy on the indictment."

"So you went behind my back!"

"No, Sir! I wanted to ensure I wasn't tacking on a count Judge DesHotel didn't want to see. He said he thought it was reasonable so long as I could establish an initial overt act and I can. I know we can win these cases much easier with conspiracy than without it. What's so difficult to understand about this?"

"You're not the District Attorney! I am! I decide who gets charged and who doesn't, and what charges are filed! Not you!"

"Sir, I'm leaving now. I'm asking you to reconsider before there's a huge problem in court tomorrow. Good day."

I got up and left. Then I went straight to Abner's office to let him know what had transpired. He blew a gasket, like I knew he would.

"Onslow's a idiot! Chu stay right chere. Don't chu moob. Ah'll go see him mahself. "

I waited almost an hour.

When he returned, he said, "Ah had ta call Chudge DesHotel at home. He went ballistic! Straightened Onslow out in no uncoitain toims, so he left da conspiracy charge on da indictment, but now he's out fah blood. He's fuming. For da time being, chu let me deal wit' him. He's plotting ways ta try ta run chu off. Problem is, he chust got re-elected. We gotta deal wit' him fah foē more yeahs unless he stubs his toe and gets recalled. Dat's never happened here befōe.

"Go on home. Ah'm coming ta court wit' chu tomorrow mornin' ta make chur Onslow doesn't pull a double-cross. Dis is a great case and we need ta convict all of dos bastids an' send 'em up da river fah as long as we can. Da public will be up in arms if we don't. Da whole parish is buzzin' about dis bust awready!"

Tuesday morning, Abner and I walked over to the courtroom thirty minutes before court was scheduled to begin. Monday had a been long and grueling, but at the same time, exceedingly gratifying day. We sat ourselves at the table for the prosecution. As soon as Onslow saw us, his face turned beet red. He knew either Abner or I would be there, but he didn't expect to see us both. It was a quiet demonstration of unity.

Ours were the most important cases on the docket, and today ours were the first cases called. Noé Arceneaux hired allegedly the best criminal defense attorney in all of Baton Rouge. His name was Neville T. Richard [pronounced Rē'-Shard]. Somehow he managed to get most his clients off without alienating the cops, or so they claim. He was supposed to be that charming - a regular 'snake oil salesman'.

Noé was first up. Mr. Richard read over the list of charges against his client out loud in his booming voice so all could hear, making himself the center of attention. He exclaimed, "Mr. Trudeau, I see you've thrown all of us a curveball here with this charge of conspiracy!"

Before Onslow could respond, Judge DesHotel interrupted. "Mr. Richard, it looks like you may have to bone up some on *Title 14.* I know you have a lot of experience in U.S. District Court defending clients charged with the federal version of conspiracy. What's that statute number - *Title 18, United States Code, Section 371?* I'm sure you have it memorized by now. The Louisiana statute and the Federal statute are nearly identical. Is this going to pose a problem for you, Counselor? Do you wish to withdraw?"

"No, Your Honor. It's just that this is the first time I've ever seen it charged in state court."

"Better get used to it then. I'm betting you'll be seeing a lot more of it in the future once the other district attorneys wise up to it and see just how simple it is to prove. How does your client plead, Mr. Richard?"

"Not guilty, Your Honor."

"Let the record show that Mr. Arceneaux has pleaded not guilty to all three counts. If the prosecution has not obtained an indictment on your client before then, the preliminary hearing will be held on Thursday, March 4th at 10 o'clock. However, am I correct, Mr. Trudeau, that you will be presenting all six of these cases to the Grand Jury this Thursday?"

Onslow stood with a look of bewilderment on his face, but he recovered quickly. "Yes, Your Honor. That is correct."

Judge DesHotel replied, "Just as I thought. If Mr. Arceneaux has not been indicted by March 4th, we will proceed with the preliminary hearing. Otherwise, we will have have an arraignment. Am I clear, Mr. Richard?"

"Crystal clear. Your Honor. About bond . . . . "

"I was just getting to that. Mr. Arceneaux is the alleged leader of this group of defendants. He's certainly their employer. He has two prior felony convictions. He's facing an additional charge of the Habitual Offender Act if he is convicted of his current charges, is that not true, Mr. Trudeau?"

Onslow stood again, blushing. "That's true, Your Honor."

"Thank you. You may be seated. That's what I thought.

"Continuing, Mr. Arceneaux is a man of substantial means and political clout from what I understand. I consider his risk of flight extremely high. Therefore, bond is set at $3,000,000 cash or surety. No collateral, and no promissory note."

Mr. Richard choked. He coughed several times. His face turned beet red. He exclaimed, "Your honor, this is unreasonable! He can't possibly afford that!"

"Better be careful, Counselor. You're bordering on contempt of court by raising your voice to me. Next time you'll be in hot water. 'Forewarned is forearmed' so pay heed. That is the ruling of this court. If Mr. Arceneaux has not been indicted by his next court appearance, I will reconsider this order.

"Case continued until March 4th. Next defendant!"

All the other defendants were remanded until March 4th on a $1,000,000 bond. Each one was provided a court-appointed attorney. You could see it in their eyes. If Noé couldn't catch a break with all his money and clout, they were screwed. They all knew they'd be back in prison within a few weeks. There was no hope of 'beating the rap.' Absolutely none.

When court was adjourned, Onslow looked at both Abner and me. He said, "I owe you both an apology. I thought for sure Judge DesHotel would crucify me for filing the conspiracy charge. I was wrong. Gentlemen, you just altered the way we now do business in the district attorney's offices throughout the state from here on out. Also, after reflection, I decided you all were right on another matter. Why should I provide the defense discovery until it's actually due? No more preliminary hearings.

"Sheriff, Chief, I need you all to start pulling together each of the documents necessary to charge the high bitch on Noé Arceneaux, Darnell Guillory, and Claude Martinez. As soon as they're convicted of the charges in this case, we're coming right back after them.

"Chief, I'll see you Thursday at 10 o'clock to testify before the

Grand Jury."

Abner said "T'anks" and extended his his big mitt for Onslow to shake. He had a huge smile on his face. I followed his lead.

All was once again well in the Universe of the Saint Landry Parish Sheriff's Office and the Saint Landry Parish District Attorney's Office. This was a win-win for both agencies. 'United we stand. Divided we fall.'

- Chapter 8 -
Running Out the String

I testified before the Saint Landry Parish Grand Jury on Thursday, February 26th. The grand jurors voted to return a True Bill against all six defendants on all charges, so we arraigned them on Thursday, March 4th.

The arraignment was in all reality, just a formality. The defendants were officially informed that the charges filed against them at the initial appearance all held up. The next phase was to set trial dates for all, unless a defendant elected to plead guilty before then. This is generally referred to as a plea bargain, in which the prosecution offers to reduce the charge(s) and/or the recommended penalty in return for a guilty plea. Sometimes it works the other way. The defense offers to plead guilty to a reduced charge(s).

The only defendants who had no incentive to strike a deal, were those three who were facing the high bitch upon conviction of the pending charges. The exception to that, would be if Onslow agreed to drop prosecution for the high bitch altogether. However, Onslow smelled 'blood in the water' plus he felt the boot up his ass by Judge DesHotel, so that was not on the table for discussion. Ergo, Noé Arceneaux, Darnell Guillory, and Claude Martinez would all be going to trial. They had nothing to lose. A conviction for any of them was tantamount to life in prison period. Might as well go ahead and 'roll the bones' hoping they'd get lucky. Besides, going to trial preserves the right to an appeal.

Judge DesHotel was nobody's fool. At the arraignment, he set the tone by denying Mr. Richard's motion that all six defendants be tried together in that the first count was conspiracy with each other. He had a valid point; however, multi-defendant trials have a way of turning into a three-ring circus with the defense lawyers and defendants feeding off each other. Judge DesHotel's ruling avoided the circus by staggering the trials, beginning with the younger, and least culpable defendants first, providing them with an opportunity to turn state's evidence for a reduced sentence. It was a well thought out move.

He set Delphin S. Robard's trial for Monday, April 5th. He was the youngest at age 25. He had one prior felony conviction for RSP. Besides conspiracy, he was charged with RSP again, and felon in possession of a firearm. He was a likely candidate to turn state's evidence.

Next, he set Lawrence G. Smith's trial for Wednesday, April 7th. He was 34 years old. Smith 'thought he was bulletproof' because his two prior arrests for grand larceny (auto) had been dismissed by his boss's uncle, Evangeline Parish Judge Odette Arceneaux. Ergo, he was the only defendant in the bunch who was not a convicted felon. Besides conspiracy, he was charged with RSP. Turning state's evidence could make his prison sentence substantially shorter. On the other hand, if he went to trial and lost and the judge maxed out his prison sentence before the remaining trials began, it might induce the others to throw themselves on the mercy of the court and plead out.

Third, he set Enrico M. Lambert's trial for Friday, April 9th. He was 44. He had one prior conviction for grand larceny (auto). Besides conspiracy, he was charged with RSP. He was facing some time, but not a lifetime.

Fourth, he set Darnell T. Guillory's trial for Monday, April 12th. He was 39. Besides conspiracy, he was charged with RSP, felon in possession of a firearm, and parole violation. His prior convictions were for grand larceny, murder and armed robbery. If convicted, besides facing the high bitch, the judge would probably max him out.

Fifth, he set Claude F. Martinez's trial for Wednesday, April 14th. He was the oldest at age 64. Besides conspiracy, he was charged with RSP. His prior convictions were for possession of a Schedule I substance (marijuana), murder, and burglary. He was facing prison for the remainder of his life.

Lastly, he scheduled Noé René Arceneaux for trial on Monday, April 19th. Besides conspiracy, he was charged with felon in possession of a firearm and RSP. Like Guillory and Martinez, he too, was looking at prison 'until death do us part' unless his high-powered attorney, Mr. Richard, 'pulled a rabbit out of his hat'. At this point, it wasn't looking too good for him, but he had plenty of money, and as the adage goes, 'Money talks and bullshit walks'.

The sweet part of this for us cops was, they were all cooling their heels in the clink because they couldn't come up with the jack to post bond while awaiting their speedy trials. That's because everyone and most importantly, Judge DesHotel, believed they would skip bail with the odds of 'beating the rap' being against them such as they were.

I got busy collecting the evidence necessary to prove violation of the the Habitual Offender Act by Guillory, Martinez, and Arceneaux.

For each defendant, I needed a certified, exemplified copy of the J&C [Judgment & Commitment Order] for each of their convictions. It sounds crazy, but the judge has to affirm that the clerk is the clerk, and the clerk has to affirm the judge is the judge, which requires original signatures and crimped seals from both officials for every single conviction.

That meant for each conviction, I had to track down each judge and clerk and beg their indulgences, assuming they were still alive. It was easier to do this face-to-face. Otherwise, I needed to prevail upon a lawman in that venue to do it for me. In those cases, I called the local ATF office which covered that venue, and prevailed upon their empathy. I usually got their help without too much of an argument, because ATF specialized in habitual offender cases, and were tuned in that judges and clerks alike were usually annoyed when they were approached to do go through this absurd legal, ritualistic rain dance.

Next, I needed a copy of mugshots and fingerprints taken of the defendant for each of his incarcerations at the respective prison. I obtained these personally at Angola and Parchman. Again, I prevailed upon ATF to get Arceneaux's for me from the Federal Correctional Institute at Fort Leavenworth.

The last nail in the coffin for habitual offender cases, was for a fingerprint examiner to compare the fingerprints taken by us at the time of our arrest, compared the prints taken at each penal institution for each incarceration. I went to LSP for that. It cost me a lunch at Frank's Diner in Baton Rouge, but it was well worth it.

I held the habitual offender cases in abeyance, pending convictions on the other charges. Now this was complete, I had time to catch my breath before the first trial was scheduled to commence.

Just like expected, both Delphin S. Robard and Lawrence G.

Smith flipped. They both agreed to plead guilty to all counts against them, receiving a five-year sentence for each count, all of which would run concurrently, in return for their testimony against the others. In essence that was like receiving one five-year sentence and being eligible for parole in 2-1/2 years. They would also get credit for time served in in the SLP Jail. Sweet.

Enrico M. Lambert pleaded straight-up to both counts. He did not flip. He received a four-year sentence on each count, to run consecutively. He was capped at eight years, but was eligible for parole in four. He was the first transported to Angola to begin serving his sentences.

Darnell T. Guillory went to trial on Monday, April 12th. It went like this.

First, Antoine G. Dubois testified to seeing Claude F. Martinez and Enrico M. Lambert cruising down his street in a white-over-green, 1975 Pontiac about 6 o'clock, Friday evening, February 20th. He knew Martinez by name and Lambert by sight. He saw Lambert pointing at two houses, including his own and Oscar T. Rowan's across the street.

On Saturday, after he and his wife returned from the Mardi Gras Parade, they found that their new kitchen appliances had been stolen. Also, Mr. Rowan's house had been burgled. His guns were stolen. Altogether five households on their street had been victims of burglary or felony theft. He made a police report, as did his other neighbors.

On Monday, February 23rd, he received a call from the Evangeline Parish Sheriff's Office. They said his appliances had been recovered at Noé's Automotive Shop on Highway 10 in Ville Platte. When he went there to pick them up, he saw Martinez and Lambert, sitting on the ground wearing handcuffs.

Then it clicked why they had been cruising his street the evening before the thefts. They were casing the street for places to burgle. He reported this to Deputy Washington of the Saint Landry Parish Sheriff's Office.

Delphin Robard testified next. He confessed to his participation in the burglaries and grand larcenies on Robert Street in Eunice with the defendant, Darnell Guillory, and co-defendants Claude Martinez, Enrico Lambert, Lawrence Smith, and including his boss, Noé Arceneaux.

Robard said Martinez and Lambert had reconnoitered the street for the boss, Noé Arceneaux, who sent them out to do it. Burglaries and theft were their stock-in-trade - meaning how they supplemented their income whenever they found a soft target, believed the swag could be easily fenced at a good resale value, and most importantly, they could get away clean. He also said the agreement they had on this particular job was that he and Guillory got first dibs on the stolen firearms. He also said he and Guillory were both in possession of a stolen firearm when they were arrested.

The defense attorney excoriated Robard for being a thief and rat-fink, but the damage to the defense was profound.

Lawrence G. Smith testified next. He piled on, stating that he witnessed Guillory shooting rats and other varmints many times in the back lot of Noé's shop. His testimony confirmed that Guillory was frequently in possession of a firearm in spite of the legal prohibition against it since he was a convicted felon. Smith too, was excoriated by defense counsel, but his testimony 'added another nail to Guillory's coffin' and helped to seal his fate, especially since he was a convicted murderer.

Then one-by-one, the victims of this crime spree testified to their losses.

I testified to the official court records I had obtained confirming Darnell T. Guillory's status as a convicted felon, to include his status as being on parole.

The last person to testify for the prosecution was Louisiana Parole Agent Denise Bell. She testified that she was Guillory's parole officer and that he was, in fact, a parole violator.

The prosecution rested.

After a break for lunch, it was the defense's turn.

It should have been no surprise. Guillory's only witness was his mother, who pleaded with the court to be lenient on her son because he was a poor, misguided soul who meant well.

The jury was out 15 minutes. They returned guilty verdicts on all counts.

Judge DesHotel wasted no time. He sentenced Guillory to serve five years on all four counts, each sentence to run consecutively. By 3:15, Guillory was in the paddy wagon headed to Angola. Once again, Judge DesHotel did not 'let any moss grow under his feet'.

Guillory's trial had a sobering effect on Claude F. Martinez. On Wednesday, April 14th, he pleaded guilty to both conspiracy and RSP. Judge DesHotel gave him four years on each count to run concurrently. The sentence was a little reward for not wasting everyone's time. Besides, Martinez was 64 years old. He knew he was facing the high bitch. He had long since resigned himself to dying in jail. He was back in Angola in time for supper.

Monday, April 19th. The crescendo had been building. Mr. Richard had filed motions to have the telephonic warrants thrown out. He took it all the way to the Louisiana Supreme Court in New Orleans. The court unanimously 'handed Mr.

Richard his ass and his hat', and told him to 'go fly a kite' in a manner of speaking. No doubt he knew it was a long shot, but he was desperately trying to earn his outrageous fee which he demanded in full before he even lifted his finger to defend Noé. His reputation for winning lost cases was about to be rendered asunder, and he knew it. Like everyone else, he could see it coming. He was 'shooting blanks' because he had no ammunition to save Noé from his 'just desserts'.

Noé's trial ran the same course as Darnell Guillory's, except Mr. Richard's cross-examinations of prosecution witnesses were brutal. No one got off lightly. He even maligned sweet Mrs. Caldwell's integrity. He accused her of senility, claiming that she sold her coin collection to Mr. Arceneaux but had a lapse of memory. He raised his voice at her and shook his finger in her face. He was sure she would crumble.

Judge DesHotel was outraged at Mr. Richard's lack of decorum! He banged his gavel furiously. It sounded like a machine gun going off. Just as he stopped, everyone in the court heard Mrs. Caldwell distinctly say, "Young man, you should have your mouth washed out by soap! Such baseless declarations! I censure your impudence, you vile slanderer! Your mother would be so ashamed of you!"

Judge DesHotel exclaimed, "Mr. Richard, you have gone too far abusing the witnesses testifying against your client! I will not have it! This is outrageous! I sentence you to serve one day in jail at the end of this trial for contempt of court - that is, unless you opt to have your mouth washed out with soap by Mrs. Caldwell right here in the courtroom. Which will it be, Sir?"

"Judge, you're a crazier old coot than this senile old battle-ax here! I'll take the jail time and be proud of it!"

"Too bad. You chose poorly, Mr. Richard. For this outburst, you are hereby sentenced to serve five days - five consecutive 24-hour days that is - just as soon as this trial is over. Get on with your cross-examination of this witness, and I warn you, tread lightly!"

"I yield, Your Honor. I have no further use for this, uh so-called witness."

"Nor I for you, Mr. Richard. Now I sentence you to ten days!

"Mrs. Caldwell, you may step down, with my apologies for Mr. Richard's contemptible behavior."

"Mr. Richard, I remind you that you are now sentenced to ten days in jail. Keep it up. Unless you mend your ways quickly, you'll be up to a month, along with a richly deserved bar complaint regarding your decorum in this courtroom.

"Next witness for the prosecution."

That was the highlight of the trial. The only thing Mr. Richard could do was try to discredit the prosecution's witnesses, all of whom were reputable. Noé didn't have a leg to stand on. He had no witnesses to offer up. The search warrants were valid and withstood Louisiana Supreme Court scrutiny. Nobody had roughed him up. Two of his own employees testified against him. His certified conviction records spoke volumes about his prior character. His own wife didn't even come to his rescue. In fact, she was noticeably absent.

All the evidence had been recovered. In fact, the Lafayette Parish Sheriff's Office had filed charges against Noé for the theft of the guns in Broussard, many of which were recovered in his home. They were waiting to take him to trial as soon as this case was adjudicated. Even though Noé was 'dead in the water' and would already be serving time, the DA in Lafayette Parish needed to get his licks in to show his citizenry that he meant business too. He, also, sought reelection.

Noé couldn't even come up with a manufactured defense. Truth is, he got lazy covering his tracks because of his uncle's protection. He left himself wide open. Now thanks to him, even his uncle was in jeopardy. His political enemies were circling like buzzards over roadkill. There was even talk of disbarment proceedings.

The remainder of our prosecution witnesses testified. The prosecution rested.

The defense tried to establish diminished capacity by having a psychiatrist testify that Noé was suffering from stress, causing him to make bad decisions, many of which were against his own best interests. This was the best Mr. Richard could come up with, and nobody was buying it. Mr. Richard made an impassioned plea for sympathy and lenience in his closing argument. It fell on deaf ears. Judge DesHotel maxed Noé out with 20 years to run consecutively. The courtroom erupted in cheers. Noé was whisked away to Angola, but it wasn't the last we'd see of him.

Mr. Richard was ushered off to jail to start serving his ten days. Onslow said his antics had all been a ploy to convince Noé that he was doing everything in his power to get him an acquittal. There was a chance Noé would be so angry that he'd hire a hitman. I didn't think Noé had the balls to do that. However, I did believe Delphin Robard and Lawrence Smith were in danger of inmate reprisals in Angola.

I had turned in my proposed indictments on our three worthy candidates for violation of the Habitual Offenders Act. Onslow scheduled me to testify before the Grand Jury on Thursday, April 22nd. 'No rest for the weary and the wicked don't need none.'

The Grand Jury returned three True Bills. The transportation deputies returned to Angola and brought back Messers Guillory, Martinez, and Arceneaux.

Their arraignments were held on Monday, April 26th. This time Noé didn't have any money to hire retained counsel. They each had a one-day trial beginning Monday, May 3rd and continuing through Wednesday, May 5th.

All were found guilty and received 25-year sentences to run consecutively to their previous sentences without benefit of parole. They were back at home-sweet-home in Angola on Thursday, May 6th. I prayed that this would be the last time I would ever have to deal with these knuckleheads.

I needed a break. Fortunately I didn't have many nickel-and-dime cases in my inbox awaiting my attention. I think all the publicity with the Noé Arceneaux gang and the magnitude of their prison sentences put the 'fear of God' in the hearts of our criminal element, which was a very small percentage of our citizenry in Saint Landry Parish. At least I hoped so.

I got a one-week respite.

- Chapter 9 -

Drug Enforcement in Saint Landry Parish

One of the major issues anywhere is illegal drug usage, which usually means sales of illegal drugs, and sometimes transportation and/or manufacture of same. Marijuana is still very much illegal whether it is proactively enforced or not, and pot was the predominant choice for dopers in Saint Landry Parish. Bad, but not usually fatal. However, there had been an uptick in arrests for the possession of ice, which is a form of methamphetamine. It's sometimes known as speed or crystal meth. It can be manufactured just about anywhere, and the process is extremely dangerous. Meth labs blow up all the time. In addition, it's a terribly harmful and debilitating substance, and that's why it's illegal. To the best of our knowledge at the time, we did not have an operational meth lab in Saint Landry Parish.

Saint Landry Parish was unequipped to make any type of significant drug case. Our agency was too small, with no budget for buy money, and everyone in SLP knows everyone else. Ergo, whenever we caught someone in possession, our first call was to the Louisiana State Police Narcotics Squad in Baton Rouge. In fact, you could say we had them on speed dial.

We did have one thing going for us, and it was a game changer. Our circuit court judge, Calvin M. DesHotel, handed down harsh sentences on everyone convicted of drug violations, whether it was a misdemeanor or felony violation. LSP appreciated that, so whenever we called, they responded.

The first SLP drug case I participated in was the investigation subsequent to the arrest of 20-year-old Esau J. Coates. It occurred at 9 o'clock, Wednesday evening, May 12th, 2004. Deputy Leonard K. Potts made a 'routine' traffic stop on what he thought was a potential DWI. Coates was weaving on US 190 in Krotz Springs on the east side of the parish close to Baton Rouge. He was driving a decrepit blue, 1988 Ford Escort. It was apparent that he was high on something, but it clearly was not alcohol. Deputy Potts placed him under arrest for impaired driving, and cuffed him. In conducting the search incident to arrest, he recovered a Skoal smokeless tobacco tin from Coates' right front jeans pocket. It was filled with crystal meth. Deputy Potts called a wrecker to tow the car, and transported Coates to our office, placing him in a holding cell. Then he called me as per our new in-house protocol.

I responded right away. Once I assessed the situation, I called Sergeant Royce A. Evers from the LSP Narcotics squad in Baton Rouge. He and Investigator Theodore 'Ted' Porter responded. Coates was facing a minimum of five years on the possession charge at the infamous Louisiana State Penitentiary, located in Angola, only about 80 miles east of us, assuming he were convicted. We pounded that into his head (in a manner of speaking) in an effort to get him to cooperate. It wasn't looking too good for him, either. Understanding his bleak future, he had a sudden epiphany and puked up his guts (also in a manner of speaking).

He said he bought the meth from Perry M. Broussard, age 24, in Krotz Springs, where he had just been arrested. Broussard was known both to LSP and to us as a meth head and low level dealer. He had one prior conviction in Saint Landry Parish for misdemeanor possession, for which he served a year at hard labor in our jail. During that year, he had been an integral link in our chain gang which picked up the trash along the ditches running parallel to our main highways every single weekday. He worked his skinny ass off for the first time ever in his wastrel life. Apparently it wasn't enough because he didn't learn his lesson.

We placed a recorder on one of our unlisted office telephone lines, and at our direction, Coates made a recorded consensual call to Broussard. Coates lied and complained that the ounce of crystal he just bought was tainted. He wanted to return it for some product which wasn't. They argued back and forth for a while, until Broussard finally said for Coates to bring it back, and he'd switch it out for another can, minus the amount of meth Coates had already ingested, of course.

We followed Coates (in his jalopy) back to Krotz Springs. Sergeant Evers placed a tiny transmitter under the headband of Coates' New Orleans Saints baseball cap. He activated it, and recited the standard preamble including name of informant, target, date, time, and location. We sent Coates in with the can he had purchased earlier, minus enough ice to make another valid test in the event we lost it during the upcoming swap. LSP's equipment was state of the art, and we could hear every word, every throat clearing, every surreptitious passage of gas in real time, all of which we were recording. The panic signal was "Please don't hurt me" and the arrest signal was "This will get me all the way to Miami".

Coates knocked on the door and a woman let him in.

What? He had not mentioned anything about a woman. Surprises are seldom a good omen in a dangerous setting. Coates said, "Hey Karen, I was expecting Perry." (Sergeant Evers thought he recognized her voice, and tentatively identified her as most likely being Karen Cleveland, Broussard's former live-in girlfriend.)

Karen whispered, "He's in the kitchen. He's pretty pissed at you. You better watch out."

A few seconds later, we heard Coates exclaim, "Yo Perry! Thanks man, for swapping this shit out for some righteous stuff. Hey! What's with the pistola? We're amigos, you and me. You don't need that to impress me."

"Sit down, asshole. All my shit is good. It's always good. I don't believe a fucking word you said. Gimme the tin."

"Here, brother, try it yourself."

Pause.

"There ain't nothing wrong with it, asshole. I think I'll fuck you up for trying to get over on me. You must think I'm stupid! I'll show you stupid!"

"No, man. Take a bigger hit. You didn't try enough. I wouldn't shit you. Why would I do that to you? We've always been righteous with each other."

"That's what got me to thinking. Something ain't right here. Nothing wrong with this shit. You get busted and the cops send you back over here to trick me?"

"No, man. You ever hear of cops returning your shit after they busted you? That's fuckin' crazy, man."

"I dunno. I smell a rat. I ought to just shoot you the fuck right now."

Karen exclaimed, "Perry! What's wrong with you? Are you fucking crazy? You gonna shoot this man in my kitchen? Then what? Grab your shit and run out the door and leave me to clean up your mess? This is my house! You wanna shoot someone, you do it somewhere else far away from me, and then don't you ever bother coming back."

"What's with you taking his side? Huh? You fucking this pencil-dick behind my back when I ain't home?"

"Do you even hear yourself? Get the hell out, and don't come back! I'm through with you! You're fucking paranoid, man. You been smoking too much of your own shit."

Coates spoke up. "Look maybe I came at a really bad time. Just give my shit back and I'll be on my way. Hook up with you all some other time when you're feeling better."

"I don't think so, dickhead. Sit back down if you wanna live. I gotta think."

"Okay. Okay."

(Two minute pause with nothing but breathing sounds.)

"Look, maybe Karen's right. Sorry. I am a little messed up. I'll take it back, but you owe me ten bucks for what you used. Karen, go get Esau another can."

(Near silence. Soft steps fading. Pause for another minute and ten seconds.)

(Muffled words). "Perry, where you stash it this time?"

(Louder.) "You know where. Where I always put it."

"Well, it ain't there."

"Did you hide it on me?"

"No! Hell, no! Come see for yourself."

Esau said, "Look, I can tell this is a bad time. I better go."

"You sit tight right there. You even fart and you're a dead man."

(Sound of a chair scooting on the floor. Another minute passes.)

(Muffled.) "Found it! It's in my sock drawer. You didn't look far enough back."

"Whatever."

(Sound of footsteps.)

"You know what else I found, Esau, old buddy? Huh? I'll tell you what I found. I found your fucking Bruce Springsteen tee shirt in my underwear drawer. The one you always used to wear. The one with the grass stain on the back."

"Great. I didn't know whatever happened to it. I thought I lost it. Where is it? I'll take it back."

"Ya see. That's just it. Why was it in my drawer, all nice and washed and folded up? Ya wanna know why? Because you been bonin' Karen when I wasn't here and you forgot and left it. That's what! She wasn't paying attention and she washed it and put it away thinking it was mine. You piece of shit! You're a dead man, asshole!"

Karen screamed, "Get out now, Perry, you asshole! I've had enough! You wanna know something? You got a teeny weeny dick that couldn't please a horny 14-year-old girl on your best day. You ever see Esau's schlong? I bet not! He's got a monster donkey dick that flips my switch every single time. Whenever you're gone, he quenches my fire! I love his dick! No! I worship his dick! He makes me come rivers! Get it? Now get the fuck out! Take all your shit and get! I never want to see you and your teeny weenie mouse peter ever again! Out!"

"Oh, I'll go all right. Right after I splatter his brains and yours all over the fucking wall!"

"Don't! Please don't hurt me!"

"Pray, motherfucker. Pull your jeans down all the way to the floor. I wanna see this monster dick before I blow you away."

Karen screamed, "You even think about it, asshole, and I'll make sure you never draw another breath!"

(Broussard must've looked up.)

He asked, "Where'd you get that gun, Karen?"

He sounded real nervous and more confused. That plus the panic signal was enough. We crashed the front door.

I was first, and kicked it in. Sergeant Evers, Deputy Potts, and Investigator Porter all rushed past me into the kitchen. When I entered, I saw Broussard had his Taurus 9 millimeter pistol trained on Coates. Karen Cleveland had her Smith & Wesson, five-shot snub-nose revolver trained on Broussard's chest. Coates was standing there with his jeans down around his ankles. No underwear. Porter and I aimed our guns at Broussard. Evers and Potts aimed at Karen. Then I glanced over at Coates. His eyes were big as silver dollars.

Karen wasn't joking. Even soft I'd never seen anything that enormous on a man. It was almost as big as a python, except pink. Coates missed his calling. He should have gone into the porn star business. He could have made a whole lot more money than he earned now as a WalMart buggy retriever. He clearly had the biggest dick in Louisiana, bar none. It put every other grown man to shame.

Broussard broke the silence. He said, "Well, the truth finally comes out. Esau, you big prick, I always knew you was a fuckin' weasel. You deserve to die.

"Karen, you're a fucking Jezebel, and I ought to kill you, too."

(Another very pregnant pause.)

Broussard's tone and demeanor changed. It was like he accepted defeat after all his bluster. With tears in his eyes he said, "Officers, I surrender, but before I do, you need to know that Karen is my business partner. She's even guiltier than me. She has the source. I only had Karen. Now I think about it, I bet she was bonin' him, too. I took all the risk while she fucked everyone

I know whenever I wasn't around. Ain't that some shit? I love this bitch, man, and she screwed me over!"

Broussard gently placed his pistol on the table. Investigator Porter had his shotgun and I had my pistol trained on him. Deputy Potts had his shotgun and Sergeant Evers had his pistol trained on Karen. Now Porter switched his target to Karen. I continued to aim my gun on Broussard in the event he had a change of heart and went for his gun. You know. Suicide by cop. Things were way too tense for any of us to make a sudden move.

Sergeant Evers spoke very calmly. He almost whispered when he cooed, "Set it down, Karen. You don't wanna do this. He isn't worth it. Think about it."

He kept trying to talk her down. He said, "Come on, Beautiful. You got your whole life ahead of you. Put it down, please. We got this."

She never responded. She was laser-focused on Broussard. Her eyes were burning holes in him. Her body was so taut with flexing she looked like she was chiseled in stone. We were all holding our breath. Nobody wins in a Mexican stand-off.

You could see the blazing anger in her eyes. She was way past reason.

Suddenly, she snapped off three rapid fire shots into Broussard's torso before Potts, Porter, and Evers unloaded on her. This all took place within 10 feet and two seconds. There wasn't much left of Karen's once stunning upper torso and breasts. Blood splatter was everywhere. I thought Broussard was a goner, but he surprised us all. He survived.

All the while, the listening device hidden in Coates' hat was still recording. LSP and we still use it in training classes to this day. None of us present had ever experienced anything like this.

What we finally decided is that this was a domestic dispute which erupted into a shooting in the middle of a dope transaction. Karen Cleveland was the joker in the woodpile. No one saw this coming, especially Broussard, otherwise he never would have surrendered his gun.

End of a very sad story.

We recovered 46 ounces of methamphetamine in 46 Skoal tins, and $1,578 in cash in Karen Cleveland's rented, furnished house.

She was buried in her hometown in Tupelo, Mississippi.

Coates was sentenced to five years on probation. We all knew he couldn't stay clean. Judge Calvin M. DesHotel warned him loud and clear what would happen if he violated his probation. He put the admonition in writing in Coates' J&C. The slightest violation would be his ticket to Angola forthwith.

It only took two months. No matter what, Coates couldn't enjoy prosperity, even blessed with Louisiana's biggest dick. He got caught 'holding' again, and Judge DesHotel dropped the hammer. Coates had no one to blame but himself.

By that time, Broussard's injuries had healed up. He'd been shot in his left shoulder, left upper arm, and chest. Two shots were through and through with no damage to his bones or arteries. The other broke his arm. Now he's serving 23 years in Angola. By the time Coates was incarcerated, Broussard had probably told every inmate he'd ever spoken with that Coates was a snitch. We told the prison administration too, recommending they keep Coates in solitary confinement.

I keep expecting to be notified that Coates has been murdered. So far, so good. Either Coates leads a charmed life, or he's been turned out as somebody's bitch. Time will tell.

That was my first drug bust in Saint Landry Parish. Not the ending I had hoped for, nor the kind of excitement I had relished.

June was fast approaching. Life as the chief deputy returned to my new norm. The weather was steamy hot. Nothing new there. The pace was somnolent. It was too hot to fight, and almost too hot to fuck. I couldn't complain. That's just the way it is in Louisiana.

I had waited and waited for Abner to tell me what he decided to do about the person(s) who firebombed his house the night of the election, but he never brought it up. Abner and I see each other daily, go to lunch together most weekdays, and socialize together frequently when we're off duty. We talked about everything except that. Finally over lunch one day, I brought it up.

"Ah know who done it - Peter 'Peckerwood' Perkins and his liddle brudder, Amos. Peter used ta be a deputy who woiked in da chail. We hoid he was sneakin' in all kind of contraband. Of course, da inmates paid him and den dey owned him. Dey kept demanding more'n more. Foist it was cigarettes. Den it was booze. Den cellphones. Den weed. 'Don't do what we say and we'll rat chu out.' Dat sort of t'ing. He got caught smugglin' in an ounce of weed. Ah busted 'im redhanded mahself. Ah wanted ta th'ow his ass in chail.

"Cheriff Neicase didn't wanna go public. He was afraid it would reflect poorly on da SO, and it would have. He tol' me ta kick 'im loose. Den he fired 'im. He tol' Peckerwood he was blackballed from evah woiking in law enforcement again, at least in Louisiana, an' he was true ta his woid. Peckerwood tried four or five agencies, but dey all toined him down. Now he woiks in da fambly bidness mowin' grass and trimmin' da booches. He's a chithead.

"He t'ought he was payin' me back wit' dat Molotov cocktail. Amos is on'y 16, and on da simple side. He had damage in da womb. He was chust doin' what his big brudder tol' him ta do. Ah spoke wit' his daddy, Leland Peters. Leland's a good man. He tol' Peckerwood raght in fronta me dat he stub his toe one mōe time, he was t'rough wid him. Since den, Peckerwood been mindin' his Ps and Qs. Far as Ah'm concoined, it's over wit' unless he stubs his toe again. Den Ah'll come down on him like da Wrath of God. Look, don't spread dat around. Ah'm gibin' him anudder chance."

Case closed on Peckerwood, at least for now.

- *Chapter 10* -

Homicide

Life had settled down to a dull roar by the end of May. The big events for Hannah and me were the Rayne Frog Festival in Acadia Parish, and the LSU Tigers baseball game at Alex Box Stadium against the Ole Miss Rebels, which we attended with Abner and Marisol. The Tigers won.

The weather in South Louisiana is moderate from November through March. However, no matter the season, it's always humid. That goes without saying. In April it starts to get hot - as in 90+ degree hot everyday - and it doesn't usually abate until November.

During the summer months, I always look forward to the aperiodic, massive afternoon thunder and lightning rain storms, which drop a couple of inches of rain in just an hour or so. The storm itself is an awesome display of heavenly fireworks, and it always mesmerizes me. On the downside, once in awhile the wind will blow down a large tree or a telephone pole, which was usually half-rotten anyway from the inside out but nobody knew. On the plus side, the temperature drops for an hour or two of sweet, blissful comfort. Then the sun returns; the temperature breaches the 90s; and, the humidity rises to 100%. What? Have you ever wondered how the humidity can be 100% but it's not raining?

That's the way it is down here. Nobody thinks a thing about it. They're 'used to it.' Very few ever voice a complaint. What would be the point? 'It is what it is.' I had lived on the Mississippi

Gulf Coast for 25 years, so I had acclimatized to the steamy heat. Even so, for some reason the humidity always seemed muggier here than on the coast. Maybe it was because in Opelousas there were no sea breezes. Could be I was just delusional.

Maybe the weather was the reason Saint Landry Parish seemed to be relatively crime-free. Maybe it was like Abner said. It was just too hot to fight or steal or screw someone else's woman. Maybe it was because the people were just plain nicer. Race issues were virtually non-existent here, pleasantly different from the big cities with all the loudmouths stirring up hate and discontent. For the most part, black and white folks got along just fine. A Yankee from Boston or Chicago would probably say I was wearing rose-colored lenses and sugarcoating my observation. Gilding the lily, as it were. They'd be wrong.

Tuesday, May 25th, 2004, was your typical sultry spring day. Absolutely nothing was going on. The air conditioning was not up to the task of cooling our building, at least today. I was in my office weeding out documents I had saved but no longer needed. The office shredder was doing it's job superbly, creating thin strips of confetti from missives which were once of great internal import, or so I thought.

I had the radio tuned to the local AM station, where the LSU Tigers baseball team was being extolled or crucified depending upon on the perspective of the caller. It was nothing but drivel, white noise, while I murdered time aimlessly. Normally I would have been tuned into the FM classical music station, but today the programmer was playing dreadful selections. No doubt he unwittingly ran off potential newcomers to classical music with his abominable choices for today.

I could have gone on home to do something useful, such as

watch the internecine aerial combat at my hummingbird feeders out by my patio, which were filled daily by me with pink sugar water. I could even treat myself to a savory cigar simultaneously. It was late afternoon and Abner wouldn't give a hoot. He was already out and about taking care of sheriff business somewhere, which when you think about it, includes nearly everything which occurs in his parish. All the problems fall into his lap. Bottom line. I didn't have anything to do, but force of habit would not allow me to call it a day.

The dispatcher, Thelma Vidrine, patched a call back to me. She said, "Chief, this sounds like a real bad one. Soon as I hang up, I'm sending unit 21 to respond. Remember who that is?"

"Oliver V. Dedeau?"

"Oliver V. Dedeau is correct."

Thelma rang off and I picked up the receiver. I said, "Chief Barnett. Who's calling please?"

"Dis Eugene Raoul Pierre, Chief. Dey calls me Frog Legs. Ah'm at mah daddy house. He at 12220 Highway 361, chust before chu get ta Highway 107 in Big Cane. Ah'm a quatter-mile past him at 12236.

"Somebody done kilt mah daddy and stoled some of his valuable chit. Dey locked mah boy, Rupert - dey calls him Booger - in da storm cellar. Booger didn't come home atter school and Ah was woirried about him. See, he simple - 16 yeahs old and still in da fift' grade. He ain't gonna nevah be right. He got off da school bus at my daddy house, but Ah didn't know. He saw da killer, and dey locked him down dere while dey do dey doity woik. Can chu come right away? Ah don't know what else ta do."

"What's your daddy's name?"

"He name Nicodemus Jean Pierre. He 82 yeahs old. Why

somebody do dat awful t'ing? He nevah hoit nobody."

"You said they. Do you know if it was one person, or more?"

"Booger seen one. Dat's all Ah knows."

"Okay. Mr. Eugene just stay where you are."

"Call me Frog Legs."

"Okay, Frog Legs. Don't touch anything. We're on our way."

"Okay. T'anks. Please hoiry."

"Will do. See you in a few."

I hung up. Then I told Thelma to get ahold of the sheriff and ask him to meet me out there if he could. I jammed on my Stetson, ran out the door, and fired up the Jeep, which I had really learned to appreciate. It added a new dimension to driving I hadn't felt since I was a 16-year-old kid learning how to drive for the first time. Not only that, I could go anywhere, and park with ease in any parking space no matter how tight. It was a hoot to drive.

A million thoughts were racing through my mind. I'd responded to a number of murders as a police officer, but had investigated nary a one. My job had been patrol, not investigations. The wall erected between Patrol and Investigations was distinct and inviolable. Most homicide dicks thought they were rock stars and the patrolmen were their adoring fans. Most of the time all we thought was we wished we could have been there to arrest or even shoot the culprit, but were thankful the blood and guts were someone else's responsibility and not ours.

I had only worked on two murders as an ATF special agent. One of those was a car bombing. The other was a gangland slaying of an 18-year-old youth who testified in court against a fellow gangbanger. It was both payback and a warning to others not to cooperate with the 'pō'-lice'. Parties unknown sneaked up on him when he got off from work at midnight as a parking lot attendant, and gave him a double tap to the back of the head with a 9-millimeter Glock. It was captured on a surveillance video, but it was dark; the image was blurry; and hoodies concealed the faces of the two assailants. I knew exactly who did it, but could never prove it. Neither could the homicide detectives in the big city in which it occurred. (The trial took place in the U.S. District Court in Biloxi, but the slaying was in a major city elsewhere out of state.) The big city dicks worked hard on the case and were just as frustrated as I. Two years later, they told me that one of our two suspects had turned up dead as a victim of a gangland slaying. Poetic justice. At the time, I hoped his partner was 'sweating bullets,' worried about his own demise.

The results were exactly the same on the car bombing - knowing but not proving. The murder occurred the same weekend the victim's husband, a convicted murderer serving 25 years in Parchman, had gotten a weekend pass from the penitentiary, if you can wrap your arms around that! What the heck? I never could. Villainous parties unknown surreptitiously placed a bomb constructed with the explosive compound PETN [pentaerythritol tetranitrate], under the front seat of the victim's car. It was rigged to go off when the ignition switch was turned on.

ATF tracked the explosive via taggants, hidden markers within all explosive compounds, which identify the specific explosive, allowing it to be tracked from manufacturer, to wholesaler, to retailer, to purchaser, and in this particular case, to the construction site where it had been reported stolen three months earlier, along with several cases of dynamite. When the vic, who was alone, sat in her car and turned on the ignition, kablooey! 'It was all she wrote.'

She was still alive when first responders arrived, but her pelvis was split wide open and her insides were mush, hanging outside the bottom of her torso. Interestingly, her husband had already checked himself back into prison before she died.

What was the motive? Most likely because the vic was having an affair while hubby was doing time in the joint. We confirmed that a specific somebody snitched her out. The problem was, we could never tie either the husband or the snitch to the explosive device. Hubby most likely paid somebody to do it. He was mobbed up with the Dixie Mafia, and certainly had all the right connections.

Why then, did he get a pass from prison and make himself suspect number one? Did he plant the bomb himself? Did he have to pay the killer first? Had he hoped to watch her die? We never found out.

We conducted at least a hundred interviews, including with the lover who was quaking in his boots. Not long afterwards, he took a powder. Nobody was talking. We had no leverage. We even polygraphed several ex-convicts who we thought had involvement. Two failed, but refused to answer questions after the examination and we didn't have enough evidence to charge them.

The case went unsolved after nearly a year of running out every conceivable lead. It wasn't my case. I was just one worker bee. The entire Gulfport ATF office, the local sheriff's office, and the ATF National Explosive Response Team, who conducted the crime scene search and forensics, all worked on it. Even so, I had hundreds of hours invested in working this one murder. I had hoped I would find and connect the missing link. It was wishful thinking.

So, my track record was zero for two as an investigator of homicides and I was nervous about resolving this one. Homicide investigation was a little out of my wheelhouse, but I owned this new one, like it or not. It was all mine. My duty was to catch the killer(s) and prove the case beyond a reasonable doubt in a court of law. Saint Landry Parish had not suffered a homicide in more than two years, so whatever I did would be under intense scrutiny by the public and the local press, reflecting favorably or poorly upon the sheriff's office.

I didn't know exactly where the victim resided, having only been in Big Cane once before, but I saw Oliver's cruiser, and pulled up to the crime scene. The residence was a small, one story, wooden dwelling painted white with black trim. It had a hip roof with gray asphalt shingles. It was a rectangular, approximately 40-by-30-feet, 1200-square-feet farmhouse, situated on three or four acres of level farmland. It was bordered by a metal post and wire farm fence in the back.

The lot also included a white wooden outbuilding to the left of the house. The batwing doors were propped wide open, as if they were seldom ever closed. I could see a faded, blue and white, 1960 GMC pickup truck parked inside. A 50-year-old old John Deere tractor, with small, close-set front wheels was parked next to it. The driveway and parking area in front of the outbuilding were gravel, which I could tell had recently been re-graveled. Everything looked to be in pretty good repair. I could also see several goats and one donkey grazing in the backyard.

Deputy Oliver V. Dedeau was standing next to his cruiser. He introduced me to Frog Legs and Booger, using their nicknames. Oliver said he had just arrived, and had not entered the house where the incident took place. He had been waiting for me.

Frog Legs was a wiry, 52-year-old, dark-skinned black male, with gray fringe creeping over his large ears. He stood 5-feet, 6-inches tall, tipping the scales at 130 pounds. When he opened his mouth, I could see his blue gums with large alabaster white teeth, which had a few vacancies where some were missing. His small, deep-set, brown eyes were piercing. His tongue and full lips were bright pink, and his lips had a thin blue border. He hadn't shaved, but he really didn't need to because he only had a few scraggly whiskers.

He was wearing a white tee shirt under baggy faded overalls about two inches too short, with white athletic socks peeking out from scuffed brown, well worn Jethro Bodine boondockers. His sunburned, now caramel-colored Panama hat with a cracked hole on the top front of the pinched crown, including a few dirty fingerprints along the brim and the bright blue satin hatband, set off his ensemble. His grief was written all over his craggy face. I could see the dried tear tracks on his cheeks, and they pierced my heart.

Oliver introduced us, and we shook hands. Frog Legs' hands, like his feet and ears, were over-sized, like they belonged to someone six inches taller, and he had a grip like a one-way vice. Frog Legs introduced me to Booger.

Booger was what we usually referred to as a big old strapping boy before the libtards turned that description into a racial slur. Call him a hulking, muscular, 16-year-old, dark-skinned, black youth. He stood 6-feet, 3-inches tall, weighing in at 220 pounds of ripped steel like Mr. T [Laurence Tureaud from the television series *The A-Team*], except he didn't have Mr. T's TV personality's surly attitude or gold necklaces. Booger had a close-cropped burr haircut with a hairline which naturally receded more than an inch on either side. He was a nice-looking, healthy kid, except for that dull, somewhat vacant expression mentally handicapped people tend to be cursed with.

Intellectually, he was about six-years-old. Fortunately, he was as friendly as Casper the Ghost. He was dressed just like his daddy, except he was wearing worn-out black, hightop sneakers and a filthy green-and-yellow John Deere baseball cap with the backside of the crown made out of plastic mesh for warm weather wear. He was even wearing it brim forward. Refreshing!

I made a conscious decision right then to learn as much as I could from the witnesses before examining the crime scene. Some might consider this 'putting the cart before the horse' but I opted to do it this way anyhow. I had no delusions to believe the victim was still alive, and I wanted to 'pick the brains' of my mentally handicapped witness and his grieving father while they were still in shock and everything was fresh in their minds. Not only that, I thought Abner would show up at any minute. Perhaps Inspector Clouseau or Lieutenant Theophilus Kojak would have chosen to conduct their investigations differently. No doubt they had more experience in homicide than I, at least in the motion pictures and television.

I asked, "Frog Legs, can you tell me what happened?"

He replied, "Ax Booger. He wa' here. All Ah done was free him from da cellah and check on Daddy. When Ah pulled up [in his 1976, olive green Ford F-100 pickup truck, parked up next to the outbuilding], Ah hoid da awfullest bangin' an' hollerin' comin' from da cellah, wich is over dere (pointing to a horizontal metal door setting on a concrete ledge about six inches off the ground on the left side of the house.) Ah see'd da padlock still be unlocked.

"Ah opens it up, an' Booger done nearly knocked me off mah feet rushin' out. He scairt of da dark.

"Den Ah axed, 'Booger, what chu doin' down dere?'

"Booger, chu tell da pō'-lice da rest."

Booger had his hands jammed deep into his pockets. He seemed to be studying a dung beetle which was crawling between his size 15 sneakers. He looked up with mournful, puppy dog eyes, and said softly, almost in a whisper, "Ah done wrong. Ah got off da school bus heah 'stead ob at home. Ah woirried mah papa and mah mama. Ah wanted ta see PawPaw 'cause sometime he hab candy. Ah likes Tootsie Roll Pops, 'specially da rād ones. Dey costs a dime at da Jiffy Sto' down at da co'ner, but PawPaw buys 'em by da box and den dey on'y costs a nickel. Dey's a hunnert in da box, too!

"Dey was a big black pickup truck in da yard when Ah got off da bus. It parked over dere (pointing next to the shed) and it all new and shiny. It hab two wheels on bof sides in da back."

"Do you know what brand?"

"It say F-O-R-D."

"What else can you remember?"

"Da nigga mean."

"So he was black?"

"Yeah. An' real mean. He an' PawPaw ahguin' loud."

"Do you know why?"

"Da mān say PawPaw owe him money an he wont it now. PawPaw say 'Ah don't owe chu a goddam t'ing.' Dat what he say when Ah come up and open da doe."

"Then what happened?"

"PawPaw say, 'Boy, chu need ta toin aroun' an' go back

outside. We talkin' grownup t'ings.'

"Den de mān say, 'Boy, chu better do what he say or Ah filet chu lahk a fish.'

"Den he pull dis big knife outta it case and point it at me. Da point touch mah neck. Den PawPaw yell at da mān. He yell, 'Bustah, get outta mah house now! Ah'm done wich chu.'

"Den da mān laugh an' say, 'Shut up, ol' mān, or Ah'll cut chu too.' Den he tell me, 'Come heah, boy. Chu go outside and open dat cellah doe for me.'

"PawPaw say, 'Don't do it boy! I'm gettin' my chotgun' but da mān point he knife raht chere (pointing to his Adam's apple) on mah t'roat an' he say, 'Hoiry up boy befōe it too late' so Ah went outside.

"We walks over ta da cellah an' he say 'Open it up, nigga' so Ah takes off da lock, 'cause we ain't nevah lock it. We chust use it ta keep the doe closed. Ah takes it off and he choves me down da steps an' slams da doe shut and puts da lock on. Ah be yellin' and bangin' on da doe 'cause dey black widow spidahs down dere, but he chust walk away. Den Ah hears da screen doe slam.

"Dey was yellin' at each udder, but Ah couldn't unnerstan' wat dey say. Ah chust keep bangin' on da doe and yellin' fah dem ta get me out!

"Den it get all quite. Den Ah hears da screen doe slammin' chut. Ah hears a motah staht up and some drībin' away. Dat's all Ah knows 'til Daddy get me out."

"Do you know the name of the bad man?"

"All Ah knows is dey calls him Bustah da Cussah 'cause he say lots of swear woids. He a big, black as naght nigga lahk me but not as tall, exceptin' he mean an' Ah'm nice. He point he knife at my t'roat an' say he gonna filet me lahk a fish. Ah hates dat mān!"

I asked, "Frog Legs, you know this man?"

"Ah knows him. He da buy and sell mān. Chu sells ta him low an' he sells ta chu high. Dat how he make his livin'. He have a stō in Bunkie over in Avoyelles Parish. He call it Bustah's Buy & Sell. It on US 171 chust nort' of Highway 115 on da raght side. He a bad mān. He cut mō dan one people wit' dat big knife he always carry, an' he done some time foe it, too."

"What's his last name?"

"Devereaux. Bustah Barnard Devereaux. He daddy daid now but dey called him da mayor of all da niggas in dat part of Avoyelles Parish back in da day. Anytime one of da white plantation folks need hands ta woik da fields or a barn need to be put up, dey tell he daddy, Ole Mān Willy Nilly Devereaux and he get dem many niggas as dey need. Den all da woikers hadda pay Willy Nilly a nickel fah each owah dey got paid. Pay up or get blackballed and don't nevah get anudder chob. Get mād about it and get chur t'roat slashed.

"Willy Nilly fast wit' dat knife, too. Mos' of da time, back in dem days, unless it real bad, da white folk didn't intafere in nigga bidness. Dat how Willy Nilly got so powoful. Cause he a killah. Bustah try ta act like he daddy, but he not dat smart. Besides, nowadays, white folk get involved in black folk' bidness, chust like chu doin' now. Dat why Bustah get locked up so much."

(Just then, Oliver's radio sprang into life. Thelma told him to tell me Sheriff Ladner was tied up and wouldn't be coming. Oliver responded in the affirmative, and I acted like it didn't matter, but I was a little worried. Abner wasn't one to kiss off a major crime scene in his own parish.)

"That's good to know.

"Frog Legs, you ready to take us inside? Booger you stay right here."

"Yassuh, Chief.

"Booger chu stay put."

Frog Legs led Oliver and me in through the front door. There was some shade on the verandah, but it was sweltering inside the house in spite of all the windows being wide open. The parlor was the only room with a ceiling fan and it was 'going balls to the wall'. I quickly assessed that this was a two-bedroom, parlor, one bath, and kitchen house.

Nicodemus Jean Pierre, black male, age 82, bald with thin white, wooly hair, 5-feet, 5-inches tall, and 120 pounds of bone and gristle, was lying flat on his back in the kitchen on the linoleum floor. He was wearing overalls and a blue chambray shirt with the sleeves rolled halfway up. He had on a new pair of Army surplus combat boots. His arms were splayed out and his eyes were wide open. I could see he had the beginning of cataracts. His throat had been slashed across the jugular vein. A pool of blood 3-feet in diameter surrounded his head and upper torso.

His no-name brand, single-shot, 12-gauge shotgun with no serial number, was laying on the kitchen table, broken open for loading. It had to be at least 90 years old, because back then, the cheaper guns, shotguns in particular, oftentimes had no markings or serial numbers. That being said, this gun had been well cared for. The wooden stock and fore-grip had recently been refinished by sanding and coating with a reddish stain. The metal parts had all been buffed, and re-blued by a non-professional, because there was a little streaking in the finish and a few thin spots. (I recognized the amateur bluing job because I had blued an old .22 rifle once myself. There's definitely an art to it.) If there had ever been a speck of rust on this firearm, it was long gone now.

The chamber was empty. I snapped the barrel closed, cocked the hammer, and test-fired it. It functioned perfectly.

A really old, as in antique old, yellow and blue soft cardboard Western brand ammunition box with red lettering, containing 11 number 6 shot in waxed cardboard shells was half open. Four yellow shells had spilled out onto the table. From all appearances, Mr. Pierre had been attempting to load his shotgun when he was murdered. The salt and pepper shakers and napkin holder had been knocked off the wooden table and were lying on the floor away from the pool of blood.

I looked all through the house, opening doors and drawers, looking under the beds, between the box springs and mattresses, searching the closets for hidden openings, behind pictures hanging on the walls, essentially 'anywhere a mouse could go' or anyplace else I could think of, looking for signs of a disturbance or ransacking. I was thorough, taking my time, but didn't see anything out of order, or unusual empty spaces, or any other anomalies.

What I did see, which blew my doors off, was a handmade, wooden framed shadow box about a foot tall and nine inches wide. The frame was flat and about an inch wide. It was made of poplar wood. 'Pfc N. J. Pierre, US Army' was carved neatly into, and centered on the bottom section of the frame.

The top left of the display had a 3" black and white photograph of Pfc Pierre in his Army, olive drab dress uniform, wearing an Ike jacket and garrison cap at a jaunty angle. It was probably taken at the end of World War II. To the right of the photograph was a 92nd Infantry Division (Colored) Army Patch. It was a round, OD green ball, circumscribed with a black circle, with a black buffalo featured in the center.

Below the picture and patch were three medals evenly spaced in a row. From left to right was a Silver Star, European-Africa-Middle Eastern Campaign Medal with three combat stars, and a World War II Victory Medal.

Frog Legs was watching me as I studied this homemade testament to his daddy's valor in the war. Pointing to the Silver Star, I said, "This is really an honor. Do you know anything about it?"

For the first time since I had been on site, Frog Legs smiled. He replied, "Daddy got drafted in 1943. He be 21 yeahs old den. Everyone else dat age done been drafted, but Daddy woiked on Mr. Cecil B. Twyman's plantation, and he be da mān in chahge of da Draft Boahd. Daddy be Miss Esther's poisonal soivant and she be Massa Twyman's wife. Dey was bot' old, but Miss Esther got polio and be confined to da wheelchair. Daddy take care of hoi and drive hoi wherever she wanna go in hoi big black DeSoto. Dey even bought Daddy a fine black suit and Flōsheim shoes, an' white shoits, an' black ties, an' a black fedora to wear when he be at woik. He look fine, like a mān in da movies. Chu know - Hump'rey Bogard.

"In da summer of 1943, Massa Twyman tell my daddy, 'Nicodemus, Ah got bad news. Ah don't have no choice. People's done noticed dat all da healthy mens yo' age done been drafted and dey knows you be Miss Esther's soivant. Dey's making a stink and Ah got no choice. Ah gotta draft chu. When da wah ovah, come back and chu can have chu chob back. Chu a good mān and we hate dis, da way t'ings are.' Den he give daddy 20 silvah dollahs and tells him to keep all his woik clothes. Da Twymans da finest white folks in all of Saint Landry Parish dat evah was.

"Daddy done all his Army trainin', den dey ship him ta France. Dey put him in a all colored Infantry Division, but Daddy a truck drivah, not a infantryman. Dey issue him a carbine, not a rifle. It smaller and not as powahful as a M-1.

"One day, Daddy and some udder sojers was in a convoy in France. Dey was s'posed ta be in a area dat had awready been cleared of Goimans, but it woin't. Dey was ambushed. Most of da mens was kilt, but Daddy grab his carbine and kilt eight Goimans and wounded t'ree mo'. Dat's why dey give him da Silvah Stah."

"You seem to know a lot about the Army. Did you serve?"

"Ah did. Me and my oldah brudder, Cletus. He t'ree years oldah dan me. He drafted in da Army in 1967. He infantry too. He on patrol in Vietnam an' step on a mine an' it kilt him. He on'y in country six weeks. Den Ah gradiated from high school in 1970, and Ah joined up for t'ree yeahs. Dey made me a doe gunner on a Huey helicoptah. Ah went ta Vietnam too, but Ah didn't get wounded and get no Poiple Heart, but Ah did oin crew chief wings and a Air Medal an' a Good Conduct Medal.

"When Ah got out, Daddy say, 'Frog, chu got a good edication. Chu needs ta find a good chob, so Ah goes ta Opelousas and got on wid the Post Office. Atter t'ree yeahs, I got transfoied ovah chere. Ah be a rural route lettah carriah foe 40 yeahs.

"Anyway, atter da wah, Daddy come home, an' he go back to woik foe Miss Esther. She up and died in 1949. She caught da cancer. One t'ing Daddy always do fah hoi was he'p polish hoi silvahware. Atter she pass away, Massa Twyman keep Daddy on to be he driver.

"Den he healt' staht failin' an' he gib Daddy Miss Esther's wooden box of silvahware and da silvah bowl. Da bowl hab da letters C-B-T and E-M-R and 5/3/1878 cahved on it. Da date cahved inside a haht lack a balentine. He even gib Daddy a signed papah sayin' da silvah a gif' so nobody t'ink Daddy done stoled it. Daddy say it woith hundreds o' dollahs when he gib it to him, and now mebbe woith a t'ousand or mō, Ah t'ink.

"Ah ax chu. Chu see dat silvah in dis house anyw'eres?"

"No. I did not. I don't even see where it's missing from."

"Da bowl be kep' on top of Daddy's dressah. He use it ta put t'ings from his pockets in when he undress ta go ta bed. Dat why chu didn't notice it missin'. Da silvahware box be kept in da bottom drawah of da hutch wit' da tablecloth on top. If chu didn't know dat, chu wouldn't miss it, 'cause da mān put it back all neat lahk. Momma on'y use dat silvahware foe special occasions such as Christmas or birfdays. Daddy always kep' it polished. Dat meant a lot ta him 'cause Massa Twyman gib it to him foe faithful soivice, like he done in da Army, on'y foe lots mō yeahs. He didn't look at da silver like somet'ing ta sell foe money. He would die foist befō' sellin' it.

"Dat what happen. Daddy nevah borrah no money from no mān he whole life. Buster a big fat liar. He been atter dat silvahware for yeahs. Daddy always tell him no. Now dis time Bustah kilt him foe it. He t'ought he could get away wit' it because Booger slow, but he ain't dat slow. No Sah! He lock Booger in da cellah 'cause he know Booger kill him if he see Buster try to hoit Daddy."

I had searched every inch of this house and did not see the box of silverware or where it had been stored. I asked Oliver and he said the same thing. I asked Oliver if he knew Buster Devereaux. He said he did not, but he had heard of him. Then I asked if he knew where Buster's Buy & Sell was. He said he did.

I asked Frog Legs if he would mind taking a seat in the parlor or on the verandah while we finished working the crime scene. He pulled out a corncob pipe, stuffed it full of Bull Durham from a small cotton bag with a yellow draw string, and struck a kitchen match to it. After a few puffs, he said he would be in the swing on the verandah.

I got out my homemade CSI kit. This crime scene didn't really require much in the way of specialized knowledge. I took photos; made a crime scene sketch with measurements; took some blood samples (which was unnecessary because the coroner would do that and I knew it, but did it anyway); and dusted for fingerprints in the vicinity of where the bowl and silverware had been before the theft. I also took photographs of the interior of the house, plus a few exterior shots of the property to include the cellar door and hatch. It didn't take 45 minutes altogether.

I called the office and spoke with the oncoming dispatcher, Ingrid Davis. She ran Buster Bernard Devereaux through LA OMV, NCIC, and NLETS. The OMV query came back with a photograph, which she put on my desk with the record checks. Buster was a black male, 61 years old, 5-feet, 11-inches tall, 210 pounds, short black hair, Fu Manchu mustache, a gold cap on his top front tooth on the right side, and a tattoo of a black widow spider with a red hourglass on his inside left wrist.

He had a lengthy rap sheet. The salient convictions were:

(1) 1970. Aggravated Assault. 10 years incarceration in Angola. Served 5;

(2) 1977. Strong Arm Robbery. 5 years incarceration. Served 4;

(3) 1984. Felon in Possession of a Firearm. 2 years incarceration. Served 2;

(4) 1995. Burglary. 4 years incarceration. Served 3;

(5) 1999. Grand Larceny. 5 years incarceration. Served 4.

While I had Ingrid on the phone, I asked her to send an ambulance for the corpse. Then I asked for the names and telephone number of the sheriff and chief deputy of the Avoyelles Parish Sheriff's Office [APSO].

I hung up and asked Oliver what he knew about the APSO. He said relations had always been cordial there between us. He knew the sheriff, Clinton W. Boyd, personally, and he was everything you'd ever want your sheriff to be - fair, honest, competent, intelligent, easy-going.

Oliver said he didn't know much about Chief Harmon L. Bergeron. He knew he was from West Monroe originally; that he'd been a starting linebacker on the Northeast Louisiana State University football team; and that he was real quiet; never said much. Pretty much stayed in the shadows. So far as he knew, both were well-liked by the deputies up there.

I decided to try the chief first. He wasn't in, so I asked for Sheriff Boyd. He picked right up.

"Sheriff Boyd speaking."

"Sheriff Boyd, this is Chief Deputy Marvin Barnett down in Saint Landry Parish. Hope I didn't catch you at a bad time."

"Not at all. What can we do for ya, Chief Marvin Barnett?"

"We just had a murder in Big Cane. Pretty sure the perp is one of your headaches."

"Good grief! Who's your victim?"

"An old man named Nicodemus Jean Pierre."

"Oh, Lordy! I know him! A very fine, honorable man. Used to

work for the biggest cane plantation in these parts, owned by a Mr. Cecil B. Twyman. Now a big corporation called Confederation America owns the Twyman place and dozens of others. Nicodemus got the Silver Star in WWII. You have any idea how many coloreds were awarded a Silver Star back in those days?"

"Couldn't have been many."

"You got that right."

"What happened?"

"An ex-con named Buster Bernard Devereaux slit his throat. Stole a wooden box of silverware and a silver bowl bequeathed to Nicodemus after Mrs. Eunice Twyman died. My major problem is the witness is a retarded 16-year-old black kid named Rupert Pierre . . . "

"You mean, Booger. His daddy is Frog Legs."

"That's him. Booger identified Buster the Cusser as the killer and said he was driving a new, black Ford dually pickup truck. Booger didn't actually witness the murder because Buster locked him up in the cellar first."

"Doesn't matter. Hold just on a sec.

"Beverly, get Rufus on the horn. Tell him to see if Buster's truck is at his shop. If not, tell him to check his digs, but to be discreet about it. No lights or siren or any Rambo shit. Make sure you tell him that, and to get right back to me asap."

"Yes, Sir, Sheriff."

"Okay. I'm back. We'll know something in a few minutes.

"Somebody should've waxed Buster a long time ago. In fact, it shoulda been me some 10 or 11 years ago. He pulled a knife on me when I was arresting him for drunk and disorderly. I clocked him with my blackjack, and then stomped a mud hole in him to make damn sure he never ever lifted his hand against a peace officer again. Pretty sure he learned his lesson because he's never resisted arrest since. I shoulda shot him but I wasn't thinking straight. It happened so fast. He got a year in my jail, and I can assure you, it was not a pleasant year for him, but if I woulda killed him back then, Nicodemus would still be alive today."

"Sheriff, you did your job. Nobody could see this coming. Even Nicodemus was taken by surprise. He let Buster into his house, but things got outta control. When Buster killed him, Nicodemus was trying to load his 100-year-old single-shot 12-gauge. What concerns me is nobody actually saw him cut the old man's throat."

"You said silver was missing. You got before and after statements from a kid too simple to deliberately lie. You got Buster's criminal history, but the biggest thing you got is Judge Calvin DesHotel. He's nobody's fool. In fact, if your DA will indict this as a capital crime and the jury convicts, your judge will give him the needle.

"In the meantime, we need to find Buster and recover the silver. That will be the ultimate nail in his coffin. We got to find it fast, or he might melt it down to conceal original ownership. Then you're standing around with your dick in your hand. Hold on a sec . . . ."

Dern! I never considered he might melt down the silver! These were antiques worth a whole lot more than the silver content!

"Chief, Buster just pulled up and went in his business. He was carrying a large cardboard box but my deputy couldn't see what was in it. I told him to sit tight and keep an eye on the truck. How long it take you to get there?"

"What is it - 20 miles? Say 20 minutes."

"See you there. I'll have five deputies with me."

"Leavin' now. See ya soon."

I told Oliver to wait for the ambulance and then to meet me at Buster's shop. I told Frog Legs I hoped I would see him at his house later tonight, but most likely tomorrow. Then I hopped in my Jeep and cut a chogie for Bunkie. On the way, I radioed the office and said I was en route to Bunkie to meet APSO deputies to arrest my suspect murderer.

I pushed the safe limits of the Jeep and arrived at 7:05. Sheriff Boyd and his posse were standing by. He sent two deputies to the rear door. Then Sheriff Boyd and three deputies and I entered through the front door.

Buster was alone, and we caught him off guard. He ran to the back door, where he was knocked on his can by Deputy Jared Bouvier, a giant of a man if I've ever seen one. While I was rushing to the rear of the store, I saw the Pierre silver and dozens of other items in an open cardboard box which I surmised were probably also stolen.

Deputy Bouvier jerked Buster up and slammed him against the wall, face first. Then he cuffed Buster and began searching his person. He retrieved a loaded, two-shot, .38 caliber derringer from his right trouser pocket. He also unsheathed a large hunting knife which had traces of blood on it.

Sheriff Boyd said, "Buster, it looks like you've been a naughty boy again. Shame on you. Looks like you're headed right back to Angola where you belong, asshole. Hopefully this time you never come back."

"Fock chu, Cheriff! Soon as Ah gets mah telephone call, Ah'm calling mah lawyah an' da FBI and tell dem chu violated mah civil rights for da last time."

"Good luck with that, buddy boy."

Then Sheriff Boyd turned to me. "Did you see IN PLAIN SIGHT what you were looking for Chief Barnett?"

"I did, and a whole lot more. Could you have Deputy Bouvier keep an eye on Buster while you and I have a little private conference?"

"You bet. Let's step outside."

We went out front and I said, "I truly appreciate everything you all have done. I'm betting all the other swag from that cardboard box is stolen too, but some of it may be from your bailiwick. I suggest we use the Pierre loot as probable cause to get a search warrant to toss his entire business and truck. It would be nice to search his house, too, but so far we don't have the PC [probable cause]."

"Well, I don't disagree, but we both know that even if everything in this store is stolen from Avoyelles Parish, your murder charge trumps it all."

"True, but there's always a chance some of the loot was taken from an Avoyelles Parish resident he murdered that we don't know about yet. I'd hate to lose it if he gets a lawyer who contests the search. I can always get a telephonic warrant from Judge DesHotel if your circuit court judge is a weenie."

"No. You're right. Judge Dixon isn't in the same league as Judge DesHotel, but I know he'll sign a warrant, but it'll take an hour."

"We could begin taking photos of what we do see while we're waiting to get the warrant signed. It could be a long night for some of your boys, but this could be a great news story, which can only enhance the reputation of your department and ours.

Plus, I bet Buster has far more enemies in your parish than mine. This is a big bust, worth a lot of ink to the local press."

"You're right again. I'll let you fill in Deputy David Jefferson so he can write the affidavit. He's done this several times before. Have you got leg irons and everything else you need to transport Buster back to Opelousas?"

"No, but Deputy Oliver Dedeau is in a marked unit with a shield and everything else we need. He should be here shortly.

"You know that knife is my murder weapon, and I'd like to glom onto the derringer too, if you don't have any heartburn with that."

"No problem. I know where it is if we need it."

"Thanks. I plan to take Buster back with us as soon as Oliver gets here. That okay with you?"

"Sure is. Don't leave before saying goodbye. I'm gonna call our favorite reporter and get him out here while you're feeding Jefferson all the details he needs for the warrant."

"Roger that. Let me go find him."

David Jefferson knew his job. We drafted his affidavit and got it signed and were 'ready to rock and roll' in 45 minutes.

Eventually Oliver showed up. Either the ambulance was slow getting to him, or he took time out to eat first. After he poked around and glad-handed the sheriff and other deputies, he trussed up Buster good and snug, stuffed him in the backseat of the cruiser, and made his way back to our jail.

Sheriff Boyd escorted journalist Arnold Campbell and photographer Rose Anne Givens from the Marksville *Chronicle* throughout the store to see the stolen property which had been recovered. Roseanne even took a photo of Buster in the back of Oliver's cruiser. I collected the two weapons and the Pierre silver and followed him shortly thereafter.

It was 9:05. I finally pulled into my driveway at 11:25 p.m. After a slow, lazy start for the day, my plate was full to overflowing.

- *Chapter 11* -
Initial Appearance

It really was a blessing to be a police officer again instead of a federal agent. The reason being, I had patrol officers available to do the grunt work, which otherwise would have been my responsibility. As an example, I didn't transport my prisoner, or book him, or lodge him in jail myself, nor was I responsible for getting him before the judge for his initial appearance, or any other court appearances for that matter. Even so, my workload due to this case would consume nearly all my waking hours in the weeks to come and I knew it.

I did call District Attorney Onslow K. Trudeau Tuesday night to give him a heads up that court Wednesday morning, May 26th, would be a little more exciting and perhaps more demanding than usual. Buster B. Devereaux would be making his initial appearance before Judge Calvin M. DesHotel for the dastardly murder of Nicodemus Jean Pierre, and the theft of his silver tableware. This was the only felony case on the docket and it was a biggie, possibly attracting the interest of the press. All the other cases on the docket were misdemeanors or traffic offenses. Onslow told me to bring everything I had, and to meet him at his office at 9 o'clock, an hour before court was to commence.

I made a copy of everything I had, and gathered up my available evidence, which included Buster Devereaux's sheathed knife, Bond Arms .38 Special caliber derringer (including the two bullets), and Nicodemus Pierre's stolen silver bowl and mahogany box with the eight place dinnerware setting, plus the ancillary utensils such as serving spoons and forks, butter knife, etc.

Onslow looked over everything while I explained the initial telephone call from Eugene Raoul Pierre, a/k/a Frog Legs; unwritten witness statements made by him and his mentally handicapped 16-year-old son, Rupert Pierre, a/k/a Booger; the crime scene investigation; arrest; and execution of a search warrant on Buster's business and pickup truck (after our sighting of the stolen silver in plain sight).

He studied Buster's rap sheet and asked, "What's the story here? Five felony convictions in Avoyelles Parish and five incarcerations in Angola. Geez Louise! How come he's not serving 25 years for being an habitual offender?"

"I don't know. I can try to find out. I didn't get the impression from Sheriff Boyd over there in Avoyelles that Buster got any sweetheart deals. In fact, just the opposite. Maybe their DA or Circuit Court Judge just don't cotton to that particular statute."

"Or more likely the last two DAs didn't push the SO to work a little harder. One would think, after the first felony conviction, the sentences would be harsher, not milder. Something smells a little fishy here."

"Perhaps, but not with the current regime. Sheriff Boyd told me he almost shot Buster when he pulled a knife on him several years ago. He beat him down instead. Now he's sorry he didn't put him down for good when he had the chance. Buster is one of his more consistent problem children when he isn't in prison."

"Whatever the reason in Avoyelles Parish, we will prosecute Buster on the high bitch over here. Also, I want to charge him with capital murder assuming all our evidence measures up to the scrutiny. I feel certain Judge DesHotel would sentence him to death were we to secure a conviction.

"You know, we haven't had a capital murder trial here since 1962, when Gerard LaRue Stone got convicted of raping and murdering the Ellison twins. They were 16 years old, and he lured them into his car by promising to take them to a Mardi Gras parade over in Hammond. Instead, he stopped by the Dairy Queen here in town before hitting the road, and bought them both a chocolate milkshake. They waited in the car while he ordered them at the window and brought them back.

"He laced the shakes with a sedative. They lost consciousness, and he drove them to an abandoned farmhouse just north of Grand Coteau where he stripped and bound them and had his way with them for a day-and-a-half. He did terrible things to those girls before strangling them with a piece of rope. He finally got the hot seat in 1965. By then most folks except for residents of Saint Landry Parish had forgotten all about it. At least that's what my dad said. Early on though, Stone nearly got lynched by an angry mob when word got out he was the culprit. I wasn't born then, but my folks told me about it after someone mentioned it when I was in the 3rd grade."

"Gosh. I need to go look that up."

"Did the ambulance take the body to Baton Rouge for the autopsy?"

"Sure did. Deputy Coroner Arnold Dawkins said they'd do it this afternoon. Also, just so you know, I plan to go to LSP after court to hand-carry the silver for a latent print exam. I'll also take the knife and sheath, and a specimen of Pierre's blood to their forensic chemists to see if they can make a match. First though, I'll drop off my film to get it developed at Rosenbaum's Pharmacy on my way out of town. Anything else you can think of that you need right away?"

"Yes. Just so you know, we can't charge Buster with the derringer. You can't prove he had it in his possession when he was in Saint Landry Parish. He could have put it in his pocket after he returned to his business. Right now, it's a violation which could be pursued by Avoyelles Parish, but I don't want you to return it to them just yet.

"You're a retired ATF agent, so think like one. I want a trace on it to see where it originated. No doubt it was stolen, but from whom? I want a ballistics check on it too, to see if it's been used in a homicide, and if so, where? You know what to do. If everything comes up a wash, give it back to Avoyelles."

"You got it. What else?"

"Find out everything Avoyelles turned up in Buster's store, truck, and house assuming they searched it too after you left. See what they can pin on him, if anything. Also, find out what any other parish could charge him with, assuming they've identified the owners of stolen property from other venues. Hell, they may have even found more stuff from Saint Landry! Doublecheck all our burglary reports from the last year to date."

"Will do."

"Okay, moving on. Today, the only charges I'm filing on Buster is what you wrote up - the murder of one Nicodemus J. Pierre, and the grand larceny of his silver you recovered. Judge DesHotel will most likely schedule a preliminary hearing for Friday, June 4th. We'll present what we have to the Grand Jury on Thursday, the 3rd. That means the 4th will be an arraignment instead of a preliminary hearing. I hope we will have everything we need to pursue capital murder by then. I've never tried one before, but Lord knows Buster has it coming."

It was time to go, so we walked over to the courthouse. I was stunned to see Eugene R. Pierre sitting in the front row bench behind the prosecutor's table. He was wearing clean, pressed overalls with a sharp crease, and an ironed white dress shirt with a purple and yellow, diagonally striped LSU tie tucked in under his bibs. He had on brown, buff-shined boondockers, an unbuttoned black suit jacket, with a clean, beige straw Panama hat resting in his lap. I could see he had a leather tether tied to a buttonhole in his bibs, running down into his breast pocket, most likely fastened to a silver pocket watch. Of course, it could be tied to a bank lockbox key securing his U.S. Savings Bonds. Who knows? His wooly hair was neatly combed with a pomade and parted down the left side. He certainly was spiffy. As the old saying goes, 'He cleans up nice.'

He smiled slightly and nodded at me as I took my seat on the right side of the prosecution table. Onslow took his seat on the left (inner aisle side) of the table, setting down a three-inch stack of court files on the table assembled in docket order.

It was a typical court day, in that most of the seats occupied in the gallery were taken up by defendants, not witnesses. Likewise, the defense attorneys whose cases were not first up on the docket were seated in the jury box. There were three, besides the first attorney up to bat, who was seated at the defense table.

Most traffic offenders did not hire an attorney. That's because they usually charged more money than the fine itself, and most folks got convicted anyway. The best you could hope for was traffic school to erase the points against your driver's license, but you had to pay for that too. Easier to pay the fine, take the points, and move on.

The circuit court clerk, Mrs. Muriel Richman, was sitting at the clerk's desk, in front of, and below the judicial bench, which was set up high, closer to heaven, nearer to all the celestial beings, where lightning and thunder originates.

We had two deputies functioning as bailiffs. Deputy Enos C. Ray standing to the left of the bench, white, lean, and tall, with wavy brown hair and a trim goatee. Deputy Josephine F. 'Wonder Woman' Jackson, was standing at the public entrance at the rear of the courtroom. Wonder Woman must have been descended from the Watusi tribe of Africans. She was 38 years old, with flawless ebony skin, 6-feet, 4-inches tall, and 185 pounds of well-defined muscle. Her uniform was tapered to accent her profile. If Judge DesHotel's dignified and august presence were not enough to keep the public at bay, both of his bailiffs certainly were.

I had glanced at the docket displayed on the wall outside the courtroom next to the batwing doors on my way in. It had the typical array of misdemeanor and traffic cases. I counted 11. Buster's case was in last place. We would be here awhile, but I had expected that. Judge DesHotel often liked to save the best for last.

At 9:55, Deputies Hiram Boniface and Clint Gifford brought in Buster, the man of the hour, attired in green and white, two-inch wide horizontally striped jail clothes with white shower clogs. He was trussed up like a Thanksgiving turkey with a belly chain connected to his handcuffs and his leg irons. The look on his ugly mug screamed 'all pithed off.' He had a mouse under his right eye. No doubt he showed his ass to the jailers when they were processing him. Too bad. He knew the drill by heart. He'd repeated it many times in the past, just not in Saint Landry Parish. They placed him in the jury box in the farthest corner away from the defense attorneys. When he sat down, he feigned sleep.

Then at 10 o'clock on the dot, Judge Calvin M. DesHotel made his entrance from the door behind his bench. Deputy Ray called the court to order and we all rose. Deputies Boniface and Gifford had to jerk Buster up on his feet by his chains. Judge DesHotel waited until then for decorum to be restored. Then he sat, banged his gavel, and told us to take our seats. The deputies shoved Buster back into his seat. Court was now in session.

The cases ahead of us didn't take too much time. Two public drunks pleaded guilty and were each sentenced to five days in jail. Six traffic offenders paid fines. One traffic offender's case was dismissed. The other two cases, one for shoplifting and the other for defacing public property, were postponed for two weeks.

In my experience, that usually meant they hadn't paid their attorneys in full yet. You could usually tell whenever the defense attorney made an innocuous comment about Mr. Green not being available for court today due to circumstances beyond his control.

One by one, all the defendants except for the two drunks going to jail and Buster, made their ways out of the courtroom as quickly as possible. It was like they were anxiously traversing a graveyard late at night during a thunderstorm. Besides that, who wants to hang out at the principal's office after your spanking?

After the prelude to felonious crime, the courtroom resembled a ghost town, bereft of honest citizens. Buster Devereaux's case was called. He was represented by an impeccably tailored attorney from New Orleans named R. Geoffrey Godfrey, Esquire. (Don't forget the esquire! He was sensitive to the slight. Also don't call him by his first name, Robin. He didn't like that either.)

Mr. Godfrey, Esquire was a slick, suave, 50-ish, Yankee

transplant from someplace up East. He was attired in a French-cut, charcoal-colored sharkskin suit with a French blue shirt which sported a white collar and white French cuffs with flashy gold cufflinks. So far, so good.

His tie was red, orange, and yellow with a paisley design. He was wearing moss green, alligator hide, low quarter shoes with a high gloss shine. His blond locks were coiffed in an Elvis Presley bouffant hairdo complete with lamb-chops. Except for his suit, he had more colors in his ensemble than a kaleidoscope. Truthfully, I didn't know what to make of him. Avant-garde? Circus clown? Colorblind? What?

I heard he was from New Hampshire, but maybe that was just because he obtained his law degree from Dartmouth. At any rate, he was purported to be the Louisiana version of F. Lee Bailey in the flesh - a veritable rock star of the courtroom. Supposedly he was even better than Neville T. Richard, who had represented Noé Arceneaux. Of course, Mr. Richard had served ten, 24-hour days in jail for contempt of court. Nevertheless, no matter which attorney were better, to the unwashed coonass and redneck Southerner, Mr. Godfrey had a funny accent.

I noticed during our several courtroom appearances, everyone except for Judge Calvin M. DesHotel seemed to be mesmerized by Mr. Godfrey. It was as though he had just transformed a glass of water into wine. You know, like a secular Jesus. A deity or Righteous Brothers level rock star of the courtroom. Grandiose. Awe-inspiring. Not a mortal who awakens in the morning with bad breath like us.

That was not my perception. I saw a pompous ass who was full of himself. At the same time, I wondered if he had any family or true friends, not just the fair weather type that money can buy.

I wondered how long it took him to get dressed in the morning, and how much it cost. I wondered if he had any warmblooded pets. I wondered if he were happy, or just an empty vessel. Enough already!

Mrs. Richman called our case. Deputy Boniface assisted Buster out of his seat and led him to the defense table. Judge DesHotel said, "Counsel make your appearances known for the record before the court."

"Onslow K. Trudeau representing the state, Your Honor."

"R. Geoffrey Godfrey, Esquire, of New Orleans, retained counsel for the defense, Your Honor."

"Mr. Trudeau, I see that the defendant is charged with the murder of one Nicodemus Jean Pierre, up in Big Cane, and the grand larceny of his silver bowl and tableware. Is that correct?"

"Yes, Your Honor."

"Mr. Buster B. Devereaux, tell me something of your background. I regret to admit that I don't know a soul from Bunkie."

Mr. Godfrey started to answer the question for Buster, beginning with, "Your Honor . . . ."

"Hush, Mr. Godfrey! You'll have your turn momentarily.

"Mr. Devereaux, tell me a little about yourself - where you reside, your occupation, marital status, how long you've resided where you are, and so forth. I'm not asking you to utter one word about your pending case. These are very serious charges you're facing. I want to know your roots in the community in an effort to assess your flight risk. The two attorneys can dig into the particulars of the case when we get to trial, assuming we get that far. You understand?"

"Yasser. Ah borned an' raised in Bunkie. Mah daddy

somet'ing ob a plantation fōman dere. He daid now. Ah lived dere mah whole life. Ah owns mah own bidness. It called Buster's Buy an' Sell, right on da main drag in Bunkie. Ah has a house next dōe. Ah been dere a long time. Ah cain't rightly say how many yeahs, but at least ten.

"Suh, Ah been in prison befōe. Ah ain't gonna lie, and Ah ain't nevah runned away from nuttin' or nobody. Chu tells me when ta come to cōte, Ah be dere. Chu got mah woid on it. And oh! Ah ain't got no wife. Nevah have, but no doubt Ah could mebbe have some chillins, but dem womens hab mō boyfrien's dan chust me, so none ob dem kids peoples says is mine is fō coitain mine. Unnerstan' what Ah'm sayin?"

"I do. Thank you.

"Mr. Godfrey, you may elucidate further if you so choose."

"Your Honor, my client is a respected businessman in Bunkie and environs. Everyone in the area there knows him. If he's incarcerated pending trial, he will most likely lose his business, which is his sole means of supporting himself. That's why I'm pleading for a reasonable bond, one he can post, especially since the facts surrounding this case are far from certain. He's had run-ins with Sheriff Boyd and several of his dubious deputies over in Avoyelles Parish in the past, and it's to Mr. Devereaux's credit that he still continues to reside there after all their harassment; however, that's the land of his nativity. He would never deign to live elsewhere."

"Sir, have you ever represented Mr. Devereaux before?"

"No, Your Honor, but he's never been accused of murder before, either. This is a horse of a different color. If convicted, he could well spend the rest of his life in prison."

"Indeed. Thank you, Sir.

"Mr. Trudeau, your comments, Sir, please."

"Your Honor, Mr. Godfrey just made my plea for me regarding bail.

"Mr. Devereaux has five prior felony convictions, and he served a prison sentence for each one! He has every reason to flee because of the severity of the charges pending against him, plus he knows how strong the case is against him!

"What he didn't know until this very moment, is that I plan to indict him for capital murder and the Habitual Offender Act. We will seek the death penalty.

"Just for the sake of argument, suppose the jury finds Mr. Devereaux innocent of murder. Without a doubt, he still will be convicted of being an habitual offender. How could he not? That's a mandatory sentence of 25 years in prison without benefit of parole. He's 61 years of age now. If he lived long enough to serve his entire sentence, he would be 86 years old.

"The most salient point however, is that we seek to execute him. What man would not flee were he facing the death penalty? The prosecution cedes the floor, Your Honor."

"Mr. Godfrey, I'm afraid Mr. Trudeau just checkmated you. I'm detaining Mr. Devereaux without bond pending his preliminary hearing, which is scheduled for Friday, June 4th. Make it 1 o'clock. That's assuming he hasn't been indicted beforehand. If he has, we will have an arraignment instead. You can ask for bail again then, but don't hold your breath unless the charges are reduced or dropped by the district attorney. There being no further business before the court, it is hereby adjourned!"

Onslow and I followed Mr. Godfrey out of the courthouse. Eugene R. Pierre followed us out. We all watched Mr. Godfrey drive away in his shiny black, 2004 Bentley Continental GT with a red leather interior. He had a vanity license plate, of course. It read WINNER.

I introduced Eugene Pierre by his nickname to Onslow, who asked Frog Legs to follow him over to his office. I excused myself, stating that I had many leads to run out. I told Frog Legs I would stop by his house tomorrow sometime if I could. He smiled and thanked me.

Then we parted ways.

- *Chapter 12* -
Running Out Leads

First stop was Rosenbaum's Pharmacy to drop off the film. I ordered five copies of each print.

Then I made a beeline to the LSP Laboratory in Baton Rouge. Fortunately I got there before they all went to lunch. I met with the Assistant Director, Dr. Amy B. Cherry. She said the latent print examinations on the silver and from the hutch would be completed by Friday. A ballistics examination on the derringer would also be ready by Friday too, if I got it to her by COB. Otherwise, it would be Monday. The DNA test results would take a week, assuming Abner would approve the $1,984 to pay for the examination.

I called Abner on my cellphone and let Dr. Cherry speak to him personally. Abner agreed, but I could tell it was like swallowing a peach seed for him. That was a huge chunk of change coming out of our budget which we hadn't planned on. At least we had a rainy day fund. Neither of us knew a DNA test was so expensive. However, there was no away around it if we wanted to guarantee a conviction, especially against the legendary F. Lee Bailey of Louisiana fighting for the defense. Don't believe it? Watch his glossy television ads. Read the billboards.

Next stop was at ATF ten minutes away. I caught Special Agents Hector V. Gutierrez and Brian Jerome 'BJ' Coates in the back parking lot. They were headed over to Frank's Diner for a late lunch, so I tagged along. Frank's has the best home fries I've ever eaten. Everything else there is scrumptious, too.

Afterwards back at the ATF office, Hector examined the Bond Arms .38 caliber, stainless steel derringer. He said, "This is really a very nice piece. Well constructed. Classic design. Costs $200 bucks, which is a lot of dough for just two shots, but it's very well made and accurate up to five or six yards."

He filled out the paperwork to initiate a trace. He promised to put a rush on it, and said if he got lucky we'd have the results in a week. Of course, being a recently retired ATF agent myself, he didn't tell me anything I didn't already know. At the same time, if he knew somebody in HQ he could probably get my request moved to the top of the stack. I thanked him and left.

I dropped the derringer off at LSP before heading up to Marksville, the local seat of government in Avoyelles Parish.

It took me an hour and 45 minutes, arriving at 4:15. Sheriff Clinton W. Boyd was out, but Chief Deputy Harmon L. Bergeron was in. I was extremely happy to make his acquaintance, being he was my peer. His dominating size suggested it was true he had been a collegiate football player, like Deputy Oliver V. Dedeau had reported. Imagine a blond Paul Bunyan in a lawman's uniform.

Also, I noticed he wasn't wearing an issue semi-automatic pistol like nearly all officers today. Instead, he was wearing a blue steel Smith & Wesson, Model 29, .44 Magnum revolver with a six-inch barrel, in a traditional brown, hand-tooled leather, western-style holster and belt with 24 loops filled with brass cartridges. Bravo for Chief Bergeron! I was favorably impressed with his panache.

What is today's Army motto? 'Be all you can be.' He was every bit of that. Whenever Chief Bergeron entered a rowdy barroom, it would be just like a scene in the television series

Gunsmoke, featuring James Arness starring as U.S. Marshal Matt Dillon in Dodge City. His size and cool cucumber demeanor alone would vanquish many an argument and misbehavior without him even raising his voice.

I had also been told by Oliver that Harmon was quiet, and he wasn't exaggerating. I introduced myself, finding him to be cordial but reserved. He led me back to his office and told me to have a seat, so I did. Then he sat in his rolling chair behind the desk. I glanced around his office to get a better feel for the man. It was fairly spartan, but not bereft of clues with respect to what was important to him. I saw two flashing green lights. The first was the official Northwestern Louisiana State University Football Team photograph for 1992, professionally matted and framed, hanging behind his desk. There was a wallet-size portrait of him in his uniform, wearing number 50, wedged in the lower left corner.

Facing his desk on the hallway wall where he could see it whenever he was seated, was an official photograph of the 1992 NLSU Cheerleader Squad in a matching matted frame. It too, had a wallet-size photo in the lower left corner, featuring a stunning blond cheerleader. That was the other flashing green light, and clearly the most important of the two. How many guesses would you need to surmise that this was Mrs. Bergeron while she was still a young maiden?

To break the ice, I asked, "You get your degree in law enforcement?"

"I did. You?"

"Yep, at Louisville, but it was many moons ago and I didn't have a double major with the greater being in Division I football."

That drew a slight nod and smile of acquiescence.

I continued. "I'm here because Buster Bernard Devereaux had his initial appearance for murder and grand larceny in Saint Landry Parish this morning. He's represented by a high-priced attorney named R. Geoffrey Godfrey out of New Orleans. We plan to indict Buster for capital murder, grand larceny, and for being an habitual offender before his preliminary hearing comes up, which is scheduled for Friday, June 4th.

"Did you all recover any additional stolen property besides the Pierre silver, either from Avoyelles Parish, or elsewhere during your searches?"

There was a long, thoughtful pause. At last Harmon responded. "We seized a truckload of his inventory, which as you know, is all used merchandise. I hate to say it, but so far we haven't married up the first item to one of our reports of stolen property.

"Sheriff Boyd had me issue an alert on NLETS to all parishes in Louisiana, requesting law enforcement agencies to respond if they have reports of high-end property being stolen, which they have not yet recovered. So far, not one agency has responded, but the message only went out an hour or two ago.

"Another thing. There should have been a logbook of both incoming and outgoing inventory, but we couldn't find it anywhere. In fact, as you may or may not know, being a transplant from Mississippi, Louisiana law requires an inventory book for a Buy and Sell. [I was impressed. Harmon had done his homework on me.] I thought it might be on a computer, but I soon discovered Buster is computer illiterate. He has a hard enough time operating a flip-phone. If we can't locate that log book, it's doubtful we'll identify many stolen items."

"You all check his house?"

Another pause. "Yes and no. He lives on the second floor of his business. The house where we thought he lived is in fact, his deceased daddy's old place. It has operational utilities, which Buster pays for in cash, just like everything else we checked, but we're fairly certain he doesn't sleep there anymore.

"So, within the Buy and Sell, it was next to impossible to separate private space from public space. If he hadn't had an unmade antique brass bed upstairs with dirty clothes piled on the floor everywhere next to it, we'd never have known the difference. He has merchandise everywhere, a lot of which is high end stuff. Pretty sure he sells guns too, but we didn't find any, nor does he have a dealer's license from ATF.

"You'd think a rat's nest like that building would be filled with vermin but it wasn't. Amazing. Maybe he employs a pest control company.

"Another thing. Bunkie doesn't have a bank. We only have one bank in all of Avoyelles Parish. It's called the Avoyelles Fidelity Bank [AFB]. It's headquartered here in Marksville, with three other branches. The nearest branch to Buster is in Mansura, which is 16 miles away, so I checked. Buster doesn't have an account in any of the four AFB branches. They claim he never has. That includes safe deposit boxes too, because I asked.

"We haven't located any banking records for him anywhere. No bills or invoices. No receipts. Nada. He had about $1,500 in cash on his person as you well know, but where does he hide all the rest? He's got to have tens of thousands of dollars in cash, but we haven't located it yet. Otherwise, how could he hire such an expensive attorney? Buster is not just some 'step and fetch it' cotton picker. He may not be well-educated, but he's a smart, crafty, conniving thief, and now he's a murderer, assuming he wasn't already one and we just didn't know it.

"We went back through everything again today looking for any business or financial records. We didn't even find a light bill or a receipt for his property taxes. Of course, we'd like to ask the IRS if Buster or his business pays income taxes, but you already know how cooperative they are. Ditto for the state revenue folks. The truth is, I bet he doesn't and never has.

"When's the last time anyone has ever seen an IRS revenue officer poking around? Buster's been in and out of the joint so many times, plus he's earned his living all his life by being a hustler, so he's probably not even on file with Social Security, especially if he wasn't born in a hospital, and a lot of these black folks weren't. They were birthed by a midwife. On the other hand, he does have a valid D/L, so maybe he is of record. I don't know."

"He probably is, but your point is well taken. What about relatives?"

"Both parents, two brothers, and one sister all deceased. Supposedly he also has a sister named Annette d'Iberville, who allegedly moved to someplace in Mississippi years ago. Nobody's seen her in 40 years. No one even knows if that's her legitimate last name, or if she's even still alive. Nobody by that last name lives anywhere around here.

"Also, Buster's never been married so far as we can tell, but there's at least six or seven local women here who claim he's the daddy of at least one of their children. As promiscuous as they all are, how could you even be sure without DNA testing? Besides, Buster isn't known to be near and dear with any of them, and he would never trust anyone with his money, especially a whore. He's never been known to be generous or philanthropic.

All I can say is, we'll keep on digging."

"Good deal. I'll check our files tomorrow morning for stolen property when I get back to the office. I'll pass along any leads I develop.

"You know, none of this is what I expected you to tell me. I'm completely baffled. Why would Buster suddenly up and kill Nicodemus Pierre over three thousand dollars' worth of silverware? Heck, he even left a witness! He's smarter than that. None of this makes any sense. As evil as he is, it seems out of character even for him."

"Agreed. Maybe that wasn't the real reason. Maybe it was something else and he snapped and afterwards he just decided to take the silver. I dunno.

"Sorry. All my life living in a parish no bigger than Avoyelles, you think you know everyone's secrets. I thought I knew everything there was to know about Buster, but I was wrong. I'll keep digging."

"Harmon, think about it. If Buster relies on cash only, how's he paying for such a high-priced lawyer? He's not getting out of jail to go retrieve it, and he certainly knows that by now. He doesn't trust a soul. Also, Godfrey knew from the very beginning his chances of getting Buster out of jail were slim to none. Would Buster trust Godfrey to go get his money?"

"Doubtful. What if Buster paid him a retainer in advance?"

"Nope. Godfrey said in court he'd never represented Buster before - that this is a first because he was charged with murder.

"Something else baffles me. I can't fathom Buster being separated very far from his stash. It has to be close to or in Bunkie, and it has to be away from prying eyes. It has to be secure, and nobody can know where it is."

"Agreed. You would think so, just like his business ledger, which the state occupational license examiner can ask to review at any time without prior notice.

"I'll have to put more thought into it, and see if I can't figure it out. If any of our other denizens knew where Buster's stash were hidden, they'd have stolen it by now. It's gotta be someplace where it won't get wet, and its gotta be fireproof, especially with all these old wooden buildings. My guess is it's in a safe located in a building somewhere in Bunkie not normally associated with Buster."

"Good thinking. Oh yeah. Today I requested that ATF conduct a trace for the original purchaser of the derringer Buster had in his possession. I hope to hear something within a week."

"Let me know. Were APSO to charge Buster, possession of that derringer as a convicted felon, and possession of stolen property from the Pierre household are the only two charges we have. Of course, we never would so long as Saint Landry is charging him with murder and the high bitch."

"Understood.

"Okay, Harmon, very glad to make your acquaintance. I'll stay in touch. In the interim, don't hesitate to call me if you need anything in Saint Landry. My regards to Sheriff Boyd."

"Same from here to Sheriff Ladner."

I was bummed out on my way home. I didn't even stop by to see Frog Legs like I had promised. Shame on me. It was hard for me to believe that none of the merchandise in Buster's store except for the Pierre items was stolen. Time would tell. Besides, it didn't affect my case. It was rock solid. Tomorrow would be a new day with new problems and new opportunities.

Thursday morning I went to work a little early so I could catch

Abner. I knew on workdays he always ate breakfast at Grand-mère Benoit's Diner. That's where I found him, in the back corner booth where he usually sat. Today, he was all to himself.

"Well, look at wat da cat chust dragged in! Where chu been mon ami?"

"I was gonna ask you the same thing. I haven't laid eyes on you for two days."

"Dat's becuz Ah knew chu had ever'ting under control.

"Listen! Chu keep dis to churself. Marisa had a tumor on her lef' breast. Ah took hoi ta Baton Rouge Cheneral Hospital ta have it removed and check it fah cancer. Che's clear, but che don't want anyone ta know, at least chust yet. Ah'm chure che'll tell Hannah when che's ready."

"Mum's the word. I hope she's feeling better. Breast cancer is a scary thing."

"Chu got dat right! T'ank God we dodged a bullet.

"Tell me about dis Buster Devereaux dude. Dat wuz awful. Nicodemus Jean Pierre wuz a kind, honest man. Ev'ryone loved 'im. Ah feel lahk chooting dat piece of chit mahself. His boy Frog Legs, and his poor wife, Hoimoine, got dat retarded boy, Booger, ta raise up an' Nicodemus shared da load wit' dem. He loved dat boy, too. Now Booger got ta get on da witness stand and tell whut happened wit' dat yankee carpetbagger cross-examinin' him an' tryin' ta confuse him.

"Don't t'ink dat won't happen, eidder. Dat's wat he gotta do ta keep Buster outta da 'lectric chair. He get dat boy all confused and den he says Nicodemus sold him dat silver, and Nicodemus wuz alive when he lef' da house and nobody can say udderwise. All it takes is chust one churor to vote not guilty. Dat's why chu have da high bitch in chur hip pocket, to make chur he never gets outta prison if he beats da capital murder rap. Makes my blood boil!"

"Abner, I never considered that. Now you got me worried. I'll have to see what Onslow thinks. Also, there's one major issue in this case that Chief Harmon Bergeron and I haven't figured out yet. It'll make all the difference in the world if we can."

"Wat's dat?"

"Nobody can find Buster's money or his business ledger. They already know Buster doesn't bank or have a safe deposit box in Avoyelles Fidelity Bank or any of its branches. They're the only banks in Avoyelles Parish. Also, they've been told Buster operates cash only for everything. No bank account or credit cards.

"And, as you well know, by law he has to have a business ledger to keep track of all purchases and sales. They've searched his business, residence, truck, and deceased daddy's residence, and come up empty on that, including his stash of cash. Of course, he needs the cash to pay for his lawyer. You got any idea where he could hide his cash or ledger? Logic dictates that they've gotta be close at hand."

"Whooeee! Dat's a tough one since Ah don't know dis scumbag. Ah gotta t'ink on dat, since Ah know chu all already looked in all da reg'lar hiding places.

"Wait! Ah got it! Chu check Cheneyville in Rapides Parish? Dat's only eight miles nort' from Bunkie on US 71. Dey got a stand alone bank dere called Farmers Savings Bank [FSB]. Dey don't do no checking accounts. All dey do is savings accounts, loans, and certificates of deposit. Dey prob'ly got safe deposit boxes, too. Chu get whatever chu need from Onslow and get up dere fast as chu can. Chu gotta beat dat yankee attorney dere before he closes dat account out, da greedy bastard! If he went dere yesterday, all da money be gone. Mebbe dey got da business ledger, too."

"Thanks, Abner! I'm a gone pecan."

I hurried over to Onslow's office, all out of breath. He asked, "What's up?"

"We've been trying to locate Buster's money, financial records, and business ledger. We think it's in the Farmers Savings Bank in Cheneyville. I need a Grand Jury subpoena."

"Marvin, you were a Fed for way too many years. We don't do Grand Jury subpoenas in Louisiana. We do court orders. Here, let me get you some blanks."

He handed me a stack. I sat at his clerk's desk and threaded a blank form into her electric typewriter. It didn't take long. I was asking for all deposits, bank records of any sort, to include accounts, loan applications, loans, certificates of deposit, both issued and redeemed, and the contents of any safe deposit boxes belonging to Buster B. Devereaux. Onslow reviewed it, smiled, and picked up the telephone. He called Judge DesHotel's clerk, Mrs. Enright, and said I was coming over with an application for a court order for bank records and deposits related to the Nicodemus Pierre murder case.

Judge DesHotel was waiting for me. It only took him 30 seconds to peruse the document. Then he signed it and crimped his seal on it. He said, "Good luck. The return is due by the initial appearance date at the latest."

"Thanks, Judge. It'll be back well before then." Then I dashed off.

En route to Cheneyville, I called Harmon. I told him what I had done and where I was going. He said he'd call a detective pal from the Rapides Parish SO, named Ralph E. 'Little Ralphie' Denton, and give him a heads up. We agreed to meet at 10 o'clock in the bank parking lot.

Little Ralphie and Harmon were both waiting for me when I arrived. We went inside and spoke with the bank president, Arthur H. Llewellyn. He studied the court document, and satisfied that all was in order, took us back into his office. He logged onto his computer and said, "I thought so. Mr. Devereaux has been a customer here since 1995. At first all he had was a safe deposit box. He doesn't have any loans or CDs with us and never has. Last year he opened a savings account. He's a most peculiar fellow."

He pushed a button and his printer started spitting out documents. He handed them to me. Buster had $53,677.62 in his savings account. His safety deposit box, number 29, had at least 50 entries. Of course the bank had one of the keys to open it, but Buster had the other key, which we never found.

Mr. Llewellyn fetched a high speed metal drill and went to work boring out that lock. From observing his proficiency with the drill, I surmised that he'd had to do this more than once. Number 29 was one of the large boxes on the bottom row. The drilling didn't take long. Then Mr. Llewellyn reached inside the vault sleeve and placed the deposit box on the table before us. We opened it and pulled out the business ledger and 11 banded wrappers of $100 bills, totaling $110,000!

We seized the ledger and the cash, to include a check for the contents of the savings account, giving Mr. Llewellyn a receipt signed by all of us. We thanked him and departed. I took the money and Harmon took the ledger. Harmon promised he would make a photocopy for himself and mail the original to me.

I returned to Opelousas with wind under my sails. The first thing I did was check for messages. I had three.

The oldest was from Deputy Coroner Arnold W. Dawkins. It was brief. Death was by exsanguination, meaning from loss of blood. Otherwise, Nicodemus J. Pierre was a healthy 82-year-old male at the time of his demise. Dawkins was releasing the body to the decedent's son, Eugene R. Pierre, for burial. Arnie was dropping a copy of the autopsy report in the mail to me, and I should have it by Friday. Call if I have any questions.

The second was from Rosenbaum's Pharmacy. The photographs were ready for pickup.

The last was from Onslow. All it said was, "Come see me ASAP!"

I had planned to go anyway, but now I put it to the top of my to-do list. I picked up the phone and called Harmon. I was in luck. He answered.

"Hey, man. Whatcha want?"

"Headed over to the DA's office. Just wondered if you've had a chance to glance through Buster's inventory book."

"Sure did. I was going to call you. I've already identified eight seized items as stolen. In fact, one was from Saint Landry.

"Let's see. That one is an 18-karat gold necklace with a one-carat solitaire ruby setting, and a pair of gold post earrings, also with one-carat solitaire ruby settings. It's a matching set. They're displayed in a solid cherry case, inlaid with abalone shells.

"The ledger says that on November 12, 2003, Buster paid $50 to an Erastus White, of 11211 Highway 29, in Whiteville, for the set. Can you believe the chutzpah of that prick? The really good news is, Buster makes each seller provide identification and sign the inventory book.

"I'm just getting started, but it looks like we really hit the jackpot. I'll put out detailed lists on NLETS as I make more identifications."

"This is great news! I'll check it out right away. The DA left me a message to see him ASAP, and I think this will help calm his nerves. I'll be in touch."

"Well, 'my cup runneth over' in a manner of speaking, so I'll be sequestered here in the office for several days more than likely. Adiós."

"Adiós."

I called out to our whiz kid, day shift dispatcher Thelma Vidrine. "Thelma, run Erastus White, 11211 Highway 29, Whiteville for me. Everything you've got. Then check for any theft or burglary reports probably from that area in late October up to November 12th. I'm looking for a theft or burglary report of a matching set of ruby earrings and necklace."

"How fast you need it?"

"Soon. Like yesterday. I got a call to go see Onslow right away."

"On it."

Thelma sauntered into my office five minutes later with a big smile on her face. She placed a handful of computer printouts on my desk. She waited to see my reaction.

The first document was a copy of a police report dated November 9, 2003, by Deputy Elmer N. Bavier, called in by Dr. Enos R. Thibodaux, of 14352 Highway 29, Whiteville. His house had been burgled. Besides the ruby ensemble, he was also missing a mahogany-cased, Parker, side-by-side, 16-gauge shotgun, which was appraised at $8,300. The ruby set was appraised at $3,100. He was also missing an antique cloisonné vase valued at $400. There were some other, less expensive items, but those were the biggies.

The other documents were on Erastus (NMN) White, Jr., DOB May 18, 1981, black male, 5-feet, 7-inches tall, 140 pounds, POB Rapides Parish, LA. He had never been issued a Louisiana driver's license, but he did have a Louisiana photo identification card with the same address as listed in Buster's inventory book. This was one horribly ugly kid. His face resembled a gargoyle. If I had a face like his, I'd shave my ass and walk backwards. Poor kid never had a chance from the moment he was delivered from the womb. He had three priors.

The first, dated in 2000, was for trespassing and possession of a half-ounce of marijuana. He served three months in jail.

The second was in 2001, for speeding, reckless driving, no driver's license, and possession of a stolen automobile. The auto theft charge was dismissed because it belonged to his grandpa. Erastus paid a $100 fine for the three traffic violations, and served four more weeks in jail.

The third was for burglary of a medical clinic in October of 2003. It was still pending adjudication.

I thanked Thelma, gathered up my file with the new documents, and the large, bulging evidence envelope full of cash and the cashier's check, and rushed over to Onslow's office. I caught him as he was preparing to leave for a late lunch. He sat back down and waived me in.

"At last! Tell me what you seized. It must be the mother load."

I tossed the evidence envelope with the eleven paper straps of 100 Benjamin Franklins, and a check for $53,677.62, on his desk. He poured it out and counted. "Wow!"

I beat him to the punch before he could utter another word,

reporting "We also recovered his Buy & Sell inventory book! It's loaded with incriminating data, all handwritten by Buster and signed by the thieves he bought stolen property from. Right now, Avoyelles is in possession of that. So far, Chief Harmon Bergeron has married up eight seized items from it, which includes jewelry stolen over in Whiteville. Look at this report by Deputy Bavier."

Onslow studied the police report carefully.

"I know Dr. Thibodaux! His son, Warren, and I were both in Kappa Alpha Fraternity at LSU. He went on to become a petroleum mining engineer at Exxon. Dern! We gotta recover that Parker shotgun!

He paused, collecting his thoughts.

"Well, the urgency of my call was this. Apparently just a few minutes after you all left the bank, Mr. Godfrey showed up. He had a notarized statement signed by Buster, allowing him to take possession of all his worldly assets in custody of the bank. Godfrey was, as they say, 'a day late and a dollar short.'

"He called here in a rage, absolutely livid! His position is that we had no legal standing to seize those assets because they have nothing whatsoever to do with our murder case. He contacted Judge DesHotel's office demanding an immediate hearing on a motion to vacate the seizure of Buster's money.

"You know why he was upset, don't you? I bet you a dollar to a doughnut hole, that $150,000 of that seizure was earmarked to cover his fee. Anyway, Judge DesHotel scheduled Godfrey's motion for 3 o'clock, May 28th."

"That's Friday. That's tomorrow! We've got so much to do! We're not ready yet!"

"That's why I was in a panic when I left that message for you, but I'm not anymore.

"The Thibodaux jewelry demonstrates that the seized money represents the fruit of Buster's crimes, to wit: possession of stolen property. How hard is it to prove the ruby ensemble was worth far more than $50, or that it didn't belong to Erastus White, Jr.? I bet we wind up with far more stolen property worth more than the $150,000 Buster had stashed away.

"I'm cutting a subpoena for Chief Bergeron to appear in court tomorrow for this hearing. I want him to bring photographs of Buster's business as well as items seized. He doesn't need to take more pictures. Just bring the ones from the search warrant. I do want separate photos of items connected to specific theft reports, like your rubies. Also, I want him to bring the business inventory ledger. He will be our star witness regarding the search.

"You, Sir, will be the star witness regarding the seizure from the bank . . . and between now and then, I want Erastus White, Jr. in jail for possession of stolen property. I don't care if you're the arresting officer or not, but I want you to be the interviewing officer. We need a confession, and he sounds like just the man to make it.

"Call Chief Bergeron before you fax him a copy of the subpoena. You can give him the original tomorrow when he gets here. I'm cutting a subpoena because he's entitled to a witness fee of $50 a day to help defray expenses, unless his sheriff won't let him keep it.

"Any questions?"

"Nope. I'm all over this like white on rice."

I went back to the office and had Thelma fax the subpoena to Harmon. Then I called him to let him know what was going on. He said he'd meet me at my office Friday with the ledger and the ruby necklace and earrings ensemble."

- *Chapter 13* -

Building the Case Even Stronger

I went back to the office. The first thing I did was ask Thelma who was riding Beat 9 (Whiteville area) today. She said it was Deputy Elton D. Crabtree, and his call sign was SLP 29. He was one of our younger road deputies at 25 years of age. He was also an Air Force veteran of the War in Iraq, and real squared away.

I grabbed my file and went out to my Jeep. It was 1:30 and I hadn't eaten, so I patronized the new KFC and gobbled up a two-piece meal, regular recipe, with cole slaw, pork and beans, a biscuit, and a medium Pepsi. After I had eaten and washed up, I fired up the Jeep and headed towards Whiteville, a man on a mission.

I keyed the mike and said, "SLP 29 from SLP 2."

"SLP 2 from SLP 29. Come in."

"SLP 29, switch to F-2.

"10-4."

"SLP 29 on F-2."

"What's your 10-20?"

"I'm 10-5 [meal break] at Melanie's Diner in Grand Prairie."

"Do you know Erastus White from Whiteville?"

"10-4. They call him Dingus because allegedly he's very well-endowed in that particular arena. What's he done now?"

"I want him for burglary on that Pierre case. I'm leaving Opelousas now for Whiteville. Can you meet me there?"

"10-4. Dingus won't be at home, but I'm pretty sure I know where to find him."

"Where's that?"

"He hangs out at a rundown pool hall called Tee [meaning little] Richard's [pronounced Rē'-shards] just north of Whiteville on Highway 29. You can't miss it. It's on the east side of the highway. Concrete block building painted hot pink. Always has flashing neon lights if it's open. Be prepared, though. About the only time a white guy ever goes in there is if he's the pō'-lice, but knock on wood, so far I've never had a problem there. Tee Richard takes care of his own problems."

"Okay. I'll meet you there. Wait for me."

"No problem. You need to know a few things first."

"Go ahead."

"Dingus has a brother a year older than himself named Leland, but they call him Popeye. They look just alike except Popeye's right eye is cocked to the right. They hang together. Both are runners and they're crazy fast, as in Olympic speed athletes. Both are known to carry a knife. If Dingus broke in a home, he probably did it with Popeye.

"Also, unless you feel like a wind-sprint, we probably ought to get a couple other deputies to help us out. I guarantee we'll wind up with two 10-15s [prisoners] if we find Dingus. Rob Beauchamp, SLP 22, is riding Beat 7 today, and Gerald Kershaw, SLP 19, is on Beat 8.

"Also, sometimes Popeye and Dingus borrow their pawpaw's car. It's 1974 Pontiac Lemans, white over forest green with some gray primer on the body. It runs like a scalded dog, but it can't outrun this marked Crown Vic with the police interceptor. Doubtful you could keep up with him in your Jeep, though."

"10-4. Ha. Ha. That's why you're going to be there, Mr. Dale Ernhardt, Sr. Where's a good place we can all hook up?"

"There's an old Gulf service station right in town on the main drag. It's open and has clean restrooms. It's got plenty of space in the back lot for a powwow."

"10-4. Dispatch are you copying this?"

"10-4, SLP 2. I'll reach out for 19 and 22 and have them meet you at the Gulf Station. Also, I'll conduct record checks on Popeye and put it on your desk."

"SLP 2 copies. Thank you. Switching back to F-1."

I smiled to myself. What a comfort it was to have competent road deputies at your disposal. They generally had all the skinny on the public they served on their designated beats.

At our briefing, Elton provided us with the lowdown on the White brothers and Tee Richard's pool hall/tavern. We decided Elton and Rob would enter through the front. Elton got that honor because this was his beat. Gerald and I would enter through the back, after we checked the two-holer outhouse in the rear parking lot. Elton said anymore, the outhouse was used as a place to hide and smoke weed they procured in the tavern, rather than as a place to relieve oneself.

Sure enough, upon our arrival, we noticed PawPaw White's white over forest green Pontiac Lemans parked two spaces to the left of the front door. It was much nicer than I had imagined. It even had chrome spoke rims and tires with three-inch whitewalls.

It was still afternoon, so there were only four cars parked in the lot. I made a conjecture that the cherry red-over-black, 1968 Cadillac Coupe Deville convertible parked in the closest space belonged to Tee Richard.

We all entered at the same time. It was dark inside, filled with smoke and the odor of stale beer. It took more than a few moments for my eyes to adjust. Two patrons, both old men, were huddled at the bar nursing their draft beers and watching a rerun of *Ironside* on TV. A much younger man and woman were scrunched together in the back both. The man had his hand up her skirt. Her boobs were enormous and in danger of making an escape from her blouse, which was skin tight and partially unbuttoned. Her mind was elsewhere. Her eyes were wide open, staring up at the ceiling. She had a glassy look on her face. I sensed that Nirvana had nearly arrived. Initially, I thought she was stoned on drugs, and she well could have been. Then I realized that she was high on digital manipulation with more than just a little help from her energetic friend.

The other two patrons were the black brothers White. Dingus was a moment too late reacting to our entrance, having just made the winning shot, trash talking, and scooping up the cash on the rail into his right trouser pocket. Popeye was more alert, and he started to take a powder for the front door, but Elton stuck out his foot and Popeye tripped and crashed to the concrete floor. He was cuffed and tossed for weapons before he knew what befell him. Dingus turned to run through the back door, but Gerald was already there and cut him off. He shoved his head, face down, into the felt of the pool table and cuffed him while he squirmed and made threats he couldn't begin to carry out. Why is it the little guys are always the ones doing all the trash talk? The drama was all but over before it even got started.

The proprietor/bartender, Tee Richard, watched, but he never uttered a word or took action. In fact, he didn't even seem to be ruffled. Elton walked over and asked if either of the brothers White owed him money for drinks. He shook his head no and replied that they were square.

Once we got them outside and we could see and breathe

again, Elton gave Popeye a thorough toss. He pulled everything out of Popeye's pockets and laid it on the hood of his cruiser for all to see. Popeye hit the jackpot on the jailhouse lottery. He knew it and it pissed him off. Today, he would be singing the *Jailhouse Blues.*

Elton recovered a switchblade knife from his hip pocket. That was felony number one. His wallet contained his D/L, three photos of the same black female in various nude poses, two business cards, and $83 in folding money. Elton also found keys to PawPaw's Lemans, a packet of double-wide cigarette papers, two books of matches, and a half-ounce baggie of weed. Uh oh! Felony number two. Our spin of the jailhouse one-armed bandit turned up triple cherries again. Popeye was going to prison whether he was involved in the burglary or not. Poor Popeye!

Gerald tossed Dingus. He found a working man's rusty, three-dollar Barlow pocket knife, and a roll of currency bound with a thick rubber band in his right trouser pocket, plus a few unsecured bills and coins. The cash added up to $171, plus $2.81 in loose change. He also recovered Dingus' state-issued ID card but no wallet; a nail clipper and house key on a ball chain with a rabbit's foot; and, an amber, plastic medicine bottle with a white twist-off lid containing 23 tablets of an opioid labeled as Vicodin, a Schedule II drug. The name of the patient on the label was Valerie Epps.

Elton exclaimed, "I know Valerie Epps! She lives in the Frenesius Assisted Living House. She's an 80-year-old white lady who recently fell and broke her hip. She's my MeeMaw's best friend! You SOB!"

I jumped in the middle of them before Elton could do any serious damage to Dingus. I didn't blame him one bit, but I had to save Elton from himself. "Gerald, you take Dingus to the office. Rob, you do likewise with Popeye. Elton, you go interview Valerie Epps and find out what happened. Make sure she's okay. Take a written statement. Then you meet us at the office, too. One more thing. Everyone listen up."

I took the Miranda Warning card out of my wallet and read it loudly and slowly so we all could hear it for the record, before any questioning occurred. I said, "Okay. It's done. Everyone heard it. I appreciate everyone's help. The black brothers White are officially under arrest. See you all at the office."

Both prisoners were waiting for me out of sight or normal earshot of the other. I decided to start with Dingus since his signature was on Buster's ledger. Also, because he was younger than his brother and he was probably the assistant burglar, not the burglar-in-charge. I told Gerald to bring Dingus in my office and witness my interview.

When we were ready, behind a closed door, I said, "Erastus White, this is Deputy Gerald Kershaw. My name is Chief Deputy Marvin Barnett. I read your rights to you at Tee Richards', so I won't belabor the point unless you tell me you want me to. If you understand your rights, I need you to sign this rights waiver."

I slid the waiver and a ballpoint pen across the desk and he signed it. Then Gerald and I signed and dated it as witnesses, including the minute it was signed. Then I placed it in my file.

"Erastus, I understand they call you Dingus. What would you like me to call you?"

"Erastus."

"Erastus it is. Have you eaten today? Are you thirsty or hungry?"

"T'oisty."

"How about a grape Nehi?"

He nodded his head.

I reached into my drawer and handed Gerald three singles. I asked, "Deputy Kershaw, could you go to the break room and get Erastus a grape Nehi? I'd like an Orange Crush, and get whatever you would like. We'll wait until you return to proceed. Thanks."

He returned with the drinks, including an RC Cola for himself. We all had a sip. Then I continued. "Erastus, tell me about that necklace and earrings you stole from Dr. Thibodaux's house in Whiteville back in November."

"Chu know about dat?"

"I do."

"Who ratted me out?"

"Who do you think?"

"Dat whut Ah wanna know. Who?"

"Maybe no one. Maybe a birdie told me. Maybe you left behind fingerprints. Maybe your brother did too."

"Dat whut Ah tol' Popeye. He say he careful, but he pigheaded an' don' lissen ta me cuz Ah younger dan him. Now he done fucked us up good, but it wuz he idee."

"What did you all do with the loot?"

"Sold it."

"Everything?"

"Most of it. Not da shotgun, dough. We kep' dat."

"Where is it?"

"It under my baid."

"What about that fancy vase?"

"Took dat to da flea market. Got ten dollahs."

"What flea market?"

"Da one dey has da t'oid Sataday each mont' over in

Washin'ton at dat ole high school. Dat where we sell ever't'ing 'cept foe da shotgun an' necklace set."

"How much did you all make at the flea market?"

"Fōty dollahs."

"Who'd you sell the necklace and earrings to?"

"Dat fat fuckuh ovah at Bustah's Buy 'n Sell in Bunkie. He cheated me. He only gib me fi'ty dollahs. Me and Popeye split ever't'ing fi'ty-fi'ty. Ah ain't sellin' nuttin ta dat niggah no mō."

"You mean Buster Devereaux?"

"Yeah. Dat him."

"Who's the boss? You or Popeye."

"Ah lets Popeye t'ink he be since he older, but he ain't. He fuck up too much."

"How far did you go in school?"

"Me and Popeye bot' gradiate from da little school."

"What's the little school?"

"Whiteville Grade School. It stop atter da eight' grade. Den if you wanna go farder, you goes to Washin'ton High."

"So you can read and write?"

"Yassuh, 'cep foe da big woids."

"Okay. I'm gonna sit right here and type up your statement. Then you read it and make any changes. Then I'll swear you to it and you sign it and we witness it. That sound okay to you?"

"Yassah."

I got busy and turned on my word processor. I typed Erastus' statement in short, simple, sixth-grade words, double-spaced. I made two deliberate errors for him to find. If he didn't, I'd find them for him. Then he could strike, correct, and initial the corrections. This is the way you have to do it if your suspect is uneducated. Otherwise the defense attorney would do his best to establish that his client was too illiterate to understand what he swore to and signed.

When that was all done, and Gerald was preparing to take Erastus to jail to book him, Erastus asked, "Wat happen now?"

"Well, you're going to jail. You knew that already. Tomorrow morning you and your brother will have your initial appearances in court, and the judge will set your bond. If you or your pawpaw don't have enough money to post it, you'll sit in jail pending your trial. Then you win or you lose. You win, you get out. You lose, you go to Angola."

"How much time Ah gotta do?"

"I really don't know. I've only worked here a few months and I don't know the judge all that well. I'd hate to guess. Best thing is for you to ask your court-appointed lawyer tomorrow. I can tell you that I appreciate your cooperation and if you continue to cooperate, you'll get less time to serve. Understand?"

"Yassuh."

"Well, good luck to you, Erastus. I don't think you're a bad guy. I just think you made some bad choices. When you get out, knuckle down and get a job working on one of the plantations as a farmhand. Earn your own money instead of stealing other folks' stuff. You know that. Your pawpaw knows that. Okay?"

"Yassuh."

Deputy Elton Crabtree had been patiently waiting for me to complete this interview. He said, "Dingus has a part-time job as a janitor at the nursing home in Whiteville where Mrs. Epps resides. She just got that prescription filled today for 24 tablets. She signed this statement [which he handed to me]. What do you want me to do?"

"The easy thing would be to return her medicine to her, but

we can't be sure it hasn't been altered, and anyway we need it for evidence. Tell your contact there at the nursing home to call her doctor and ask for a new prescription. If the doctor has heartburn with that, have him call you or me to verify exactly what happened."

"Roger that."

Then I walked over to the other room where Deputy Rob Beauchamp was guarding Popeye. "Rob, would you bring Popeye to my office and sit in the interview with me?"

"Of course."

I went through the same opening ritual with Popeye as I did for Erastus. Popeye was being a little snotty and said he preferred being called Popeye. After Rob brought us all cold drinks, I opened my file and examined the NCIC, NLETS, and OMV computerized printouts on him. It seems that Leland (NMN) White had two misdemeanor arrests for drunk and disorderly. He had one conviction for grand larceny, for which he was sentenced to five years on probation. He had only completed two. That meant he was still on probation, thus buying himself an additional charge for probation violation, otherwise known as PV.

"Popeye, we're interested in talking about the burglary of Dr. Thibodaux's house in Whiteville last November. What have you got to say for yourself?"

"Dat not me. Some udder nigga do dat."

"So you're going to let your little brother take the fall for it after you took half the proceeds from the sale of the stolen goods?"

"If he done it, den he hab ta take da fall all by hisself. Not me."

"I'm sorry you feel that way. Being the big brother, I thought you would cowboy up. Set the example. Erastus has already 'fessed up. Guess we'll have to do this the hard way and compare your fingerprints with the prints we recovered at the scene. Then we'll check with the proprietors of the flea market and see what they recall. They work extremely hard keeping thieves out of their fairs so it won't become a den of thieves. I'm charging you with that burglary, and putting you in jail while I wait for the results of the investigation.

"Then because you wouldn't own up, when it comes time for sentencing, I'll ask the judge to max you out at 20 years. When you go off to prison, I will make sure the warden and his guards keep a close eye on you.

"You know, they still have a chain gang, and I'll make sure you're on it - digging ditches, clearing the swamp, hunting for cottonmouth snakes with a stick, dodging alligators, feeding mosquitoes with your tasty red blood, hoping not to get malaria, shitting in the bushes, picking cotton with the same fingers you pick your nose, cutting down trees, burning brush, and all sorts of other disagreeable things - for 20, very long, brutal, sweaty years living with bigger inmates who love to have anal sex with smaller guys like you. How's that sound to you?"

"Sound lack you da mudderfocker."

"That's me. Do yourself a favor and tell me the truth. Get out in five or six years instead of 20. Besides, you know your parole is going to be revoked anyway, and then there's the switchblade and the weed. You know what your new nickname is going to be? Everyone's gonna call you Sad Sack, because everything you do just gets you in deeper shit. You're a sad sack, Popeye. 'Fess up and give yourself a break."

"Nope. Ah's gonna go ta trial. Chu cain't prove jack shit on me."

"Have it your way. It actually makes my job easier.

"Deputy Beauchamp, take Sad Sack to booking. Charge him with burglary, illegal possession of a switchblade knife, illegal possession marijuana, and parole violation.

"Sad Sack, I'll see you in court tomorrow morning. Just remember, I gave you a chance to cut your time in half while you're dodging cottonmouths and gators draining that swamp, not to mention big brute butt-fuckers at night."

"Fuck you."

"We'll see who's getting fucked. Remember, you did it to yourself."

Rob cuffed Popeye behind the back, lifted him by the stack and swivel, and perp-walked him over to booking.

I took the aerosol can out of my desk drawer and squirted a lavender scent in my office to help erase the odor of Popeye. It was too late to return any of my missed calls. I was bone tired anyway. I looked to see if Abner was still in his office but he was gone. I still hadn't paid Eugene Pierre a visit like I said I would. His daddy's funeral was on Saturday. I had planned to go, so maybe I could pay my respects then. In the meantime, Friday would be a another long day. I started to go home, but I knew what had to be done right now. No time to waste. I asked Janine Compton, the afternoon shift dispatcher, which deputy was working the Whiteville area. She said, "LeRoy Broussard, Jr., SLP 17. He's on a stolen auto call now."

"As soon as he clears, you tell him to meet me at Whitaker's Gulf Service Station in Whiteville. I'm headed there right now."

"You got it, Chief."

"Also call my house. If my wife doesn't answer, leave her a

message that I had to make a quick stop in Whiteville, and I expect to be home in two hours."

"Will do."

I grabbed my murder file and headed out the door. I got in the Jeep and called 10-8 [in service]. I was so hungry I could eat the asshole out of a bastard rat, but dinner would have to wait.

It took me 45 minutes to arrive. LeRoy was waiting for me in his unit. He was eating a corndog and drinking a Mountain Dew he had purchased inside. He wiped some mustard off his lips and asked, "How's it going, Chief?"

"LeRoy, I'm having more fun than the law allows. How about you?"

"Like Phil Collins sings, 'It's just another day in Paradise.'"

"Good. Hey, you know about us arresting Popeye and Dingus last shift?"

"Does a hobby horse have a hickory dick? Ever'body knows. Wish I had been there."

"You know where they live?"

"Yep. They live with their pawpaw, Grinstead White. He goes by Toot Toot because he farts so much. They live in that green shingle shack with that old Farmall tractor parked out front. It's only a half-mile or so up the highway."

"What kinda guy is he?"

"They say he was a hellion when he was young. Now he's just a broke dick dog. He doesn't cause anyone trouble anymore, unless he's been drinking too much watermelon wine. Then he can be a little cantankerous."

"Where's he get that?"

"Oh, he makes it hisself when watermelon's in season. He fills as many gallon jugs as he can get his hands on. Then he starts drinking and doesn't finish until around Thanksgiving.

"Who all lives with him?"

"Just his old lady, Miss Peach, and his two grandsons. Also that chihuahua he calls Mr. Bo Weevil."

"Think he's at home now?"

"He was when I passed by earlier. He was out on the front porch smoking his pipe and nursing a 40-ounce Blatz beer."

"Hope he's still there. Dingus has a stolen Parker shotgun worth $8,300 under his bed and I need to pick it up."

"Let's go. He won't give you any trouble."

"I'll follow you."

We made haste and arrived two minutes later. From the looks of things, Toot Toot hadn't moved. We drove up and walked over to where he was sitting in an old wooden kitchen chair. There were two empty 40-ounce Blatz beer bottles standing next to the one he was currently nursing. Mr. Bo Jangles was sitting in Toot Toot's lap, licking his [own] balls.

Toot Toot said, "LeRoy, what chu all wont now? Ain't all chu pō'lice done did all you need ta do fuckin' wich mah fambly?"

LeRoy replied, "Toot Toot, this is Chief Barnett. He needs to pick up that shotgun your boys stole." Mr. Bo Jangles hopped off his lap and licked my hand. I wondered if it tasted better than his balls.

"Mah boys ain't stole no got-dam shotgun. Ah dares chu all ta find it."

"Thanks, Toot Toot. That's exactly what we wanted to hear. You wait right where you are, and we'll go fetch it. Be back in a minute."

LeRoy opened the screen door and we let ourselves in. Miss Peach was in the kitchen fixing their supper consisting of smoked pork sausage, collard greens, cornbread, and peach cobbler made from canned peaches. She looked up and said, "Lawdy, LeRoy, chu all ain't fixin' ta take mah ole mān ta jail too, are chu? It nearly suppah time. Ah needs mah mān. I cain't survive widout him. Who else gonna pay dem bills? I ain't got no money, an' Ah'm too old to shake mah ass ta make some now."

"No, Ma'am. We just stopped by to pick up a shotgun Dingus hid under his bed."

"What? Ah don't know nuthin' about no shotgun! Come. Let's go see."

We followed her into the boys' bedroom. The outside of the house was rundown, but the interior, though poorly furnished, was as neat and clean as any house I had ever been in. I could detect the odor of Pine Sol throughout the house where she'd been scrubbing the pine floors.

She pulled on the cord to the naked overhead lightbulb as soon as we entered the room. I got down on my hands and knees and looked under the double bed both boys shared. Sure enough, a beautiful wooden gun case was under there, shoved up against the wall. I pulled it out and laid it on the taut quilt on top of the bed. I unfastened the latches and opened it up. The most beautiful shotgun I had ever laid eyes on was inside. It was all any of the three of us needed to see. I closed the case, fastened the latches, and we prepared to leave.

Miss Peach broke into tears. She placed her hands over her eyes and said, "Oh Lawdy, Lawdy! What dem boys done been up to now? Dey knows bettah dan dat! Ah'm so ashamed. Lawd, please hab mercy on dem."

I said, "Miss Peach, this gun belongs to Dr. Thibodaux here in town. You know him. We'll see he gets it back. We're both sorry for your troubles. We'll see ourselves out. Thanks for your hospitality."

We stepped outside and Toot Toot said, "Guess dem boys' done chit da bāde now, huh?"

I replied, "Looks like it. Thanks for your understanding."

We drove back to the Gulf station and pulled into the lot side by side so we could talk face to face. I said, "Appreciate all your help. Your presence made this much easier than it might have been."

"No problem. Happy to be of some assistance. Good night, Chief."

"Good night, LeRoy."

Then I drove home, calling it a very good day. I wondered what Hannah was fixing us for dinner. I hoped it was one of my favorites.

- *Chapter 14* -

Logging in More Time in Court

May 28th. I woke up bone-tired Friday morning. I knew I'd be in court all day, making and returning calls in between. Hannah was off today, so she was making me country ham and biscuits, to include fresh strawberries for breakfast. I sat around long enough to drink three cups of black Community Coffee. Then it was time to gird my loins and prepare to slay dragons. I picked up the crime scene photographs from the pharmacy on the way in. No surprises there, unless you thought some might be blurry, but none were.

I began working the phones as soon as I arrived at the office. First call was to Dr. Cherry at the LSP Lab. We hit the jackpot on latent fingerprints. Buster's latent prints were on the Pierre silver bowl, as well as on the top of the bottom section of the hutch where the silverware had been stored. She said the DNA results should be in on Tuesday. She also said the ballistics test on the derringer came out clean. It hadn't been used in any murder which was on file. I could pick it up at any time. I asked if she could Fed Ex it to me. She said it would go out today.

Then I called Special Agent Hector Gutierrez from ATF. He said he would call Firearms Branch and check the status of the Bond derringer firearms trace. He called back a few minutes later. He said the gun was purchased at Leonard's Gun Shop in Krotz Springs. The purchaser was Delmar H. Crenshaw, white male, DOB November 20, 1964, address 1322 Pecan Grove Road, Krotz Springs, in Saint Landry Parish! Our case! Not someone else's. Purchase date of May 2nd, 2000. Hector said the report was put in the mail to him yesterday, and he'd forward it to me as soon as it arrived. I thanked him again.

I asked Thelma to conduct a records check on Crenshaw, to include an Auto Track report, since I figured he didn't have a criminal history. She had 15 minutes before I had to leave to go to court. She came back in five. No arrests. No traffic citations. Class A CDL license. US Marine Corps veteran, honorably discharged in 1986. No bankruptcies. No divorces. No tax liens. No law suits filed against him. Current holder of a concealed carry permit. Married to Janice Mae Crenshaw, née Brooks, age 38. Employed as a route supervisor for McKee Foods, purveyor of Little Debbie's Snacks, located at 4000 Highway 105 in Melville, about eight miles north of Krotz Springs. He was, in other words, a solid, upright, American citizen, clean as a whistle, or so it would seem. My kind of guy.

I asked Thelma who was riding Beat 1. She said, "Deputy Edward D. Cate."

"Good. Send him to interview Mr. Crenshaw. Tell him I want to know what happened to the Bond derringer he bought from Leonard's Gun Shop in Krotz Springs on May 2nd, 2000. Get a detailed, sworn, signed statement. I want it on my desk when I return from court. Also if this inquiry turns up leads anywhere in the vicinity of his beat, ask him to pursue posthaste."

"Will do, Chief."

"I'm off to court."

I stopped by to check with Onslow first. He was ecstatic with the arrests of the black brothers White. He said he would ask the judge to appoint Clarence Bateman to represent Erastus on his new charges, since he's already his appointed counsel on the pending burglary case of a medical clinic in Whiteville. He mentioned that case had been postponed three different times, and Judge DesHotel said no more. Either Dingus pleads guilty by this coming Monday, or be ready to go to trial.

I asked, "Which medical clinic did he burgle, and what did he steal?"

"Moreau's Medicine Shoppe in Whiteville. He got caught by Deputy Larkin Rivers coming out of a small backroom window at 3 o'clock in the morning. He stole prepackaged, labeled prescriptions for two different customers.

"It's really pretty funny. Dickhead must have been in a big hurry. Either that or he can't read. He thought he had narcotics, but what he actually stole was a box of suppositories and a small prescription bottle of 10-mg Viagra. He didn't have a flashlight when he was apprehended, so he must have been fumbling around in the dark. Something spooked him, and he decided to boogie. When he climbed out of the window he fell right smack dab into Larkin River's outstretched arms, who had watched him enter the building."

"Well, the reason I wondered is because, in addition to the burglary of Dr. T's house, I charged him with possession of a vial containing 23 tablets of Vicodin, which you know is a Schedule II drug. The label identified the rightful owner as Valerie Epps, a resident of the Frenesius Assisted Living House in Whiteville, which is also where Erastus works part-time. Also, I've been advised that the brothers White are always together. Ergo, Leland was probably waiting outside the shop and slipped away when Erastus got busted."

"Well, Erastus is looking at some serious time. What's the deal with his brother, Leland?"

"Besides the burglary of Dr. T's house, he's charged with

possession of a switchblade knife, a half-ounce of weed, and probation violation for a conviction on grand larceny two or three years ago."

"Then he's also looking at a long vacation in sunny Angola. 'Birds of a feather flock together'."

"One other thing. This should tickle your funny-bone. Saving the best news for last, we recovered Dr. T's shotgun. It's in pristine condition so far as I can tell."

"Hot damn! He'll be thrilled when I call him."

"Are you and Chief Bergeron prepared for the 3 o'clock hearing?"

"I am. Sure Harmon is, too."

"Good. Let's head over to court. We have a long docket this morning. Hope you ate a hearty breakfast."

The courtroom was packed. I sat in the back pew just like in church. Today the jury box was stuffed to overflowing with green and white horizontally striped, shackled inmates. Dingus was at one end and Popeye was at the other. Dingus looked scared. Popeye looked homicidal. Was his nose flatter this morning than last night? It sure looked it. Wonder if he was clocked by a guard or an inmate. Had to be one or the other.

The truth is, I really didn't need to be here for their initial appearances like I did in Federal Court. Old habits die slowly. Today was just an exercise in patience.

Dingus was called first. Sure enough, Clarence M. Bateman was appointed to represent him. Bond was set at $5,000. It might as well have been $5,000,000. He didn't even have the money to post a $500 bond. He was remanded into the custody of the SLPSO Jail. It would probably be five or more years before he tasted freedom again. He should get the following adage tattooed on his arm. 'Can't do the time? Don't do the crime.'

Popeye's case was called next. Miss Alice N. Coursey was appointed to represent him. She was young, beautiful, and new to the Public Defenders Office. I felt sorry for her. Popeye was a handful even when he was on his best behavior. He was remanded without bail due to the PV. Good for the public, but bad for him. It didn't really matter anyway. Like Dingus, he had no money to post any bond.

Both had preliminary hearings scheduled for Monday, June 7th. Meant we would have to present their cases to the Grand Jury by Friday, June 4th.

I tracked down Abner after court. We ate lunch at Miss Esther's Roundtable Buffet. Great food. It was all you could eat for $8. We did our very best, but were way overmatched. We got caught up on current events.

We also decided that tomorrow we would take the wives and go together to Nicodemus's funeral. Abner said if we'd never been to a black funeral, we were in for a treat. The entertainment and the food would be first class, assuming I liked gospel music and southern fried chicken. It was too early in the season for watermelon, but he said there'd be oodles of fresh cantaloupe, muskmelons, and strawberries, not to mention bread pudding with rum sauce, chess and pecan pies. I was already stuffed from lunch, but just talking about all those things I love to eat made me hungry all over again.

When I returned to the office, Deputy Cate was waiting for me. He handed me his report. I thanked him sincerely, but asked him to tell me what he learned before I delved into it.

"Chief, this Crenshaw fellow seems to be a first class citizen. He said the Bond derringer was a wedding anniversary gift paid for by his wife. He's not a screwball. As it relates to firearms, he owns three plus the derringer. They include a Winchester .22 bolt-action rifle; a Marlin .30-30 lever action rifle; and a 12-gauge Remington pump. The Bond was his only handgun.

"He always kept it in the glovebox of his old white, 1986 Chevy C-10 pickup truck. He'd only shot it a half-dozen times. He still has a half-box of Federal hollow-point bullets he bought when he purchased the gun.

"He doesn't know for sure when it was stolen, because he seldom got in his glovebox, but he knows it was sometime after Thanksgiving. The gun was in the glovebox then, because he was rooting around for his spare sunglasses and he saw it. This occurred in the old Washington High School parking lot where he and the missus went to the flea market.

"Then a couple of weeks before Christmas, he was back in the glovebox again, looking for a roll of Rolaids. That's when he noticed the gun wasn't there. When he got home, he asked his wife if she had taken it out, but she hadn't. He looked everywhere he might have put it, but no luck. He was going to make a police report but didn't, and then he forgot, so I had him file one during my interview."

"Good thinking. Does the glovebox have a lock?"

"Yep, but he never uses it."

"Do you know if he still has the box the gun came in or a receipt from the purchase?"

"He has 'em both."

"I suppose he never filed an insurance claim."

"Nope."

"Okay, the gun's clear. Not on record by LSP as a murder weapon. As soon as we're done with the Buster Devereaux case, you can call him and we'll release it back to him, or you can sign it out and take it to him. Your choice.

"In the meantime, check to see how often he goes to the flea market. The reason is, Buster Devereaux goes there too, and both of my two defendants from whom Buster purchased a stolen necklace and earrings set, sell stolen goods there. They're brothers. Erastus "Dingus" White and Leland "Popeye" White. Looky here at their mugshots. This is what they all look like.

"I want you to make three six-packs [photo array with two rows of three mugshots of similar-looking individuals] and have him take a close look at them. See if he recognizes any of them. It wouldn't surprise me to learn that one of the White brothers stole the derringer out of Crenshaw's truck at the flea market and sold it to Devereaux. I know it's a long shot but maybe we'll get lucky. Copy?"

"On it, Chief, I'll let you know if we get lucky."

After Deputy Cate left, I began tackling my inbox, something I'd neglected since Tuesday. Fortunately, there weren't any time-bombs or sticky wickets. This was my lucky week. I was just finishing up when Harmon arrived. Thelma showed him in. He stood in the doorway of my office for a full minute looking in, studying anecdotes of my life displayed on the walls just like I had studied his.

My office was fairly spartan, too. All of my most important I-Love-Me pictures and trophies were hanging on the wall of our den at home. Here at work, I had used more discretion. The framed Louisiana certificate proclaiming my appointment as Chief Deputy of Saint Landry Parish, was hanging on the wall behind my desk. An antique color print of a map of early Saint Landry Parish was on the wall facing my desk. A framed bullseye target with the center blown out from 60 .38 Special wadcutter rounds, tabulating the maximum score of 300, fired during qualification at FLETC during New Agent Training [NAT] dated July 26, 1978, was hanging on the left wall as you entered.

The right wall had a framed print of three pelicans on wooden dock piers in a South Louisiana bayou.

I had three smaller framed photographs on the credenza behind my desk. The one in the most ornate frame was a picture of Hannah in her wedding dress.

The next one was a picture of our son, Irvin, in his football uniform after the last game his senior year in high school. His white pants and blue and white jersey were covered with mud. He was holding his helmet by the face mask. It was a Red Grange type of photograph. Iconic for the late 1980s era.

The last one was a black and white photograph of me in my Army dress greens, flanked by my parents. It was taken when I returned from basic and AIT on Thursday, November 30th, 1968. I was wearing my Expert Rifleman Badge, of which I was very proud. My folks were smiling from ear-to-ear because I was in the Army National Guard, unlikely to be deployed to Vietnam. I was smiling because the six months of intense training was finally over. Besides, I was still a slick-sleeve, and had to salute everything that moved whenever I was in uniform.

We had plenty of time, so Harmon took his old sweet time trying to assimilate the personal clues I had on display. These depicted significant events I was willing to share about my personal life at work. Finally, he stepped in. We shook hands. He took a seat in the old overstuffed, maroon leather chair with brass studs that I had commandeered from the parish warehouse. I was told it had graced the Saint Landry Parish President of the Board of Supervisors Office back in the 1940s. If so, it had weathered well, all the ravages of time.

Harmon said, "Your son likes football. Did he play in college?"

"He was a walk-on, tried out, didn't get much of a shake, and got cut. He morphed into rugby. Even played rugby in the Army when he deployed to Korea. I've tried hard to get into rugby, but for some reason it just doesn't flip my switch."

"No. You like shooting, and are very good at it."

"I was at one time. My skills have eroded somewhat, but I am well aware of my limitations, and I stay within them. I love baseball too, but I was never very good at it. 'Rode the plank a lot.' Shooting was always my thing."

"Your wife is beautiful."

"Thank you, as is yours.

"Ready for court?"

"Can't wait. I've already identified 26 stolen items from Avoyelles, Saint Landry, Rapides, Evangeline, and Natchitoches Parishes, and I still have another 152 items to try to place. In fact, as it relates to Saint Landry, I have a stolen Rolex watch from Arnaudville, and a bonafide, authenticated Jim Bowie fighting knife stolen from Eunice. I've got pictures and copies of the ledger entries here for you. (He handed me a file for both recovered items.)

"Do you have any heartburn if I hang onto the ledger while I'm going through everything? I brought you a xerographic copy to use in the meantime."

"You keep it until you're all done with it.

"Regarding that Bond derringer, it was stolen from a guy named Delmar H. Crenshaw from Krotz Springs. He's pretty sure it was purloined from his truck at the Washington Flea Market the Friday after Thanksgiving. He didn't realize it was missing for a week or two. We took a police report from him today. Before I knew this, I had the LSP lab check it for ballistics and matches of expended projectiles recovered at crime scenes. It came back clear, so after Buster's trial we will return it to the rightful owner.

"By the way, we also arrested the brothers Erastus and Leland White from Whiteville, for the theft of that ruby jewelry ensemble. During the same burglary, they also stole a vintage Parker shotgun appraised at $8,300. We recovered it last night."

"Outstanding. You all have been busy beavers. Look, you mind if we head on up and meet with your district attorney? I'd like to know how he wants to present our evidence."

"Of course not. Let's do it."

"Onslow was hard at it when we arrived. I made the introductions.

Harmon handed Onslow the ledger, and a three-ring binder containing his indexed file with copies of police reports married up with photographs of the stolen items and a xerographic copy of the relevant page from the ledger.

Onslow took his time to study each pairing. Then he looked up and said, "This is absolutely perfect. Awesome. It's exactly what we need.

"I hate to give up this much discovery information before it's required, but I can see no other way to get the judge to quash Godfrey's motion, compelling us to turn over Buster Devereaux's financial assets to him.

"The way this works, Godfrey will present his motion first. Then I will put you, Marvin, on the stand to confirm everything you all seized from the bank as a result of the court order. Then you, Harmon, will go on the stand to discuss the search warrant on Devereaux's property, to include what you all seized, and how many items you have already identified as stolen property. The judge might have his own questions. Then he'll decide yay or nay. I feel pretty good about getting a favorable decision. Any questions?"

Harmon asked, "Will you ask me questions one by one, or will you just ask me to provide a narrative regarding what we did and what we've identified so far?"

"Do you have a preference?"

"I'd prefer that you ask me to explain what we found and let me run with the ball."

"Done, but if Godfrey interrupts and asks you a question, do not answer right away. Give the judge or me the opportunity to object before you respond. Okay? Look at me before responding. Godfrey's got a reputation as a slimy lawyer, and he will do his best to get you confused and 'all pithed off'. Assuming we get a favorable ruling, and I believe we will, Godfrey and Devereaux are toast. Any questions?"

"No. Thanks."

"Marvin, you have any questions?"

"Nope."

"Good. It's time to go."

We walked over to the courthouse. The courtroom was vacant. Nothing else was on the docket this afternoon. Nobody to witness the proceedings. This should be interesting.

At 2:55, Deputies Carl T.F. Witherspoon and Harold W. Lacy brought in the shackled Buster Devereaux. He looked like he'd lost a few pounds. Then at 2:59, Mr. Robin Geoffrey Godfrey,

Esquire, made his entrance. He looked like a million bucks. He even had a manicure! You know, all GQ with his expensive threads and coiffed hairdo. He ignored us and we ignored him.

At 3 o'clock, Mrs. Richman came in, followed by Judge DesHotel. He sat, banged his gavel, and pronounced court in session. Mrs. Richman read the docket number. Counsel made their appearances for the record. Then Mr. Godfrey was called to plead his motion.

He stood behind the defense table and said, "Your Honor, Mr. Devereaux's case is about the murder of one Nicodemus Jean Pierre, allegedly at the hands of my client. It's also about the alleged theft of Mr. Pierre's silver tableware, which I understand the sheriff's office recovered from my client's business. Even if we concede that those two allegations are true, which we absolutely do not, it has nothing whatsoever to do with my client's banking assets. He had not made any deposits into his account, nor unlocked his safe deposit box for three days PRIOR to the demise of Mr. Pierre. Therefore, the defense requests that the prosecution surrender the contents of the safe deposit box, and that my client's bank assets be returned in full."

" Very succinct. Thank you, Mr. Godfrey. Mr. Trudeau, what say you?"

"Your Honor, the state wants to call two witnesses in rebuttal."

"So be it."

"The state calls Saint Landry Parish Chief Deputy Sheriff Marvin L. Barnett to the stand."

I stepped up to the witness box and was sworn in by Mrs. Richman. Then I took a seat. Onslow approached the witness stand and said, "Chief Barnett can you tell us about your application for a court order to seize Mr. Devereaux's assets at Farmers Savings Bank in Cheneyville, in Rapides Parish, on Thursday, May 27th, 2004?"

"Yes, Sir. Mr. Pierre was murdered on Tuesday, May 25th, at his home in Big Cane, and his silver tableware was stolen. I got a lead that the assailant was one Buster Devereaux from Bunkie, in Avoyelles Parish. I called Avoyelles Parish Sheriff Clinton W. Boyd and asked for assistance. He checked and determined that Mr. Devereaux had just returned to his business, which is called Buster's Buy & Sell. APSO set up a surveillance and waited for me to arrive. We raided his business simultaneously, front and rear, and deputies from APSO placed him under arrest. I was one of the officers to enter through the front. That's when I saw Mr. Pierre's silver tableware in plain sight.

"At that point, in consultation with Sheriff Boyd, it was decided to obtain a search warrant for the business, in the event that there were other stolen items within. APSO obtained the warrant, and while they were conducting the search, one of our deputies took custody of Mr. Devereaux, and lodged him in our jail. I returned myself just a few minutes after he arrived.

"The following day, Wednesday, May 26th, I met with APSO Chief Deputy Harmon L. Bergeron. He made the comment that the search of Buster's Buy & Sell, his house, and his vehicle had not resulted in the location of any financial records, cash, or his business ledger, something which any legitimate business would have.

"In fact, by state law Mr. Devereaux was required to maintain a business ledger, and any state or local officer could request to inspect it at any time. Chief Bergeron said the lack thereof was hindering his determination of the origin of any of the merchandise he recovered, all of which were used items.

"Furthermore, he stated he had ascertained that Mr. Devereaux did not have an account or safe deposit box in any of the banks in Avoyelles Parish, which only has four, all of which are branches of the Avoyelles Federal Bank.

"On Thursday, May 27th, I mentioned this conundrum to Sheriff Abner Ladner. He replied that Cheneyville was only seven miles from Bunkie, and it has a bank, so I checked to see. I obtained a court order compelling the Farmers Savings Bank to release any assets, documents, and any safe deposit items to me. We discovered that Mr. Devereaux had $53,677.22 in a savings account, plus $110,000 in cash and the ledger for Buster's Buy & Sell, stashed in his safe deposit box, all of which I seized. I brought the money back here, and Chief Deputy Harmon Bergeron of the Avoyelles Parish Sheriff's Office, took custody of the ledger."

Onslow stated, "Thank you Chief. That will be all."

Mr. Godfrey asked, "Judge, may I cross?"

"Proceed."

"Chief Barrett, what on earth induced you to get a court order for Farmers Savings Bank? What evidence did you have?"

I paused waiting for an objection from Onslow, but there was none. "Sir, Mr. Devereaux is in a cash-only business. He only had $1,500 on him at the time of his arrest. That was the closest bank."

"So this was purely speculation on your part. You had no probable cause."

Onslow jumped up, "Your honor, this wasn't an application for a search warrant or an arrest warrant. The application for a court order does not require probable cause. They are used for a myriad of things, like obtaining telephone toll records, educational documents, banking records, and the like. Mr. Godfrey knows that."

"Agreed. Mr. Godfrey, do you have any other questions for this witness?"

"No, Your Honor."

"You may step down, Chief Barnett. Call your next witness, Mr. Trudeau."

"I call Chief Deputy Harmon Bergeron from Avoyelles Parish."

After he was sworn in, Onslow asked, "Chief Bergeron, what is your role in this investigation?"

"Well, I was out of town the night the search warrants were executed on Mr. Devereaux's property, but as the chief deputy, I inherited it all, including the investigation to determine where all of Mr. Devereaux's inventory had originated, especially since we found no financial or business records, and no currency. By state law he must keep a ledger of all incoming and outgoing merchandise, yet there was none in his business, his home, or his motor vehicle. I checked all of our banks, but I never thought about checking in Rapides Parish. It made sense, though, because the bank in Cheneyville is, in fact the closest bank to Bunkie.

"Once I got my hands on the ledger, I was able to identify 26 stolen items of the 152 we seized, and that was in just one day. This is the file I created which matches a photograph of the seized item, the corresponding police report of the theft, and a copy of the page in the ledger where Mr. Devereaux logged it in."

Onslow asked, "May I show your file to the judge?"

"Of course."

"Judge, I demand to see the ledger first!"

"By all means, Mr. Godfrey."

Godfrey poured over the file at the prosecution table like it was a best selling novel. His face turned beet red and became contorted. Finally, he surrendered the ledger to Onslow, who presented it to Mrs. Richman, who handed it to the judge. It only took him two minutes to make up his mind. When he looked up, he was suppressing a grin.

He passed the file down to Harmon. Then he cleared his throat and said, "It is the order of this court that the Saint Landry Parish Sheriff's Office maintain custody of the ledger and all the assets recovered from the Farmers Savings Bank. Is there any other business before the court today?"

"Yes, Your Honor."

"What is it Mr. Godfrey?"

"Your Honor, I'm stepping aside as Mr. Devereaux's counsel."

"I see. And why is that?"

"To be quite frank, he can no longer afford to retain my services."

"So that's what this motion was all about."

"Pretty much, Your Honor. This is a difficult case. It requires a great deal of attention that now I must divert elsewhere to remain gainfully employed."

"I see. How many pro bono cases do you have right now?"

"One or two."

"Which is it - one or two?"

"Well right now, just one. The other case was resolved two days ago."

"Okay. Well then, Mr. Devereaux is now your second. He needs an attorney of your caliber if he has any hope of ever being a free man again. You are hereby appointed to represent him. File the paperwork with the clerk's office before you go home today.

"Court is hereby adjourned."

It was Friday afternoon. Everybody bailed except for Mr. Godfrey, who remained seated with a look of disbelief on his face. Buster had already been hustled off back to jail. Mr. Godfrey was all by his lonesome, looking forlorn.

Outside, Onslow said, "Great job, fellows. Keep up the good work. Marvin, why don't you take Harmon to the clerk's office so he can be reimbursed. I have a date with a fishing hole. See you all Monday."

I got Harmon squared away at the clerk's office. I told him, "I'll jump on those other two cases come Monday. I'll let you know what we come up with."

"Good deal. Let me know. This is the gift that keeps on giving."

"You got that right. Adiós."

- *Chapter 15* -
Arresting More Thieves

Saturday, May 29th was the day to honor a good man and pay our respects. It would be an outdoor event in the heat of the day, high expected to be 93 degrees Fahrenheit with typical humidity of 92%. Also a 60% possibility of a semi-tropical thunderstorm with heavy rain beginning around 3 o'clock. We dressed in typical Louisiana chic for this time of year. Black suits and dresses were too hot. Besides, if a summer deluge came down, fancy outfits could be ruined.

Hannah wore a lightweight, white sleeveless cotton blouse with a short, baby blue, full gathered skirt to allow the air circulate around her bare legs. She had a gauzy, white shawl to protect her shoulders and arms from sunburn, not to mention oodles of sunscreen. She wore dressy-looking, beige, open-toed canvass shoes with a slight wedge heel, but no socks or nylon stockings; however, she did have a matching French pedi and mani. She capped off her ensemble with a beige, wide-brimmed, low-crowned straw hat with a bright blue silk hatband, and green-tinted, oversized sunglasses with black frames.

Me? I wore western cut khaki trousers, freshly buff-shined, brown Tony Lama cowboy boots (with rounded toes and low heels) and a matching brown leather belt, a white, long-sleeve, pleated tuxedo shirt with black studs for buttons open at the throat, no tie, and a beige, straw Stetson cowboy hat. The trousers were full-cut and pleated, which allowed me to conceal my off-duty, stainless steel, snub-nose Smith & Wesson, five-shot, .38

Special revolver in the right front pocket. Nobody but Hannah and Abner were the wiser. I knew Abner was packing too. It comes with the office. No doubt there were others we didn't know about, but Louisiana is a conceal carry state for anyone who obtains a license.

Marisol and Abner were similarly attired as we.

When we arrived at the Big Cane AME Church, ushers provided guests with a looped black ribbon and pin to wear on their shirts and blouses, signifying their bereavement. They also passed out handheld cardboard fans courtesy of the Ichabod Johnson & Sons Funeral Home in Washington (LA) to all the ladies.

Looking around, I estimated the crowd at 500. Maybe a fifth were white. The church had seating for about 120. Not to worry. Someone had kicked in to rent four large, peaked white awnings with white, rectangular, folding tables and white folding chairs. Each table was designed to accommodate ten guests.

Also, they had six-feet tall, oscillating fans under each awning. I saw six per.

They had gigantic coolers spread around liberally under the awnings filled with ice and bottled water.

Lastly, they had somebody professionally wire several gigantic amps and speakers outside, so the the overflow crowd could hear the pastor, organist, and the choir. Somewhere in the shadows there was a big bucks donor.

We took seats in the back row under one of the awnings out of reverence. Out of reverence, two deacons ushered us inside the church, four rows back from the pulpit. Ditto for our ranking parish supervisor, Eliot T. Bradshaw and his wife, and our newly elected black parish supervisor, Ronald W. 'T-Bone' Smith, Jr., and his wife.

Nicodemus' closed casket was a simple pine box. It was sitting on a high stand up close to the pulpit. There were scores of sprays and bouquets placed next to it.

It was nearly 1:30 when the celebration of a life well-lived kicked off. It was supposed to start at 1 o'clock, but we live in an imperfect world.

Pastor Ezekiel J. Coe began the service with a lengthy prayer, followed by the choir belting out 'Go Tell it on the Mountain' a cappella, which nearly brought the walls of Jericho down. They followed up with another five gospel songs, mesmerizing everyone within earshot. In fact, by comparison, in some of the hillbilly churches in Eastern Kentucky and West Virginia, this is the point when they bring out the live, poisonous serpents to allow those who are completely possessed of the Holy Ghost, to prove the strength of their faith by handling them and passing them around. If you get bit, that indicates your strength of faith is lacking. All the true believers know that.

Of course, it's been claimed that certain snake-handling pastors milk the rattlesnakes before the service so that any of the brethren who do get bit (for lacking in faith), don't get a full dose and survive to try it another day. Aware of such, I had my eyes wide open looking for the snakes to come out, but of course it was a different state with different religious customs.

The Pastor Ezekiel Coe was a hellfire and brimstone pastor, with a booming, melodic voice, and a rhythm or cadence similar to the ocean waves. He stirred up the congregation, a number of whom, especially the larger church ladies wearing the enormous, outrageous hats, leapt from their pews, arms stretched up to heaven, begging Jesus to come back to Earth and commence the

Rapture. The choir had its cues to harmonize with the pastor at key points of his message. To say the church was rocking from its very foundation during its send-off of Nicodemus to the Pearly Gates would be an accurate assessment. I'm sure Nicodemus was humbled from his perch up on high in Heaven. For more than an hour we sat approaching hypnosis due to Pastor Coe's fiery rhetoric, and the choir's rendition of absolutely captivating, harmonizing gospel hymns.

Then it was over. The absence of sound was palpable and a little eerie.

Pastor Coe led the deacons who were pallbearers carrying the casket, and the Army National Guard Honor Guard, followed by the congregation, to the cemetery behind the church. Once assembled, the remarks were brief. The Honor Guard rendered a 21-gun salute. The 23-year-old 2nd Lieutenant in Charge, Thurlow G. "Tweety Bird" Brown, presented Eugene the folded flag. The casket was lowered into the grave. Family and well-wishers dropped dirt on the casket while the choir belted out all five stanzas of Amazing Grace. I didn't see a dry eye anywhere.

Suddenly the ceremony was over once again, but nobody moved nor uttered a word for several minutes. Eventually the congregation began to break up and return to the church and the shade of the awnings. The church ladies in charge of feeding the masses had already set up the buffet lines. We joined the queue and loaded our plates to overflowing. I filled mine with two pieces of fried chicken, a slice of country ham, and small portions of potato salad, cole slaw, candied yams, black-eyed peas, cantaloupe, strawberries, bread pudding with rum sauce, a biscuit, and a small slice of chess pie. I passed on the collard greens and chitlins among other delights.

The church ladies brought everyone a tall tumbler of freshly squeezed, iced lemonade once they were seated. They followed up with countless pitchers of the same, keeping everyone topped off. Honest Injun, I could not recall the last time I had feasted like this.

Abner kept saying, "Ah tol' chu so. Dis is da way dey do t'ings ovah heah. Dese ladies can cook! Whooeee!"

I consumed so much I was shot in the ass for the rest of the day. Why fight it? After we made our way back home, I sat out back with one of my premium cigars to top off the meal. Later that evening, we partook of a light supper consisting of iced, deveined, boiled shrimp with cocktail sauce, a tossed salad, cottage cheese with sliced fresh peaches, and a chilled bottle of pinot noir wine.

Sunday was a day of much needed rest, and of course a church service which covered all the evangelical bases. The reverent message was clearly there, but compared to Reverend Coe's service yesterday, it came up way short. I hated thinking this, but it was worship like usual - uninspiring. Like kissing your sister. Going through the motions. I pondered if I should join a black church.

I decided to talk to Abner about this next time I saw him. He would have some ideas on that, but like most of the folks in South Louisiana, he was a Roman Catholic. Protestants were still looked upon here by some folks in the same way the ancient Jews looked at the Samaritans - unwashed. Heck! It was illegal in this state until 1825 for three or more Protestants to gather for religious purposes. I changed my mind and decided to keep my thoughts to myself. Best to let sleeping dogs lie.

Monday was Memorial Day, so we were off.

Tuesday morning, June 1st. I met Abner for breakfast at his usual haunt. I got him caught up on the Buster Devereaux case and it's growing string of related thefts. I mentioned the recovery of the stolen Rolex watch from Arnaudville, and the stolen, genuine Jim Bowie knife from Eunice. The latter rang his bell loudly. This was a sacrilege! It fired him up and got his juices flowing.

"Who stoled dis knife?"

"Well, Buster bought it from a worm named Ned J. Fontenot. He may or may not have stolen it. He's supposed to be black, but in his DL photo he looks awful light-complected to me. He's a 33-year-old welder by trade, several arrests for public drunkenness and fighting. One big hiccup with a felony conviction in 1999 for dwelling house burglary. He got four years to serve at Angola and was released after two. Drives a light blue, 1992 Dodge D150 pickup truck registered to him at Daigle Woods, #23, at 2144 Highway 13, in Eunice."

"He's Creole. Half French, half black, half Indian, half polecat, half alligator. Dat's why he's so light-skinned. Bet he has blue eyes and kinky sandy hair, too."

"You nailed it. You know him?"

"Ah do know some Fontenots from around dat area, but no Ned. Betcha Ah know his mama or papa, dough. Dat address is a trailer park. Used ta be pretty nice. Not so much now. Today chu an' me are gonna go arrest dat chitbird. Dat's on Beat 12. Before we leabe, we'll call da patrol deputy ta meet us. How long it take chu ta get ready?"

"Five minutes after we get back to the office."

It only took 20 minutes to get to Eunice with Abner's lead foot. It was a straight shot west on US 190. We met Deputy Ansel B.

Caillou at the Flying J Truck Stop.

"Hey, Cheriff, Chief. Wat's up?"

"Chu know a dude named Ned Fontenot?"

"Oh, Lawdy. Wat's he done did now?"

"Chu recall a burglary back in February at da Napoleon M. Guidry house?"

"Yep. Ah took da report. Ned do dat?"

"Yep. At least he da one who fenced da stolen Jim Bowie knife. Chu recall what all else wuz stolen dere?"

"Shō do. A 1873 Colt Peacemaker wit' ivory grips. Hab a 7-1/2-inch barrel. Da grips has 11 notches on da bottom foe all da bandits da mān kilt. Choots a .44-40 bullet, w'ich a partial box of dem was stole, too."

"What can chu tell me about Mr. Guidry? He a rich man?"

"Lawdy no! He a high school geography teacher. Dese t'ings wuz passed down from his pawpaw back in da day. Ole Mān Lucius Vidrine Guidry, very famous, dey called him da Grim Reaper 'cause he done kilt so many outlaws. He wuz a depity cheriff in Cameron Parish neah Port Ahthur, Texas, back in da oily 1920s up 'til way atter WWII ended. Dey wuz a lot of smugglin' goin' on down dere back den. He lahk Wyatt Oip. He move ta Eunice wen he hung up his spoirs. He a highly respected ol' mān when he passed away."

Chu t'ink we can find Ned Fontenot at his trailer dis mornin'?"

"Mebbe, but he most lahkly at woik at Theriot's Welding Chop. If he truck dere, he dere. In fact, it not too fah from rat chere. Chu all follow me."

It was 9:25. The shop was in a fairly new industrial park off Highway 95. Sure enough, Ned's truck was parked in the lot. All three big bay, overhead rolling garage doors to the business were up, so we let ourselves in. Abner approached the service desk. Ansel made a beeline for a workstation where our suspect had just removed his welder's helmet. I followed him. Ned didn't see this coming, so he was easy to apprehend. I cuffed him, and we stuffed him in the backseat of Ansel's unit. Then Ansel and I walked up to the service desk and stood by while Abner schmoozed the owner. Introductions were made, hands were shaken, and we departed, happy campers all around except for Ned. This may have been the easiest arrest I'd ever made.

We followed Ansel to the Eunice Police Department, where we had a small office. We borrowed an interview room with a one-way mirrored glass. Ansel watched while Abner and I went in to conduct the interview.

I made the official introductions. Then I read Ned the Miranda Warning and obtained his signature acknowledging same.

I said, "Ned, you gotta know this is important if the high sheriff himself came all the way out here from Opelousas just to see you. That's because you messed up bad. Why don't you just go ahead and 'fess up to what you've done?"

"Soi, Ah cain't imagine wat chu mean. Chu probably got me confused wit' some udder lost soul."

"Possibly, but I doubt it."

Holding up a photograph of the Jim Bowie knife for him to look at, I said, "Tell me about this."

His Adam's apple started bouncing up and down like a bobber with a hooked fish. He started wringing his hands. He asked, "How much trouble am Ah in?"

"I'm not gonna lie to ya. A fair amount. You're caught. The

question is, are you gonna try to lie your way out of it, or are you gonna make amends?"

"Well, Soi, dat's a pitcher of a stoled knife. Ah stole it from da current owner, who's pawpaw stoled it from my pawpaw back in 1900-and-43, wen he arrested my pawpaw for fighting and drunk and disorderly. All Ah did was right a wrong w'ich was a long time a-comin'. Ah intended on keepin' it, 'cause it's one of on'y six or eight original Bowie fightin' knives wat still exist. Not shoi how much it's woit', but it's a lot.

"Den my ole lady up and run off with some weasel name of Eli S. fah Chithaid Billiot. Las' Ah hoid dey was in Beaumont, Texas. Bitch is carryin' my baby. At least che claims it's mine. Ah got ta drinkin' a lot atter che run off, an' callin' in sick ta woik and fell way behind on mah trailer and truck payments. Ah can sleep in my truck but Ah can't dribe my house trailer.

"So . . . . Ah needed cash. A lot of cash. Ah hoid about dis crooked fence who hab a Buy & Sell up in Bunkie, so Ah took da knife up dere, and sold it ta him fah a t'ousand bucks. It woit ten times dat, but Ah was in a bind. Da bank was gonna repo mah trailer in two mō days.

"Dat's da whole story."

"What about the Colt Peacemaker?"

"Nap Guidry said Ah took dat too?"

"It would seem so."

"Ha! Ain't dat a cryin' shame? Ah wudn't the onliest jasper wat broke in ta Nap's house dat day. He own son-in-law, Howie Doucet, was wit' me. He even had da house key and he stoled dat gun. Said he always wanted one of dem Wyatt Oip pistols. Chu want da gun, go talk ta him. Ah've done said too much awready."

Ansel placed Ned in a holding cell. Then he came back and

said, "Howie Doucet is da heating and air condtioning dude. He a one-man operation. He chop on da main drag headed eastbound. Chu all wanna follow me?"

Abner said, "Let's do it."

After a fair amount of consideration, I've decided luck is equal to or better than skill. This is just another example. Howie Doucet's service truck was parked in front of his tiny shop. He was inside, stooped over the counter perusing one of a half-dozen HVAC catalogs while smoking a Lucky Strike down to the filter. He had an ashtray full of butts. He straightened up when the sheriff and two deputies walked in.

"What can we do for you all, Sheriff?"

"Howie, chu can turn around and put chur hands behind chur back. Chu're under arrest."

Howie lost all his starch. He melted like a limp dick after sex and was totally compliant. You could see it in his eyes. He knew his goose was cooked and it was time to pay the piper.

I asked Ansel to hold up putting the handcuffs on him, while I pulled out a rights waiver and read it to him. Howie said he understood, and he signed the waiver. Then I told Ansel to press on.

I asked, "Howie, where's Mr. Guidry's Peacemaker?"

"Uh, it's in that drawer over there. Did he ask for it back? I would have gladly returned it if he had just said something."

Abner opened the drawer and recovered the gun and a partial box of .44-40s. He held them up for all to see. Howie hung his head in shame. A tear rolled down his cheek.

I asked, "Hold on a sec. Let me call and ask. Nap Guidry at the schoolhouse today or should I call him at home?"

"Ur, well, I dunno, but that won't be necessary. I'll just go ahead and return it. I didn't think he'd get so pissed off. All I done was borry it for a few days."

"How's come he filed a police report then?"

"Oh God! How's this gonna work out for me?"

"I dunno. You're going to jail today, and then you'll go before the judge tomorrow morning. At least you don't have to explain this to your boss.

"Sheriff, what would you say to you and me taking Howie back to our shop, and having Deputy Caillou take the other jaybird since he has a shield in his unit?"

"Ah'd say great minds t'ink alike. Let's go."

It wasn't even 11:30 yet. We came to arrest one burglar and hooked up two. Life is good!

It soon became clear that it was our misfortune that I suggested we transport Howie to jail instead of Ned. Howie filled his britches on our way out of town. He must have been constipated for a week. The smell was so bad, it could've brought tears to a glass eye. We must've scared Howie shitless. The jailers were going to love us. At least we had a bevy of inmates to wash and sanitize Abner's truck, but what can you do to sanitize your nostrils? Vicks Vaporub was not anywhere near potent enough for this toxic, nuclear bomb.

It didn't take long. Abner exclaimed, tears running down his cheeks, half blinded by the stink, "Marvin, chu havta get dat udder chitbird churself. Ah'm gettin' too old ta smell chit lahk dis. Ah hope da chudge tacks on anudder six months on him fah chitting in mah new truck. He's peeling da paint off da doors. Mah eyes cain't stop waterin'. Mah nose is on strike. Ah can barely see ta dribe.

"For God's sake, Howie, don't chu have flush toilets dere in

Eunice? Chu're killin' me. Marvin, if Ah die, chu charge dis polecat wit' moider!"

I wanted to laugh but the noxious odor was clearing my sinuses, too. I had planned on us dropping off Howie, and then the two of us going somewhere to eat. Now it might be days before we felt up to eating again. As soon as we drove up to the jail, Abner bailed out of his truck and handed Deputy Herman G. Whitaker his keys. He said, "Book dis chitbird fah burglary. Chief'll tell ya da rest. Den get a team of trusties out here ta sanitize mah truck." He stomped off without another word.

Deputy Whitaker responded, "On it Sheriff!"

By then, Deputy Caillou showed up with Ned Fontenot. I met with him and told him what to put on both booking slips. Then I picked up my file, climbed in the Jeep, and drove over to the Dairy Queen for a cheeseburger and large vanilla milkshake. Guess I was pretty hungry after all. I called the office and asked Thelma who was working Beat 2. She said it was Esther Marie Bienvenu, Unit 14.

Esther was a 55-year-old deputy with 30 years of faithful service. She had been the jail matron in charge of the women's side for 22 years. She begged Sheriff Neicase to put her on the road, and eventually he acquiesced. Esther was a first class matron, and he hated to trust the position to any of the other female deputies. More than that though, Esther was like your me-maw. She was 5-feet, 4-inches tall, and a little on the portly side. Not exactly fat, but age had shifted once voluptuous curves into sagging curves, like it does to most 55-year-old ladies. Sheriff Neicase was afraid the young punks would not respect her and she would get hurt. However, she had put in more than her fair share of time as a jailer, and she was long overdue her chance on patrol.

Esther had a calming personality which defused most situations. She didn't try to throw her weight around, no pun intended. She showed respect to everyone. The few times a punk decided to blow off her lawful orders, she tased the living shit out of them. Then she cuffed them, and called for backup to help her load the incapacitated criminal misanthropes into the back of her cruiser. After word of that got around, she had very few problems. For obvious reasons, she was quicker to tase than most deputies. It worked for her, and the rest of the deputies benefitted too. Besides that, it was a far stretch for a bigger, muscle-bound thug to claim police brutality.

Also, she was one of only a handful of Saint Landry Parish deputies who had used deadly force. It happened when she was one of two night shift deputies involved in a high-speed pursuit of a pair of car thieves. After a lengthy chase, the perps wrecked the stolen car. The driver bailed out with a revolver. Esther Marie shot him once in the gut and he collapsed. The other perp was unarmed and surrendered peacefully. The driver made a full recovery with the permanent aid of a colostomy bag. He was sentenced to 15 years at hard labor in Angola. The other mutt got four. That's how Esther Marie 'made her bones' on the street.

I called Esther Marie and asked her to pick a location in Arnaudville to meet. She suggested the Stripes Convenience Store at the intersection of Highways 93 and 347. It was a small establishment. I bought a bottle of water and waited for her to arrive. I stood in the shade under the front awning, stretching my legs, sipping on water, and smoking an Alex Bradley Maduro Robusto. The aroma and flavor were especially good, and soothed my nerves after the shitty (pun intended) morning I'd had.

Esther Marie rolled up like she had to pee really bad. She apologized for keeping me waiting. She said she had been tied up on a traffic accident.

I responded, "No worries. Do you need to take a break? Use the restroom? Get a drink or a bite to eat? Take all the time you need. I'm in no rush."

"Thanks, Chief. I'll take you up on that." She stepped inside. I smoked some more. Finally she returned with a smile on her face and a cherry Slurpee in her hand.

"What's up, Chief? What brings you all the way down here to Arnaudville?"

"Do you have any knowledge about the larceny of a Presidential-style Rolex wristwatch belonging to a Mr. Elmer T. Authement back on January 17th? That was on a Saturday."

"I read the squeal. I didn't take the report. I think Bubba Domingue did."

"That's right. Do you know the vic?"

"Yeah, sorry to say that I do. Elmer's hard not to know around these parts whether you want to or not. He owns at least ten sections of rice paddies and all the crawfish traps they can hold. Drives a yellow 2002 Cadillac Escalade with garish LSU stickers plastered all over it. He didn't even graduate! Flunked out after three semesters. Family money. Lives in a restored antebellum house up the road over there (pointing north) with his wife, Miss Trish, whose nickname is Pissy Trishy, pardon my French. They spawned the two orneriest, worthless, most disrespectful teenage boys in all of Saint Landry Parish. They're criminals in the making. Nothing would please me more than catching them in the middle of a felony.

"What I heard is Elmer claimed he took his watch off to wash his hands at the Phillips 66 gas station and he left it on the sink. Soon as he returned to his car, he remembered it, so he went back, but it was missing. Said he couldn't have been gone more than two minutes, max.

"Edwin 'Hanky Panky' Dubois was the only employee at the station when it happened, so naturally Elmer accused him of stealing it. Hanky Panky is a big ole country boy, generally as passive as a teddy bear, but nobody wants to be called a thief. He blew up, got fightin' mad, and said Elmer better back off because he didn't do it. Threatened to kick Elmer's a-double-s all the way to Texas, and he's big enough, and was furious enough to have done it. Anyway, Elmer called the SO in a blind rage and Bubba got the squeal. Bubba used his charm and Hanky Panky being a good guy, readily consented to a search of himself, his pickup, and the entire premises. Bubba searched for the better part of an hour. Nada.

Both Elmer and Hanky Panky claim there had not been any other customers at the time of the theft. That's about all I can remember."

"That's a whole lot more than what's in the report. I appreciate your insight. Do you know a Detweiler Chauvin, Jr.?"

"I do. He's an 18-year-old 7th grade dropout. Tall and skinny. They call him Bones. He lives with his mammy, Tootsie Labat, and a half-dozen half-siblings and cousins in a tiny house about a half-mile south of here on Highway 31. Not a bad kid. Just a product of a mostly hopeless situation. He's gotten into trouble a few times, but nothing serious. He works as a field hand whenever he can find work. He doesn't have any transportation, so he walks wherever he goes. Why the interest?"

"Does he have access to a set of wheels?"

"Oh, hell no. This kid would be lucky if he owns a second pair of overalls. He doesn't even own a bike."

"Well someone using his name sold Elmer's Rolex to a crook named Buster Devereaux. He's the guy who owns Buster's Buy & Sell in Bunkie. That name ring a bell?"

"No kidding! I bet Bones wasn't the thief, though. They would have noticed him. Maybe one of his little brothers slipped in to use the restroom, saw the watch, snitched it, and slipped away. If he was quiet, there's a good chance no one would even notice a little kid."

"How would Bones get to Bunkie to sell the watch?"

"I bet Tootsie drove him. She's got a car. It's a white AMC Gremlin. A 1978 model, I think. I bet she sent Bones in to sell the watch in case something went haywire. That way she doesn't lose her welfare check. I bet Bones didn't get more than ten bucks out of it."

"How would Tootsie know about Buster's Buy & Sell?"

"The down-and-out crowd has a grapevine too, you know. Probably better than ours. How do you want to handle this?"

"You know the family dynamics. What would you suggest?"

"We use subterfuge to get our hands on Bones. Then we take him back to the office and present his options to him. See what he says. If what I think is true, I would hate for this to be the incident which propels him into Angola. You know, turn a misguided youth into a life of crime, but that may be what happens."

"I appreciate your compassion. I'd hate that too. What about this? What if we bag the real culprit? What if we charge Tootsie with receiving stolen property and contributing to the delinquency of a minor? RSP is always a felony, and contributing is too, especially under circumstances such as these.

"Bones doesn't have a D/L. He doesn't even have a state-issued ID card. He says he's 18, and it's true this is the 18th year of his birth, but he hasn't passed the threshold just yet. He does have a juvie record, just like you mentioned, but they're chickenshit violations. Throwing a rock at a kid who was bullying him but missing him and breaking a schoolhouse window. Stealing a watermelon from a farmer.

"Our records list his DOB as June 6th, 1996, so I had Thelma call Saint Landry General Hospital where he was born, and they confirmed it. That means when he made the transaction with Buster he was a minor, and he still is for five more days.

"Dern, Chief. I'm impressed. Maybe things will work out for the better after all."

"Thanks. I hope so. So tell me where do we locate Bones and Tootsie?"

"Tootsie will be at home if her car's there. If Bones isn't working, he'll be there, too. There ain't too many places to go down here.

"Speaking of watermelon. Tootsie and all her kids got their own little watermelon patch in the backyard. Actually, it's pretty big. Besides watermelons, they grow cantaloupes, green beans, lima beans, carrots, radishes, tomatoes, okra, cabbages, leaf lettuce, peppers, cucumbers, you name it. Bones is the head farmer. Ya feel lucky, Chief? Let's check there first."

"Lead the way, Deputy Bienvenu."

We drove down a dirt road off Highway 347 to cluster of eight or nine Negro dwellings on what I would call acre-size lots. Most backyards had farm fencing. Some folks had a few goats. A couple had a milk cow. I saw a donkey, chickens, a mule, rabbit hutches, chickens, hound dogs, and several cats. All but two backyards had a sizable garden. I was impressed with what I saw. These folks were working hard to augment their meager incomes.

The terrain was flat with a smattering of hardwood trees, most of which were cottonwoods. The houses were pretty much all the same. Small rectangular brick homes on a concrete slab with a gray shingle hip roof and white trim. No garages, but they all had a covered roof adjacent to the house over the single-car gravel driveway, called a carport by some, although it was used mostly for shade for outdoor cooking and socializing rather than for sheltering a motor vehicle.

Only a couple of these houses had air conditioning by way of an old rattler hanging out of the front room window. Few of these folks were concerned about getting too hot in the summer. They were more concerned about getting enough heat in the winter. Forty degrees in the wintertime when the wind blows in a semi-tropical climate might as well be zero. Metal sheds were standard issue in all the backyards. Esther Marie said these were all Section 8 homes. I had figured as much.

Tootsie and family lived in the house at the very end of the row of houses. Her car was parked in the front yard, windows all rolled down. She was seated at a picnic table under the carport, shelling some beans. A half dozen folding lawn chairs were also under the carport. Four youngsters were watching or playing some type of tag. I could see Bones and another skinny kid working in the garden.

I had incorrectly assumed Tootsie would be old, haggard, surly, fifty pounds overweight, wearing a worn-out housedress, fuzzy house slippers, hair covered in a doo rag, and utterly disagreeable. She was anything but. She looked to be between 30 and 35 years old, smooth, milk chocolate complexion, hair neatly combed, trim body, wearing short turquoise shorts and a white, scalloped-necked, short-sleeve blouse, and flip flops. She was alert, but not defensive.

She looked up and cautiously asked, "Wat's up, Miss Esther?"

"Tootsie, I want you to meet Mr. Marvin Barnett. He's our new chief deputy, right under Sheriff Landry. He hails from Mississippi. He's responsible for the investigation of all our serious crimes."

Tootsie quietly sized me up and said, "Chu da mān who arrested Buster Devereaux. He kilt Nicodemus Pierre. Now chu comes ta arrest me."

"Why would you say that?"

"Because Ah done bidness wit' dat mān."

"What business?"

"Ah sold dat mān a gold watch my boy, Mouse Toid, found. Ah knows who watch it wuz. Who else besides Massa Elmah can affōd a watch lahk dat? Ah sold it anyway. Mah car needed brakes an' a muffler an' a tuneup an' da inshooance was due. Buster gib me $800 an' Ah spent evah last cent fixin' mah cah."

"Buster's ledger says Bones sold him the watch."

"Dat because Buster want me to gib him around da woild befōe doin' bidness wit' me. I says den he hab ta pay me one t'ousand dollahs if he want some nu-nu, too. He say no. He only gib me eight hunnert dollahs. Den he say he want Bones ta sign da book in case he get busted fah buyin' a hot watch. Den he gonna rat out Bones 'stead ob me. So Bones not guilty. Ah'm guilty. Take me."

"Who will raise your kids while you're in prison?"

"Mah mammy an' sistuh. Dat how we do. We he'p each udder out. Chu t'ink all dese kids be mine? I only got t'ree. Dat'n dere be mah sistuh's (pointing at a 6-year-old girl). Dat'n dere (pointing to the 9-year-old boy standing next to Rat Turd) be mah udder sistuh's. Rat Toid on'y 7."

"How far you go in school?"

"All da way. Ah gradiated from Saint Landry High School in 1986."

"Are you married?"

"Not anymō. Ah's a widow. Ah be married ta Detweiler Chauvin, Sr., but he kilt in Iraq in 1991, by a Ah-E-D. He a private foist class in da Army. He hab da lahf inshooance from da Army. I gets a small pension."

"What about this? How about I write a statement reporting what you just told me. You read it. Make whatever corrections are needed. Then you swear to it and sign it. Then when Buster Devereaux has his trial and I need you to testify, you tell the court what you just told me. The other thing is, you promise me never to keep or sell something which isn't yours ever again. What I'm saying is, this is your one and only pass you'll ever get for breaking the law."

"Deal. Ah promises. T'ank chu, Mistah Mahvin." Then she broke down in tears. She cried so hard, she lost her breath. After she calmed down, she read and signed the statement. She said over and over, "T'ank chu, Mistah Mahvin. T'ank chu, Soi. Ah'm so sorry. It was a turrible t'ing ta do."

As Esther Marie and I were leaving, she whispered, "Chief, you got the Midas touch. I've known Tootsie a long time, and she has never been this cooperative."

"Thanks for saying so. Wish it were true. We caught her just right. She wanted to get this off her chest. It was eating at her, which means she's basically an honest person. I don't really need her to testify. I just wanted her to give something back in return for not going to jail.

"You know, it took years but I finally figured it out. Sometimes jail's not the right answer, even if it is the legal one. From what I could see, Tootsie cares, and she's doing a pretty good job raising those kids."

"You got that right."

- *Chapter 16* -
Tying Up Loose Ends

It was Wednesday, June 2nd. I was scheduled to testify before the Grand Jury tomorrow to obtain True Bills against Bernard Devereaux for capital murder, the Habitual Offender Act, and possession of stolen property. Things were really beginning to crescendo in the Nicodemus Pierre murder case. The spinoff had resulted in four additional arrests for us in Saint Landry alone. I needed to check with Harmon to get the tally from the other parishes.

The final nail in Buster's coffin which I had been waiting for finally came in. Dr. Cherry at the LSP Lab confirmed that DNA on Buster's knife and sheath belonged to Nicodemus J. Pierre. I didn't know how Mr. Godfrey could get around that evidence. No doubt he would attack the test.

The worst case scenario would be that the results would be thrown out. We still had plenty of evidence to convict for murder, but maybe not enough to obtain the death penalty. Either way, the result would still be the same. Buster would die in prison sooner or later.

I decided to go to 10 o'clock court to see what the judge would do with Ned J. Fontenot and Howard M. Doucet. The docket was light for a change. Judge DesHotel set Ned's bail at $5,000, which he was able to post via a bail bondsman. He set Howie's bail at $10,000 because the victim was his own father-in-law from whom now he was estranged, not to mention his wife, who kicked him out of the house. Howie too, posted bond through a commercial bail bondsman. Both of their preliminary hearings were scheduled for Friday, June 11th.

Onslow wanted to know if I were ready for the Grand Jury. I said I was.

I asked how long he thought it would be before we went to trial on Buster. He replied that he was hoping it would be before the end of August. If Godfrey wanted to wash his hands of the case, we could probably go to trial by the end of July. Since he's court-appointed counsel now, he's limited in how much he can earn defending Buster. That might induce him to agree to an earlier court date. We should find out at arraignment on Friday.

After court, I called Harmon to see how things were going in terms of matching stolen property with thieves. He said so far he had identified 38 thieves with 104 recovered items. Most were from Evangeline and Jefferson Davis Parishes, followed by his own. He said he hadn't found anything else from Saint Landry. (I whispered a silent prayer of thanks.) He said he was starting to think most of the rest of the stuff was legitimately acquired.

I asked if we'd reached the $153,000 threshold on the value of stolen items yet.

He replied, "Oh hell yeah. We're at $208,000 and change."

"Good. That means Mr. Godfrey doesn't get any of Buster's money."

"You bet, so who does?"

"My guess is the insurance companies will get whatever their payouts were. It may fall well short of the actual value of the stolen property."

"You got that right. The insurance companies always come out ahead."

We promised to stay in touch.

I checked to see if Abner was in his office. He was.

"Hey, you wanna go to lunch?"

"Where at?"

"You pick it."

"How about Ottawa's Smokehouse?"

"Let's go."

I caught up Abner with everything I knew related the the Devereaux case. He caught me up on sheriff business. Things which included being over budget by $2,600 so far this year; three new marked units coming in which will be swapped out with our three oldest units; bringing in a new hire transferring over from Pointe Coupee Parish SO; the Board of Supervisors renewing our gasoline and petroleum contract with Cretin Wholesalers; Deputy Brewer's wife just delivering their new daughter named Amanda; and, it was time to go the range for annual qualifications. Bottom line: the outfit was in good shape. He was happy as a clam.

After lunch, I made my way to the firing range. Our instructor, Sergeant Ralph G. Cohen, was busy logging in a new shipment of Federal brand 9mm ammo. He asked, "What brings you out to the range today, Chief?"

"If you have the time, I'd like to go ahead and do my requals today. I've got several cases coming up in court, and I'd like to get ahead of the power curve while I have the time."

"No problem. Put on your eyes and double ears [earplugs, earmuffs, and shooting goggles, oftentimes with yellow lenses to reduce glare]. Grab three boxes of 9s, two of 00 [double-aught buckshot], two of rifled slugs, and three of .223. Use Lane 7. I'll get the targets and meet you in a few minutes."

When he was ready, Ralph and I walked down range to the

three-yard line. He stapled a silhouette target to the frame. All ten six-round drills were timed.

When I was ready, he faced the target. I ran through six strong-hand, draw-and-fire-twice drills, with a reload drill after six rounds, for a total of 12 rounds.

Next was the very same drill from the seven-yard line, except I shot double-handed, also for a total of 12 rounds.

For the third course of fire, we moved back to the 15-yard line, using a vertical barricade which was eight feet tall and eight inches wide. It simulated the corner of a building to be used as cover. The first string was six rounds standing from the right side barricade. Second, was the same thing from the left side barricade, also using the strong hand, for a total of 12 rounds.

I placed the board on the ground and we moved back to the 25-yard line, which also had a vertical barricade.

The first string was six rounds kneeling right side barricade, followed by a magazine reload, and second six round string standing right side barricade.

The second string was exactly the same, except from left side barricade.

I fired 24 rounds from the 25-yard line, for a grand total of 60 rounds.

We scored the target. I shot a 292 out of a possible 300, each shot valued between 0 and 5 points - 5 for a bullseye, and then ever larger concentric ellipses worth 4, 3, 2, 1, down to 0 outside the 7-ring.

We did it again. My second score was a 294. Ralph said, "Not bad for an old timer with a different make of gun than you used in ATF."

I replied, "We qualified four times a year on my old job.

Besides, shooting has always been a hobby of mine."

Next we did the un-timed shotgun drill. We put up a new target, and then walked back to the 50-yard line.

First drill was five slugs standing. Next was five slugs kneeling.

Then we moved to the 25-yard line. I shot five 00 buck from the shoulder.

Finally we walked up to the 15-yard line and I shot five 00 buck from the hip.

The idea with the buckshot was to learn what the spread of twelve .33 caliber balls looks like from those two distances.

With respect to the slugs, each shot anywhere on the silhouette was worth 30 points. Max score was 300. I maxed out.

Finally, Ralph who was holding an M-16 said, "You don't have an M-16 do you?"

"Nope."

"You ever shoot one?"

"Oh yeah, six years in the Army National Guard, not to mention basic training and AIT; then the ATF Academy and then four times every year thereafter."

"So you know your way around an M-16."

"I do."

"Here, only the SWAT Team and Sheriff Ladner have an M16 assigned to them. Do you want one?"

"Not really. I prefer a shotgun for law enforcement. That being said, I'd appreciate it if you qualified me on the M-16 so if I had the need to carry one, I'd be covered."

"Not a problem. I'll go set up a target. Then I'll meet you at the 100-yard line."

I filled three 20-round magazines.

First course of fire was 20 rounds prone from the 100.

The next was 20 rounds kneeling or sitting from the 100. Your choice. I kneeled using the barricade for support.

The last was 20 rounds standing from the 50. Again, I used the barricade for support.

We went down to score the target. I got a 298.

"Chief, you sure you don't want a rifle?"

"Thanks, but not at this time. I'll let you know if I change my mind."

"Good deal. Chief, do you carry an off-duty weapon?"

"Yep. The proverbial Smith & Wesson, .38 caliber, Chief Special snubby."

"That's what all you old timers carry."

"That's because we all carried revolvers back in the day when we came on the job. Didn't switch to automatics until 1992. Besides, revolvers never jam or misfire. I've had mine for 31 years now. That's because I couldn't afford one my first year on the job."

"What type of ammo you carry?"

"Standard Winchester or Remington, 158-grain, lead round-nose."

"Bring it with, and some extra ammo?"

"Of course."

"You'll need 30 rounds. You provide the ammo. There are no reload drills."

"Roger that."

Ralph set up another silhouette target.

First course was two, timed five-shot strings standing from the 3-yard line.

The second was two, timed five-shot strings standing from

the 7-yard line.

The third was the same except from the 15-yard line.

Everything within the 8-ring counted 10 points. I got another max score.

"Did you shoot up all your old 9s and shotgun shells?"

"I did. If you don't mind, I'd like four boxes each of 9s, slugs, and 00, especially since the shotgun shells come in 5-packs. Also, do you want me to clean the M-16?"

"No, this is my assigned weapon. I'll clean it, but thanks for asking.

"Hold on. Here's your range qualification card with your new scores on it, dated and signed by me. Stick it in your wallet.

"Chief, this is to cover your ass if you ever end up having to use deadly force before next year's requals. The presumption of a lawman doing the right thing when he has to shoot someone in the line of duty just doesn't exist anymore. Now it's up to the officer to prove he was justified. The new world we live in now has gone plumb batshit crazy."

"Thanks, Ralph. Appreciate it. Do you mind if I clean my guns here?"

"Absolutely not. Knock yourself out."

I cleaned my guns and went home. It had been a prosperous day, fulfilling, though not especially titillating.

Thursday, June 3rd, was game day.

Testifying before the Grand Jury was important, but not especially difficult because no defense attorney was present to try to trip you up. All you had to do was be accurate and tell the truth. Try not to get too deep in the weeds, because the defense gets a copy of your testimony and can try to use it against you during trial. An honest mistake or an incorrect guess can trainwreck your testimony in trial. Sometimes the grand jurors have questions, but they are usually well-intentioned and cordial. Today was pretty standard. As they say, 'no heavy lifting.'

Buster was indicted for possession of stolen property, the Habitual Offenders Act, and capital murder.

Then, to make the best usage of our time, Onslow decided to indict all our Buster-related defendants. I presented our cases against the black White Brothers, otherwise known as Dingus and Popeye, and Ned Fontenot, and Howie Doucet, the purveyor of noxious gas.

Erastus "Dingus" White, Jr. was indicted for the burglary of Dr. Thibodaux's house, possession of stolen property [ruby ensemble and shotgun], and illegal possession of narcotics. Previously, he had been indicted for the burglary of a pharmacy, which was still pending.

Leland "Popeye" White was also indicted for the burglary of Dr. T's house, illegal possession of a switchblade knife, felony possession of marijuana, and probation violation.

Ned J. Fontenot was indicted for burglary of Napoleon Guidry's house and possession of stolen property [Bowie knife].

Howard M. Doucet was indicted for burglary of the Guidry house too, and possession of stolen property [Colt Peacemaker].

It was indeed a good day in Mudville. This time, the mighty Casey did not strike out. [*Casey at the Bat* - Ernest Lawrence Thayer, June 3rd, 1888.] Casey hit for the cycle [single, double, triple, and home run] plus a grand slam [Buster].

Friday, June 4th, was a busy day of jurisprudence in Saint Landry Parish. The courtroom was packed. Onslow had a stack of files four-and-a-half feet deep. I sat in one of the wooden rolling chairs in the back of the courtroom reserved for deputies.

I noticed that Patrol Captain Hal Hebert had assigned two extra deputies for courtroom security as an added ounce of prevention due to the unusual number of defendants in court today.

One by one, Judge DesHotel went through all the traffic and misdemeanor cases, listening to explanations for bad or foolish behavior, adjudicating everything which could be resolved right then, rescheduling others, fining some, exonerating some, sentencing a few to jail, and generally separating all the 'fly shit from the pepper'. An hour later, we were down to eleven felony cases. Five were mine. None were scheduled for trial today, thank goodness. Otherwise we'd be here until the wee hours of the night. Even so, my cases were the last to be called.

Erastus was my first called case. He and his attorney were provided with a copy of the indictment. Judge DesHotel asked Onslow if there were any chance of a plea agreement. He replied that he expected a signed agreement soon. Judge DesHotel placed it on the docket for Tuesday, June 15th for either a guilty plea or a trial. Erastus was remanded back into custody.

Leland's case was called next. He and his attorney were provided with a copy of the indictment. This time Onslow stated no plea was anticipated. Judge DesHotel told his attorney to be ready for trial on Tuesday, June 15th. He also warned that he didn't tolerate lawyer games. He promised to drop the hammer if both the White brothers' attorneys were not prepared for trial. He also said if either case turned out to be a slam dunk for the state, and the trial ended up being a waste of his time, he would max out the defendant with consecutive sentences. Leland was remanded back into custody. He was showing his ass, and it took two deputies to jerk him up by his chains onto his toes and drag him out of the courtroom. I hoped the deputies would take some of the starch out of him behind closed doors.

Ned's case was called next. He and his attorney were provided with a copy of the indictment. Onslow said he expected a plea agreement. The judge placed it on the docket for a plea on Wednesday, June 16th. Ned remained free on bond.

Howie's case was called next. He and his attorney were provided with a copy of the indictment. Onslow said he expected a plea agreement. The case was placed on the docket for a plea on Wednesday, June 16th. Howie remained free on bond.

Finally, Buster's case was called. He and his attorney were provided with a copy of the indictment. Onslow said no plea was anticipated. Judge DesHotel asked Mr. Godfrey how much time he needed to prepare for trial. He replied that if discovery were forthcoming soon, he would be ready by the middle of July at the latest. Onslow said he would provide full discovery by Friday, June 11th.

Judge DesHotel scheduled trial for Monday, July 12th. Buster was remanded back into custody. Buster gave Mr. Godfrey a chilling look, but he didn't resist the deputies. It was as if the realization of what he was facing had just kicked in.

Court was adjourned.

I helped Onslow carry his load of case files back to his office. On the way back, I observed, "Judge DesHotel doesn't waste a moment of time. All business. You better have your shit packed tight or 'woe is me' for the offending party."

Onslow concurred. He said, "You got that right. I love the way he runs his courtroom. No silly reindeer games. Everyone knows where he stands, and that he'll get a fair and impartial shake. It wasn't always that way here. Judge Benjamin Arce was a real ass. You never knew what he would do. Sarcastic, too. Easy to offend."

"What happened to him?"

"It was the strangest thing. He and his wife were on vacation at Pensacola Beach in coonass Mecca. He was chest deep in the water when a drunk on a jet ski ran over him. Crushed his skull. Sayonara, Judge Arce.

"The drunk got eight years to serve for vehicular homicide. The grieving widow, Mrs. Bunny Arce inherited all his money. Then Judge Arce's brother, Kermit, divorced his wife, Imogene, and married Bunny. Seems like they'd been having an affair for years. Last I heard they were living on Fort Lauderdale Beach in wedded bliss.

"Returning to present day, Miss Alice N. Coursey better get Popeye under control, or she's liable to get sanctioned by Judge DesHotel. It won't be pleasant. You do know she's fresh out of law school."

"Yep. You do know Popeye's going to take us to trial. He's a hardhead."

"Probably so. I can hardly wait. He'll get 20 years if he does, and Alice will get royally reamed by the judge. Not the way you want to start your legal career."

"Nope. By the way, I thought Mr. Godfrey yielded rather quickly, today."

"No wonder. He's got a shit client with no money and a hopeless case. The best he can hope for is to keep Buster off Death Row, and that would only be a Pyrrhic victory. However, today was not a day to litigate or pontificate if you're a hot shot defense attorney. It was a day for the court to inform the defendants of the charges they're facing. It was just a formality - a wake-up call. Not a day for posturing.

"Also, Godfrey really is a good attorney, but he's not holding even a Jack high. It's all part of the vicissitudes of being a defense attorney. Most of their clients are folks they wish they'd never met. Even Ben Matlock and Perry Mason can't win 'em all.

"I need to interview Eugene Pierre's kid so I can see what to expect. He could get stage fright, making it harder to bring Buster's bloody knife into evidence. Think how important it is for the jury to hear that Buster threatened the kid with a sheath knife just before Nicodemus was murdered with one."

"The kid's name is Rupert, but he goes by Booger. Want me to go out there and line it up with his papa?"

"Yes. See if you can get them to come in Monday morning about ten. That's the 7th. Right now nothing's on the docket."

"I'll head out there right now and let you know."

"Thanks."

I was happy to take a ride out in the country. The pace is slower out there. Folks usually aren't in such a big hurry. It's not nearly as frenetic as the city. I do realize that I live in Opelousas and not New Orleans, but even in Opelousas it seems like folks get their panties in a wad way too quickly and way too frequently.

I drove past Nicodemus's little patch of heaven in Big Cane to get to Eugene's. It rattled me a little bit to see just how similar they were. Eugene maybe had an extra acre. I noticed that his daddy's goats and donkey were mixed in, living with his own like they'd always been there.

One thing that was different. The American flag was waving in the breeze from a 12-foot pole. Nicodemus didn't have a flag at his house.

Eugene's OD green, 1976 Ford pickup truck was parked in his

outbuilding, doors wide open just like his pappy's had been the day I was called out there. Life gets into a rhythm. Let's face it. 'Like father. Like son.' Also, 'If it ain't broke, don't fix it.'

Eugene was on his tractor pulling a mower around his front yard. Grass clippings, dust, and little bugs were flying everywhere. The chickens were penned up in the chicken coop while Eugene mowed. Booger was sawing a 40-foot pine tree into logs to split for firewood way in the back. A white and black mixed breed terrier was on the front verandah chewing on an old shoe. The panoramic view, minus the tractor noise, depicted the essence of bucolic bliss.

I parked and climbed out of the Jeep waiting for Frog Legs to take notice. He shut off the tractor and walked over to greet me where I was standing in the shade next to his house. Booger was a man on a mission. He never even looked up, just like the dog with his shoe. There was work to be done!

"Hey, Chief! How chu? Wont a glass of col' wadder?"

"No. Kind of you to ask. The reason I'm here is, today Buster was told in court that he's facing the death penalty. Mr. Trudeau said we need to get ready for trial. He asked if you could bring Booger to see him at his office Monday morning at 10 o'clock so he can talk to him and see what he still remembers."

"Ah can do dat, but Booger, he don't nevah forget nuttin'. Dat boy got a good mem'ry, like a elephant. He chust hab trouble loinin'."

"That's what I told Mr. Trudeau. He'd like to talk to Booger just to see for himself that he isn't scared."

"Dat boy ain't skeert. He kill Buster if he evah came around heah again. He lahk a mad bull. Chust as strong, chust as dumb, an' no changin' he mind when it made up.

"Dey gonna hang Buster for what he done to Papa?"

"Mr. Trudeau's gonna try, except nowadays they stick 'em with a needle and give 'em a hot shot like the vet does to a dying mule."

"Do it hoit?"

"I don't think so, but they strap 'em to a table so they can't get away. You could watch if you want. It's just that it might take a few years to get there because he can appeal all the way up to the Supreme Court."

"Buster done lost his appeal ta God. Dat da big one. Buster awready done choined hands wit' da Debil. He be goin' ta Hell where he be boinin' fah eternity. Dere ain't no savin' dat mān. We be dere Monday at 10 o'clock."

"Thanks, Frog Legs. I might see you there."

On the way back, I stopped at the Dairy Freeze for a chocolate shake to hold me over until supper. I consumed it in the Jeep under their awning. It brought back memories of my teenage years.

- *Chapter 17* -

Inching Forward Towards Justice

Time passed rather quickly.

On Monday, June 7th, Rupert Pierre went over his unshakable testimony with Onslow, who became a firm believer of Booger as an honest person and as a witness. He knew Booger's testimony would be electrifying.

On Tuesday, June 15th, Erastus White, Jr. pleaded guilty to all counts - burglary of the pharmacy, burglary of the Dr. Thibodaux residence, possession of stolen property, and illegal possession of Schedule II drugs. Judge DesHotel sentenced him to serve two years, five years, two years, and one year respectively in Angola, all sentences to run concurrently in return for his turning state's evidence against his brother.

The ink had not even dried on Erastus' conviction and commitment order, when the court shifted gears and began voir dire to select a petit jury to sit on Leland White's trial. It was accomplished within 20 minutes. Opening arguments were limited to ten minutes each.

Dr. Enos R. Thibodaux testified that his home in Whiteville was burgled on November 9th, 2003. Among the stolen items were a ruby necklace/earring set and a Parker 16-gauge shotgun.

Deputy Elmer N. Bauvier testified to taking the police report.

I testified to making a police call for assistance at the Nicodemus J. Pierre residence on May 25th. Certain items had been stolen. The thief was believed to be Buster Devereaux, owner of Buster's Buy & Sell in Bunkie, who had been the last known visitor in the house. I called Avoyelles Parish Sheriff

Clinton W. Boyd. He reported that Buster Devereaux had just been observed carrying a large corrugated cardboard box into his business. I met Sheriff Boyd and deputies there. We entered the business, where we arrested Mr. Devereaux, and I recovered items taken from Mr. Pierre's house. The APSO obtained a search warrant of the business while I was there.

Chief Harmon L. Bergeron testified that APSO recovered and inventoried over 100 stolen items. One of the items they recovered was a ruby necklace/earring ensemble from the Dr. Thibodaux residence in Saint Landry Parish. The business ledger from Mr. Devereaux's business indicated that he purchased the ensemble from Erastus White, Jr. of Whiteville. He notified me of this discovery on May 27.

I returned to the stand. I testified that SLPSO deputies and I located Erastus and his brother, defendant Leland White, in a tavern in Whiteville. They both attempted to flee as soon as they saw us. I watched while both brothers were searched incident to arrest. Leland was in possession of an illegal switchblade knife and a half-ounce baggie of marijuana. I subsequently learned that Leland was on probation for grand larceny.

We transported both brothers to our office. I interviewed Erastus first. He confessed to committing the burglary of Dr. Thibodaux's house with his brother, Leland. He also said he still had the shotgun they stole there, hidden under his bed in the room he shared with Leland. I subsequently recovered the shotgun exactly where he said it was.

Erastus testified next, confirming everything I just reported. He said he was testifying against Leland because the information was true. He also admitted he was offered a reduced prison sentence if he testified against Leland.

During cross-examination, Miss Coursey tried to bloody up Erastus as an unreliable witness, but it was obvious to all that he had told the unvarnished truth.

The testimony and cross-examinations were completed within an hour, max. It was a simple case. Closing arguments took twenty minutes. Jury instructions took five. The jury was out for ten. Leland was found guilty on all counts. Judge DesHotel sentenced him to five years for possession of the switchblade knife; two years for possession of marijuana; ten years for dwelling-house burglary; and, five years for probation violation, not including the three years left on his sentence. The total was 25 years. All sentences were to be served consecutively. The trial ran its course like a river rapids in two-and-half hours, soup to nuts. We weren't even late for lunch.

Before he adjourned court, Judge DesHotel told Miss Coursey he wanted to see her in his chambers in one hour. Her face turned red and she burst into tears. I felt bad for her, but the judge had warned her. She needed a lesson on how to convince her clients as to when it was 'time to fish, and when it was time to cut bait' to better serve them. In Leland's particular case, he bought himself an extra ten years for wasting the judge's time, pure and simple. He had warned them both in open court. The sad truth is, even Perry Mason couldn't have gotten through to Popeye. He was incorrigible, and he deserved every year he got at hard labor.

Leland was dragged off to jail, kicking and screaming. I could see an ass-whipping headed in his direction once they got him back inside the jail. Erastus went peacefully. Onslow said he would call the prison and advise the warden to house the black brothers White in two separate buildings to prevent a murder.

On Wednesday, June 16th, Ned J. Fontenot appeared before

Judge DesHotel. He pleaded guilty to burglary of the Napoleon M. Guidry house and possession of his stolen Jim Bowie knife. Ned had previously served two years of a four-year sentence for burglary back in 1999. Judge DesHotel sentenced him to serve ten years this time, dismissing the lesser charge for possession. He told Ned to wise up because he would get 20 years the next time he got arrested for burglary.

Howard M. Doucet was up next on the very same charges as Ned, except the stolen property was the Peacemaker. Judge DesHotel said he was a despicable person for stealing from his own father-in-law. He sentenced him to serve five years on the burglary and dismissed the possession charge.

Except for Buster the Cusser, I was all caught up on my judicial actions. It felt good to have a little breathing room.

Life returned to it's normal routine. Hannah and I had decided to go visit my brother in New Mexico as soon as the Devereaux trial was over. I could hardly wait. It had been a year since we had taken any time off. We'd both been running wide open since I had accepted Abner's job offer in November. It was high time to play a little bit.

Monday, July 12th, finally dawned. It was a blistering hot, sultry day. There was a great deal of public and press interest in the Devereaux trial because this was a capital murder case, and because Nicodemus Jean Pierre had been a military hero and a well-loved, local octogenarian.

I planned to wear my uniform to court, like always. I had asked Abner if he would object if I bought some long-sleeve white uniform shirts like he wore daily, in lieu of the pullover uniform shirt. Topped off with the Stetson, this uniform looked really sharp. He said he thought it was a great idea. The SO bought me six.

Onslow informed Judge DesHotel that he thought the trial could take up to four days for the following reasons. First, the voir dire might go on ad infinitum, selecting a jury who would vote for the death penalty if they thought the defendant truly deserved execution. Second, the prosecution had at least a half-dozen witnesses, and maybe one or two more. Third, defense counsel had a reputation for vigorously cross-examining prosecution witnesses. Fourth, because he had no idea how many witnesses Godfrey would call.

Judge DesHotel had blocked off the entire week for the trial. He also made it known that no cameras would be allowed inside the courtroom. The press could remain in the air-conditioned hallway outside the courtroom, IF they did not interfere with witnesses coming and going, and so long as they did not get boisterous. If they stepped over the bounds of propriety set by him, he would banish them outside the courthouse in the sweltering heat and humidity for the remainder of the trial.

I drove to work early. I was on pins and needles. It was only 7 o'clock, and the trial was scheduled to begin at 9. As it turned out, I was a latecomer. The town square was already jammed with two television trucks, KBRL and KANO, death penalty protesters, illegally parked cars and uniformed deputies who were having them towed to the secure lot outside of town, gawkers, street vendors, and a growing mass of curious humanity. Thankfully, I had a designated parking spot in the SO lot, and we had two deputies assigned there this week to keep all others out.

For the SO, this week was all hands on deck, working 12-hour shifts. They were making some overtime, just like during our

Mardis Gras Parade Day. The circus had come to town to watch a public hanging, or so it seemed. At any rate, Sheriff Ladner and Captain Hebert were old hands in crowd control, and they were well-prepared.

I stopped by my office first and double-checked my evidence. Then I walked over to Onslow's office. He appeared to be the picture of serenity. I asked if he foresaw any ambushes for which we were not prepared. He replied, "We have a mountain of damning evidence. So long as Booger doesn't get rattled, I think we'll be okay. If either the judge or the jury thinks Godfrey is hounding the poor boy, it's trial over for them. Go straight to the sentencing phase."

"Think we'll have a jury today?"

"I do, but it might take the greater portion of it to get there. The Board of Supervisors has approved sequestering the jury overnight at the Comfort Inn if it looks like we need it. I'm thinking that might be a good idea, but I'll wait to see how it goes today. Part of it will depend on whether the protestors get too threatening. Did you know some of those assholes came in from places as far away as New York City and LA?"

"I'm not the least bit surprised. Abner's got the Fast Response Team on standby in case they get out of control. He expects the general public to toe the line when it comes to civil behavior. Shame on anyone who steps beyond it. That's when he'll 'unleash the hounds of Hell' in a manner of speaking.

"He's also got Lafayette Parish Sheriff Winston Romero on standby to house prisoners for us if we get saturated. You know, we've really only got room for 20 jailbirds. Sheriff Romero's even offered to send us a paddy wagon to transport if we get overwhelmed. Of course, I hope it doesn't come to that."

"Me either."

"What's the lineup?"

"Eugene Pierre is up first. He'll testify about Rupert not coming home after school, and what he discovered at his daddy's house.

"Rupert will go next. He's the star witness. His testimony may take some time. Be interesting to see how Godfrey responds to his testimony.

"Deputy Oliver V. Dedeau goes next as first officer at the crime scene.

"Then you. My guess is you won't go on the stand until tomorrow.

"Then Sheriff Clinton R. Boyd is on to confirm what you found in plain view at the Buy & Sell, followed by Chief Harmon L. Bergeron to testify about the ledger and the stolen property he identified.

"Dr. Amy B. Cherry will testify to the results of the DNA examination.

"Forensic Specialist Dennis S. Robard will testify to the latent prints found on the silver bowl and the Pierre hutch.

"That'll be a wrap for us, hopefully by the end of Day 2.

"R. Geoffrey Godfrey puts on his witnesses next. I haven't seen his list yet, but I expect he'll try to introduce an expert witness who will say Rupert is not capable of separating fact from fiction. Maybe another one to discredit DNA evidence. He'll probably also introduce an alibi witness who will claim that Buster was with him during the time of the murder. He could well have another trick or two up his sleeve. I expect that will be the end of Day 3. Then Day 4 will be closing arguments. Then the jury will determine innocence or guilt. I expect that to be the easy part. If he gets convicted, then we go into the penalty phase. Execution or life without parole? Honestly, I'm not sure which way that will go."

"What do you plan to do about lunch this week?"

"I brought something to eat here in my office. I need to prepare for whatever the afternoon brings, plus I don't feel like getting mobbed by the press or the protestors. What about you?"

"Same thing. After opening statements, you've got me sequestered with the other witnesses."

"Just trying to avoid a mistrial."

"I know. Can't be helped. I brought a book of Sudoku puzzles to while away the time."

"Well, you aren't sequestered until the first witness is called. You can hear opening arguments. At least you can return to the prosecution table after you testify."

"I plan to do just that. See you in the courtroom."

"Ditto."

Our courtroom is the pride of Saint Landry Parish. It's beautifully appointed with old cypress wood paneling throughout. It's furnished with classic red oak furniture to include the public benches. The polished brass Great Seal of Louisiana hangs high on the wall behind the judge's bench. Both the American flag and the Louisiana flag are on poles flanking the bench. The former is to his left and the latter is to his right. There are two oil painting portraits hanging on the wall facing the judge. One is of President George Washington. The other is of Louisiana Governor Huey P. Long, Jr., known as 'The Kingfish', a high profile populist politician who was assassinated in 1935. Some say it occurred because he was contemplating a run against President Roosevelt in the 1936 election and he was gaining momentum. (This does not imply that President Roosevelt or any of his staff had knowledge of the plot or any involvement in the slaying whatsoever.)

The courtroom was already packed to overflowing by 8 o'clock. I went in at 9:45, and took my seat next to Onslow at the prosecution table as is customary for the lead investigator.

Mr. Godfrey was seated at the defense table. The jury box was vacant. Buster had not made his appearance yet. There were four deputies pulling security, essentially posted in each of the four corners of the courtroom. Mrs. Richman had already taken her seat at the clerk's table below the judge's bench. I saw a sketch artist sitting on the front row directly across from the witness stand.

At 9:55, two deputies escorted Buster into the courtroom. He was attired in a lizard green gangsta suit with a lavender shirt and a brilliant, cobalt blue tie. He was also wearing two-tone, lizard green and white patent leather wingtip shoes. His hands were shackled in the front, but he was not wearing leg irons or a belly chain. He had a huge smirk on his face like he was Al Capone and this was all beneath his dignity. One of the escorting deputies posted up at the entrance to the courtroom. The other posted up by the jury entrance on the left side of the room.

Judge DesHotel made his entrance from the door behind his bench which led into his private chambers at 9 o'clock sharp. Court was called into session. Counsel made their appearances for the record. Judge DesHotel called for the first 14 of 60 prospective jurors to take their seats in the jury box.

Each prospective juror was called to rise one by one. He/she stated his name, age, occupation, and highest level of education attained. Then he sat.

The only qualifications to sit on the petit jury were to be at least 18 years of age, a resident of Saint Landry Parish, and never to have been convicted of a felony. It was not a high bar, but then our Founding Fathers wanted jurors who represented all classes of society, not just the landed gentry. That being said, back then, that only included white males. Today we include both sexes and all races who meet those qualifications.

Jury duty is considered a civic duty, just like obeying the law, paying your taxes, voting, signing up for selective service if you're a male, serving in the armed forces (particularly if you're drafted), paying your obligations, testifying in court, placing your hand over your heart when reciting the Pledge of Allegiance, honoring our flag, etc. It does not include sewing an American flag across the seat of your trousers like some of the more militant hippies did back in the 1960s - a provocation guaranteed render yourself an ass-whipping in the more conservative venues, and rightfully so. Disrespect has consequences.

The prosecution has six strikes from the jury pool he could invoke without cause. The defense has eight. Any other strike must to be for cause, and the judge has to agree. Cause in this particular case would be someone who didn't believe in the death penalty, someone who personally knew the defendant or was related to him, someone who hated Blacks, someone who had already made up his mind on how he would vote before hearing any testimony, etc.

Judge DesHotel explained the procedure. He excused one potential juror because his wife was due to deliver a baby. He excused another because he was no longer a resident of Saint Landry Parish. Two more were excused because they didn't believe in the death penalty. Then the defense and prosecution took turns interviewing each of the remaining ten, of which four were selected. The others were excused.

The second group of 14 prospective jurors was called. After screening, three were selected.

Four were selected from the third 14.

One juror and two alternates were selected from the fourth pool.

The jury was empaneled. Then we broke for lunch. The jury was sequestered in the jury room. They selected their lunches off the KFC menu. The meals were brought to them for consumption in the jury room.

We returned to the courtroom. Opening statements, limited to 15 minutes each, began at 1 o'clock. Afterwards I had to excuse myself and wait in the witness room until called to testify. Bummer.

Eugene Pierre testified first. He said his son, Rupert, did not return home from school on the bus, so he went to his papa's house to see if he got off there. He did. He was locked in the cellar. He was screaming at the top of his lungs. Eugene unfastened the latch and let him out. Rupert said Buster the Cusser was arguing with his grandpappy, Nicodemus Pierre, when he stepped inside the house. Buster held a knife to his throat and put him in the cellar.

Buster the Cusser is the nickname of Buster Devereaux. Buster's truck was not parked there when Eugene arrived at his papa's house. Rupert waited outside while Eugene went inside the house. He found his papa lying on the kitchen floor. He was dead. His throat had been slit. His empty shotgun was on the kitchen table next to a box of shells.

Eugene checked the house to see if anything had been missing. He knew what to look for because Buster had tried to convince his papa to sell him a silver bowl and tableware set given to him by Mr. Cecil B. Twyman, now deceased, a planation owner his papa had worked for most of his life. The bowl and tableware were missing.

During cross-examination, Mr. Godfrey wanted to know how Eugene knew that his papa had not already sold the silver articles to Mr. Devereaux. Did he see it in the house every time he came to visit?

He also wanted to know if it weren't possible that his papa had locked Rupert in the cellar for misbehavior. Also, assuming that Mr. Devereaux had been visiting with his papa, how did Eugene know that it wasn't somebody else who came by after he departed, and that this person killed his papa?

Finally, he accused Eugene of lying because he had a longstanding feud with Mr. Devereaux.

None of this worked. Eugene was calm, and he stood his ground. He didn't get confused or rattled, and he did not contradict himself. His statement inflicted a lot of damage to the defense, not to mention that Godfrey's badgering alienated the jury. Onslow said Buster looked like he would explode during Eugene's testimony.

Rupert was led into the courtroom by a deputy. Onslow had told Eugene to sit at the prosecution table next to him while Rupert was on the stand.

Onslow patiently led Rupert step by step. Why did he go to his grandpapa's house after school? Was his grandpapa good to him? Did he give him Tootsie Roll Pops? Did he recognize the man wearing the green suit, sitting at the table in front of the judge? What is his name? Have you seen him before? Was he at his grandpapa's house that day he was killed? What kind of a vehicle did he drive? What color was it? Was it there when you got off the school bus? Where was the man when you entered the house? What did you see? Was your grandpapa angry with the man? What did your grandpapa say to you? What did the man say to you? Did he have anything in his hand? Did he point a knife at you? Where did he point it? What did he tell you to do? Did he lock you in the cellar? Were you scared? Did you see any black widow spiders? Did he hurt you? What did you do? What did you hear? How did you get out of the cellar?

Onslow said Rupert was the best witness he had ever put on the stand. Buster scowled at Rupert and tried to intimidate him, but it didn't work. The courtroom was silent like a library full of monks in a monastery the entire time Rupert testified. He mesmerized everyone present with his simple, detailed recitation. The jury appeared to be ready to convict without even hearing the most damning evidence of all.

During cross-examination, Mr. Godfrey tested Rupert's memory by various means, to include asking him to repeat after me before rattling off a long statement, and showing him a series of playing cards and then asking him what order they had been shown to him. Then Judge DesHotel told him that was enough and to move on. Godfrey was skillful in his questioning by asking questions such as what type of shoes was Mr. Devereaux wearing? What exactly did he say to you? Why did you disobey your papa by going there after school, etc.?

None of it worked. Onslow said by this time, Buster was glaring viciously and uttering under his breath at Mr. Godfrey, who was doing his best to calm him down.

Thus endeth Day 1.

Tuesday, July 13th. Day 2 begins.

Deputy Oliver V. Dedeau testified next. He reported getting the squeal from the office that a murder had occurred at the Nicodemus J. Pierre residence. He was the first officer on the scene. Eugene Pierre and his son Rupert were waiting outside when he arrived. Eugene told him his papa was lying dead on the kitchen floor with his throat cut. Dedeau decided not to enter the residence because he knew I was en route to conduct the crime scene search, and he didn't want to disturb any evidence.

He stated that I arrived shortly thereafter. Both Eugene and Rupert told us what they knew. Then he and I entered the residence, confirming that Nicodemus was indeed dead. We conducted the crime scene search of the entire premises for evidence, to include taking photographs, making a crime scene sketch, taking measurements, and dusting for latent fingerprints.

Eugene told us a silver bowl and a wooden box with silver tableware had been stolen, and the location those items had been taken from.

I had asked him if he knew Buster Devereaux. He said he did not, but he knew where his business was located in Bunkie. I called the office, explaining what had taken place, and requested an ambulance. I also called the Avoyelles Parish Sheriff's Office. I told Sheriff Boyd I was headed to Bunkie and asked him to meet me there. Then I told him (Deputy Dedeau) to meet me there after the ambulance removed the decedent's remains.

By the time he arrived, Mr. Devereaux had already been placed under arrest. He transported Mr. Devereaux to the jail and booked him. He did not interview Mr. Devereaux. He did not make any spontaneous statements to him.

During cross-examination, Godfrey suggested that Deputy Dedeau was too green and inexperienced to properly conduct a major crime scene search. Dedeau stated that he followed my lead and that, although he had never been involved in a search of a murder scene, he had conducted many other types of crime scene searches in his nine years on the job.

Godfrey continued his nitpicking during cross-examination, but Onslow said no one was paying attention, not even Buster, who by that time, was sitting rigidly still like a black stone sphinx with a scowl chiseled on his face.

Deputy Dedeau was excused. Judge DesHotel's secretary entered the courtroom and tiptoed up to the bench. She handed him a folded note. He thanked her and read it. He checked his watch and stated that even though it was only 10:30, today we would have a long lunch. Court would resume at 1 o'clock.

We were notified about this in the witness room. I checked in with Onslow because I was up next, but all he said was, "You know what to do. Don't be late. We've got this in the bag."

I went back to my office and checked for messages, but had none. My inbox was empty. I sat at my desk wondering what I should do for the next two and a half hours.

Abner was nowhere to be found. I was sitting on pins and needles. I walked down the hall and looked out the window. What I saw was an enormous milling crowd with citizens getting into each other's way. I decided to stay put, so I returned to my office, turned on my radio, and listened to classical music. I ate my lunch early. It consisted of a ham and cheese sandwich, corn chips, dill pickle, and oatmeal cookie, all washed down by an RC Cola. When I was done, I washed up. It was only 11:15.

I walked to the janitor's office in the boiler room and out the backdoor, and sat in the shade inside the wooden, fenced-in patio out of public view, which was a designated smoking area. I lit up an aromatic six-inch Churchill, Maduro Te Amo cigar, and puffed away. Soothing.

When I was done, I returned to the courtroom. It was empty. I took my seat at the prosecution table and went over my testimony again in my mind. I had it down pat. Then I waited. I had another 23 minutes to cool my heels.

- Chapter 18 -

It's Never Really What You Expect

I watched quietly as the courtroom began to fill up. I saw that Eugene and Rupert got seats midway back on the prosecution side. Once the deputies closed the doors (because the courtroom was full), another deputy escorted the jury from their room to the jury box. Judge DesHotel was the last to enter. He called the court in session and we got down to business.

I had noticed that Mr. Godfrey and Buster were having a heated but hushed discussion at the defense table. Then I was called to the stand. The butterflies in my stomach started to flutter. This was without a doubt, the most important testimony I had ever been called to give. No kidding. It was a matter of life or death. Buster deserved death, but it was no longer an abstract belief. It was becoming real.

I took the stand and took the oath to tell nothing but the truth, so help me God. Then Onslow began his questioning.

I stated my name, position, length of service with Saint Landry, ATF, and the Jefferson County, Kentucky Police. I said I spoke by phone with Eugene Pierre, after he called the office to report the murder of his father. Deputy Dedeau arrived first, and then I.

Eugene introduced me to Rupert, who said Buster the Cusser was at his grandpapa's house when he got off the school bus there. Buster was arguing with the decedent about what, he wasn't sure. His grandpapa told him they were talking about adult things and for him to wait outside. Then Buster pulled a sheath knife on him and put the tip up against his throat. He threatened to fillet Rupert 'like a fish'.

Then Buster told him to go outside and open the metal storm door to the cellar and step inside, so he did. Then Buster put the padlock back on the hasp. He left it unlocked, but Rupert was essentially locked inside.

I happened to look over at the defense table, where I saw Buster stand up suddenly and start strangling Mr. Godfrey vigorously with his bare hands. He was turning dark purple and growing limp.

Deputy Francis D. Prejean, Jr. responded quickly, and began trying to pull Buster's hands off of Godfrey's neck, but Buster was too strong. Godfrey was losing consciousness.

Then suddenly, Buster slipped around and managed to pull Deputy Prejean's pistol out of his holster, thus releasing his choke hold on Godfrey, who fell down. By then two other deputies had rushed up to assist, but they stopped short, because now Buster had ahold of Deputy Prejean around the neck with his left arm, pulling him backwards, and cutting off his oxygen. He was holding the gun in his right hand with the barrel pushed hard into Prejean's temple, using him as a shield.

Buster yelled, "Back off, or Ah'll kill dis mudderfocker, and den Ah'll kill dis pissant choke of a lahyah."

Godfrey was slumped over the defense table struggling to catch his breath. His face was a dark shade of purple. The whites of his eyes were bloodshot. He had tears running down his cheeks and slobber trickling down his chin.

The entire courtroom was in a state of frozen animation. Buster was focused on the two deputies standing nearest him like frozen statues, neither of whom had drawn his weapon because they had been responding to a fight, not a gunfight.

I was still sitting in the jury box, maybe 20 feet away. I slowly unholstered my Glock while the world was focused on Buster. Then I stood slowly with both arms stretched out to full extension, using a two-handed grip, aiming my pistol at Buster. He detected my motion, turned, and aimed Deputy Prejean's Glock at me. He managed to twist Deputy Prejean even tighter to where he mostly shielded his own body.

Buster said, "Drop da gun or Ah'll rub dis mudderfocker out! Ah means it!"

I shifted my focus for a second to Deputy Prejean. We had a split second to stare at each other eye to eye. Our brainwaves connected. Suddenly, he jerked towards the floor, exposing more of Buster's profile. I fired once, hitting him in his right cheek a quarter-inch below his right eye. Fortunately, the people in the courtroom had crouched down behind the benches. My shot embedded itself in the rear wall about six feet high without striking anyone else. Buster crumbled to the floor with a heavy thud, and at the same time Prejean jerked out of his grasp. Both he and Mr. Godfrey were covered with shards of Buster's skull, brain matter, and blood. Nobody but those two moved for at least five seconds. Everyone was still in frozen animation, to include me. Finally, I reholstered.

Judge DesHotel was the first to speak. He said, "Court adjourned. Somebody get Sheriff Ladner over here right away! Mr. Trudeau, you, Chief Barnett, and Mrs. Richman come with me to my chambers. Mr. Godfrey, you can clean up in the restroom in the Jury Room. You will need to be deposed, so you cannot leave. The jury is hereby sequestered in the Jury Room until further notice. Deputy Ray, you're in charge here until Sheriff Ladner or Captain Hebert arrive. Secure the courtroom!

No gawkers. Law enforcement only. Everyone understand?"

"Yes, Sir!"

Once all the invitees were safely ensconced in Judge DesHotel's chambers, he said, "You all can stay here as long as you want. I brought you all back here to avoid the press.

"Chief Barnett, we all owe you a debt of gratitude. I suggest you don't say anything to anybody except perhaps to your wife, until LSP arrives to take over the investigation. Even then, I recommend you have counsel. I'm sure the parish will cover the expense."

"You all are free to leave anytime you wish, but I do recommend you stay put until we get an all clear. With that in mind, Onslow, since you were present, you may need to make a press release. The court will not issue one. Chief Barnett, I suspect Sheriff Ladner will make one too, as soon as he's been briefed by you."

That's when I called Hannah. I told her what had happened, and that when the press learns where we live, they'll be camped out at the house in an effort to interview me. She said she was leaving for home now. I told her I would get Abner to detail a deputy at the house as soon as I saw him.

Abner showed up right then as if on cue. First thing he did was check to see if I were all right. He detailed Wonder Woman to my house, and took command of the crime scene until LSP showed up in force.

That night, he and Marisol came over to eat dinner with us. He brought the steaks. I furnished the fixings, beer, wine, bourbon, and cigars. They stayed until the wee hours of the morning. I knew Abner wanted to make sure we were okay.

This was the first time I ever shot someone, let alone kill

anyone. I had traded shots with the bad guys several times on the police force, but nobody ever wound up shot. It's hard to be accurate when you're running full bore into combat, especially in the darkness, and particularly so before the advent of tritium sights. I thought I might have misgivings about the shooting - many lawmen do - but I didn't. Buster had it coming several times over.

Abner wound up making several press releases. Onslow made one. LSP was in town for several days doing their job. They made two. They were all good guys. Extremely courteous and professional. Within a month, it was like this had never occurred. Business returned back to normal.

Being the kind of guy Abner was, and as a result of this incident, he created five different awards for service to Saint Landry Parish. They came boxed with a medal attached to a ribbon for formal wear, and a ribbon-only for everyday wear. Two were for valor, greater and lesser (like a Silver Star and a Bronze Star); one was for distinguished service over several years, but unrelated to valor (like a Meritorious Service Medal); one was for distinguished marksmanship (with handgun, shotgun, and rifle designators); and one was for lifesaving, putting oneself in peril while doing so (like a Soldier's Medal). Already, deputies were awarded a slanted gold hashmark for every five years of service, which was worn on the bottom of the left sleeve of our jackets.

Heroes are not made. They just are, like the sun and moon just are. Most are innocuous. One never knows when circumstances may dictate, compelling a hero to make an appearance, many times against his better judgment.

Abner went back through departmental records, giving

awards to officers who would have received one before, had they been in existence at the time of the achievement. At the same time, he did not hand them out like candy. I was the only recipient of the greater valor medal. The ribbon was red, white, and blue, and reminiscent of the one on a Silver Star. Abner spent $2,500 of his discretionary office budget, and increased pride in a job well done by all the deputies by 1,000%.

In July, Hannah and I drove out to New Mexico and spent a couple of weeks visiting with my brother and his wife.

It was time to rest. Time to let the wind blow the cobwebs from my mind.

The End

- Epilogue -

When the Wind Blows

When the wind blows

Softly

On a steamy August weeknight

In the bayous of South Louisiana

While I lie alone in my undies on top of the sheets

My clothes soaked with perspiration and sticking to me and the sheets

While my wife is three miles away tending to an ailing relative

And the kids are all grown and on their own

And tomorrow I must go back to work

And I'm thirsty

And sleep like a temptress evades me

And the cat slips off the bed

And stands tall looking out through the screen in the open window next to me

While I ponder questions I cannot hope to answer

Until the thirst in my mind wins out

And I stand up and look to see what the cat sees

And the wind blows a little harder

And I can see by the light of the waxing moon

Playing hide and seek between the turbulent clouds

And the branches on the windswept live oak trees down by the bayou

And I turn away and pad barefooted along the wooden floor to the kitchen

Where I open up the freezer on the top of the old fridge

And it's dark and I can barely see
And the wind blows
Through the open kitchen windows
And I break some ice cubes out of the metal tray and put it away
And drop three or four in a glass from the cupboard
And fill it from the faucet
And quench my thirst
Three glassfuls
And place the empty glass with melting ice cubes in the sink
And slowly make my way back to the bedroom
Checking the locked doors along the way
Which makes no sense
Because each of the windows is all the way up
To let in any breeze which might favor me with a kiss
On this sultry night
And lightning begins to flash
And thunder cracks
And booms
And doesn't let up
Again and again
Like cannons on a battlefield
And the rain starts pelting in half-dollar size dollops
As it storms
And the wind blows harder still
So I lower the windows to within an inch of the sill
Grateful
For the refreshing breeze
And I return to the bedroom
No longer half asleep

But wide awake
Where the cat is no longer to be found
Because she is cowering under the bed
Where it is safe
And the boogers can't find her
Leaving me to take care of myself
But I am in awe of the storm
And I watch
And the wind blows
And the rain pelts
And I continue to stare out the bedroom window
Mesmerized
Contemplating the fury of God
And I see the figure of a man in dark clothes wearing a wide-
brimmed hat
Holding a staff taller than he
Standing near the bayou under a live oak tree bowing
Precariously in the storm
With leaves shaking furiously
But the man's not really seeking shelter
Because the wind is blowing sideways
And he's exposed
Yet his hat stays on unassisted
And he's looking my way
But I can't recognize him
Because he's too far away
And I don't understand why he is there
In my yard
In the storm
And he appears ominous

And it sends a chill down my spine
While the wind blows
And the rain splatters on the windowsill
And I wonder if this is the Devil or the Grim Reaper
And if he is after me
And I say a silent prayer to Jesus to save me
From all my sins
And I remember the saying
That God helps those who help themselves
But don't recall ever reading that in the Bible
And I don't know who coined that phrase
But decide 'an ounce of prevention is worth a pound of cure'
And the man's still there
Watching me
So I go to the kitchen and pick up the receiver of the phone on the wall
To call the police
But the line is dead
And we've lost power but I didn't know
Because all the lights were off
So I turn quickly and return to the bedroom and open my closet door
And retrieve my H&R shotgun
A powerful 16 gauge
Which has harvested a cornucopia of game
And terminated numerous varmints
Which I bought brand new for $39 too many decades ago to remember
When I was young and very poor
But it holds only one shell

So I feel up on the shelf for my box of buckshot
And load the gun
Ready to defend myself
And return to the bedroom window
But the man is gone
Vanished
And I run through the house
And look out through all the windows
And see him not
But I remain inside
Behind locked doors
Not really safe
And I know it
And I sit on the couch in the parlor in my drawers
With the loaded shotgun across my lap
And wonder if my imagination
Had been playing tricks on me
And the wind blows
But the rain stops
And the thunder and lightning move elsewhere to frighten
other sinners
And the storm fades
And the wind blows softly
And I fall asleep on my vigil
Protected by God
A grace I didn't earn or deserve
And I awaken with a start
When the cat licks my cheek
And purrs loudly in my ear
And I check my watch

And see it's 5:43
And getting light
And I need to be at the factory at 7 o'clock to start my shift
To pay our bills
But first I put on my overalls and boots and hat
And take my shotgun and walk all around my yard
And the bayou
Searching for evidence of the apparition
And I see muddy footprints going from the bayou
To the gravel lane we live on
But that's all
So I return to the house
And the power is back on
So I put on the coffee
And feed the cat
And watch as she slips quietly through the cat door after she
had eaten
And I unload my shotgun
And put it away
And clean myself up
And fry some patty sausage
And make some sandwiches with last night's leftover biscuits
And eat
And drink orange juice and coffee
And clean up the dishes
And lock up
And crank up my old green pickup truck
And depart for work
Wondering all the while
Who was that man

And what did he want
And would he return
When the wind blows?

January 4, 2025 by Earl Snort

Making Mountains Out of Molehills

Author: Earl Snort
Publisher: TotalRecall Publications
Paper Back: 9781590954324
Ebook: 9781590956533
Number of pages: 320
Publication Date: 2019

It was 1969. Barlow Adams, age 20, was a recently discharged veteran. He was driving late at night on a lonely stretch of highway in the Trans-Pecos region of Texas. He stopped to render assistance to a motorist with a flat tire. What he stepped into was a vicious attempted rape. He rescued the victim, which catapulted him into an appointment as a deputy sheriff.

Along the way he encounters an enchanting woman who will change his life forever. In addition, he will be confronted by a gang of outlaw bikers who are obsessed with killing him while he is still learning the ropes of becoming a lawman. Will they succeed?

This is the story of a young man in the 1960's, an era which has long been forgotten except for those who lived it.

Barlow Adams Series Book 1

When Dreams Come True ~ Sort Of

Author: Earl Snort
Publisher: TotalRecall Publications
Paper Back: 9781648830006
Ebook: 9781648830013
Number of pages: 320
Publication Date: 2020

The year is 1970. Barlow Adams is a young deputy sheriff in a rural county in the Trans-Pecos region of Texas. He's a rookie still learning the ropes. Up until now, his experience has been limited to working in the jail and performing routine patrol work that is anything but routine when bad men decide to exert themselves in furtherance of their wicked ways.

In recent months, a gang of rustlers had begun to prey on the livestock of unwitting ranchers. The sheriff has decided to stop them cold wherever he finds them. He employs all the limited resources at his disposal to achieve this goal. One of those resources is Deputy Adams, who learns new law enforcement skills in teamwork, criminal investigation, surveillance, and undercover operations.

Barlow also learns something else. The crime may be solved and plans may be hatched to catch the evildoers, but, in the end, there's usually a joker in the woodpile who upsets the applecart and then suddenly Life becomes a free for all.

Barlow Adams Series Book II

A Lethal Odyssey of Cat and Mouse

Author: Earl Snort
Publisher: TotalRecall Publications
Paper Back: 9781648830785
Ebook: 9781648830792
Number of pages: 320
Publication Date: 2021

The year is 1971. Barlow Adams is a young deputy sheriff in a rural county in the Trans-Pecos region of Texas. After two years of instruction, he completed the Texas Police Officers Standard Training Course, and now he is fully certified as a law enforcement officer. As important as that is, something even more important is about to take place.

Barlow and Sarah, his fiancée, are about to be married.

They don't know it yet, but a depraved outlaw biker Barlow arrested two years ago has decided to stalk and murder Barlow and Sarah while they are on their honeymoon. The outlaw biker isn't operating on his own. He recruits criminals as savage as he is to pull off his barbarous scheme.

By the time law enforcement learns of the plot, the newlyweds have already departed. Until, and unless, they call home, there is no way to warn them.

Tick Tock.

Barlow Adams Series Book III

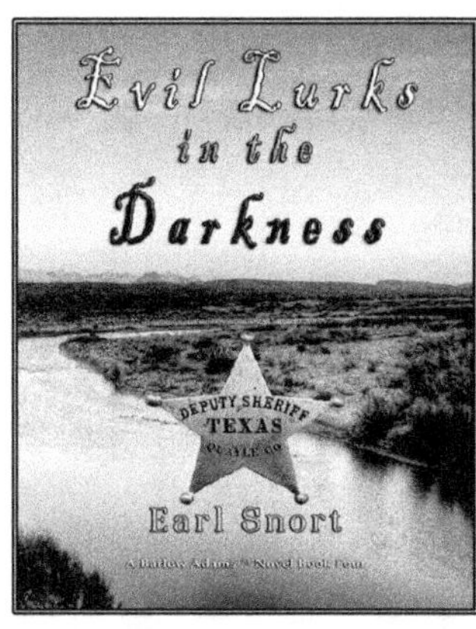

Evil Lurks in the Darkness
Even When Strong Men Stand Watch
Author: Earl Snort
Paper Back: 9781648831782
eBook: 9781648831799
Number of pages: 306
Publication Date: 2022

The year is 1972. Quayle County, located in the Trans-Pecos region of Texas, has seen an uptick of illegal alien smuggling from across the Rio Grande. The alien smugglers are determined and violent. The Border Patrol is overwhelmed with greater numbers of human trafficking cases in other areas, and therefore is unable to assist. Illegal aliens and Americans are dying alike. The small sheriff's office and the local population are left to their own devices to resolve this crisis.

Once again, Sheriff Solomon Pratt, Deputy Barlow Adams, Deputy Slick Oldman, retired Deputy Archie Willis, plus the new rookie, Deputy E.M. Gillespie, and the rest of the staff on the Quayle County Sheriff's Office rise to the occasion to vanquish the threat.

Barlow Adams Series Book IV

**Thicker Than Blood Murder,
Hide & Go Seek Texas Style**
Author: Earl Snort
Publisher: TotalRecall Publications
Paper Back: 9781648832567
Ebook: 9781648832574
Number of pages: 312
Publication Date: 2023

The year is 1973. A four-man crew of stick-up artists has been on a rampage in South Texas along the Rio Grande corridor from El Paso to Laredo. One day they stick up the bank and liquor store in Mosby in Quayle County, killing one person and severely wounding another. Mosby is a small town in a large county, with only 3,000 souls and very little crime. Deputies Slick Oldman and Barlow Adams are tasked to locate and arrest the murderers.

Barlow Adams Series Book V

***Cleaning Out A Snake Pit,
Before the Wheels Fall Off***
Author: Earl Snort
Publisher: TotalRecall Publications
Paper Back: 9781648832765
Ebook: 9781648832772
Number of pages: 356
Publication Date: 2024

It's 1974. Deputy Barlow Adams is on patrol in Quayle County, Texas, late at night. He initiates a traffic stop on a speeding truck. It screeches to a halt, and both occupants bail out, flourishing firearms. A gunfight ensues. One is killed and the other is wounded. A search of the truck reveals 60 kilograms of high-quality marijuana known as Oaxacan Highland Gold, or OHG for short. This leads to Deputy Slick Oldman and Barlow Adams being temporarily assigned to a DEA Task Force in El Paso. The stakes are high and the drug smugglers are deadly.

Barlow Adams Series Book VI

The Lawrence County Moonshine War

Author: Earl Snort
Paper Back: 9781648831782
eBook: 9781648831256
Number of pages: 200
Publication Date: 2022

This is a tale of a changeling shortly after these powers were bestowed upon him. Jack, who began life as a rabbit, fell asleep in arid West Texas shortly after wishing he had a home someplace else in a more temperate climate. When he awoke, he was a young man in a forest glen in such a place. He got exactly what he wished for! The problem was, he was wearing an Army uniform and he did not know his location. He didn't even know which century it was! Jack was suffering from a serious case of amnesia.

He soon learned that the year was 1920 and that he had been slumbering on his own property in Eastern Kentucky. He was re-introduced to his cousin, Gerard, whom he did not recognize, yet with whom he had maintained a best-friend relationship since childhood. Gerard also introduced Jack into his moonshine business during these, the early days of Prohibition. Before long, Jack found himself situated between big city gangsters and state investigators.

Lead was flying in the hills of Eastern Kentucky and Jack was in the thick of it.

A Jack Rabbit Novel

***Cleaning Out A Snake Pit,
Before the Wheels Fall Off***
Author: Earl Snort
Publisher: TotalRecall Publications
Paper Back: 9781648832789
Ebook: 9781648832796
Number of pages: 356
Publication Date: 2024

The year is 1973. Retired police officer Chester Sinclair has a dire situation. Twice within three weeks, unknown subject(s) have tried to kill him. In an effort to determine whom, he reviews 38 years of his police daily notebooks. He comes up with several possibles, but by doing so, he plows up some old ground which had been buried deep within the recesses of his mind. This is the tale of an old warrior pursued by long vanquished evildoers seeking revenge.

Stand Alone Title

Regarding the tombstone, it reads, "This site May 23, 1934 Clyde Barrow and Bonnie Parker were killed by enforcement officers." It's located near Arcadia in Bienville Parish, Louisiana.

At This Site May 23, 1934
Clyde Barror and Bonnie Parker
Were Killed by
Law enforcement officers

Erected by
Bienville Parish Police Jury

About the Author

Earl Snort is the nom de plume of a retired law enforcement officer with more than 40-years' experience toting a badge and a gun. Before that, he served in the armed forces.

He and his wife have been married more than 50 years. They have one son, also a career law enforcement officer, and two grandchildren.

This is the author's ninth foray into the world of writing fiction. After a lifetime of writing non-fiction to document investigations of true crimes, he decided to try his hand in make believe.

He hopes you enjoy this yarn and all the others.

April 15, 2025